I had no idea how I was going to get out of this...

I stepped backward, looking at Anguilla. "What are you saying?" I asked.

Dr. Anguilla looked me in the eyes and said, "When you passed me at the Her Majesty's reception yesterday, your scent smelled familiar. It was not until this morning that I recalled where I had smelled it before. It was in the broadcast studio at Livermore, and your scent was that of the Interrogator who destroyed His Excellency's new container. I accuse you of being that Interrogator."

"You're out of your mind!" I exclaimed, challenging his accusation. But I knew that I had been outed. "Your Majesty," I pleaded, "I just donated three million dollars to the construction of the Hollywood Rebirth Center!"

"My staff checked you out, Mr. LaSalle. You have pledged money, but you have not provided it. In fact, your partner is now trying to find an alternate source of funding because you have disappeared and your contact information is bogus. In fact, we would like to know where the equipment intended for Hollywood has been taken. Apparently, the shipment was hijacked."

"Your Majesty, I have not yet delivered the construction funds to Simone because I was summoned to come here by His Excellency."

"Your lies will not work here, Mr. LaSalle," the queen replied.

The queen raised her hand into the air and four Draconian guards entered the room. If I had had my 1911, I'd have taken a couple of them out before they killed me, but I had nothing to use to defend myself, and they were too imposing to try to out-muscle.

"Escort this man to the scow," the Queen ordered, "and schedule him for crystallization"

Whatever that was, it didn't sound like something appealing.

Back from destroying the New World Order's secret lunar facility and rescuing his wife's hybrid child from the hollow moon, FBI Special Agent Dan Arrow discovers that the NWO leader he killed might not be dead at all. Instead, he appears to be alive and has more up his sleeve—selling opportunities for older humans to be reborn in younger clones of themselves. Traveling to several places around the globe to investigate the NWO's new emerging agenda, Dan soon discovers more truth than fiction in modern conspiracy theories. The serpent he thought he had killed has more than one head, and the opportunity the NWO is peddling has an evil hidden agenda intended to enslave mankind. While attempting to behead the serpent, Dan escapes death in a frozen wasteland, and through Remote Viewing his wife Mona sees him captured, beaten, and dying. Can she find him in time to save his life and help him sever the serpent's last head?

KUDOS for *Dan Arrow and the Three-Headed Ophidian*

In *Dan Arrow and the Three-Headed Ophidian* by Edward S Baker, Dan Arrow is still chasing aliens from the New World Order. In this episode, Dan has to sneak into the Bohemian Grove where a meeting is being held on the alien's cloning technology, whereby older humans can be transferred into younger clones of themselves. The case then takes Dan and FBI Special Agent Mack Smith to the South Pole where Hitler, recently transferred to a new clone, and the alien queen are hiding. But every time Dan thinks he's winning, the aliens come up with something new. It's like decapitating the multi-headed hydra from mythology. Every time he cuts off one head, two more replace it. Will he ever finally defeat the New World Order and the aliens invading Earth, or will he die in the attempt? As well written, fascinating, and thrilling at the first two books, you won't want to miss all of Dan's new misadventures. A really great read. ~ *Taylor Jones, The Review Team of Taylor Jones & Regan Murphy*

Dan Arrow and the Three-Headed Ophidian by Edward S Baker is the story of FBI Special Agent Dan Arrow, his wife Mona, and their alien-human hybrid child Stella in their fight against the aliens and criminals trying to take over the Earth. Teaming up with FBI Special Agent Max Smith and the friendly alien from Ummo, Waam, to destroy Hitler, who has been reborn into a new clone, and the reptilian alien queen, Dan travels the globe trying to apprehend the bad guys. But the bad guys always seem to be one step ahead of him. From the Bohemian Grove in California to a secret hideaway in the South Pole, Dan struggles to outsmart the aliens trying to enslave and/or destroy mankind. But with the aliens' advanced technology, he runs the risk of being found out before his mission is complete. Can Dan stop the aliens and return home safely to his wife and child, or is he doomed to end up in the alien feeding tanks? Combining science fiction, mystery, suspense, and a hint of romance, *Dan Arrow and the Three-Headed Ophidian* is a fun and exciting ride you won't be able to put down. A real page turner. *~ Regan Murphy, The Review Team of Taylor Jones & Regan Murphy*

ACKNOWLEDGEMENTS

Many thanks to Faith at Black Opal Books for her confidence in my ability to weave a story and for her suggestions about point of view which are always on target. And thanks, too, to Jack, who has designed all the covers for my books—this one being especially exciting. Thanks, as well, to my wife Edna for her edits and questions that help me to see minor details that need fixing.

OTHER BOOKS
BY
EDWARD S. BAKER
AND
BLACK OPAL BOOKS

Dan Arrow and the New World Order

Dan Arrow and the Hollow Moon

DAN
ARROW

And the
THREE-HEADED OPHIDIAN

Edward S. Baker

A Black Opal Books Publication

GENRE: MYSTERY-DETECTIVE/SUSPENSE/WOMEN SLEUTHS

DAN ARROW AND THE THREE-HEADED OPHIDIAN
Copyright © 2019 by Edward S. Baker
Cover Design by Jackson Cover Designs
All cover art copyright © 2019
All Rights Reserved
Print ISBN: 9781644371053

First Publication: MARCH 2019

Published by Black Opal Books **http://www.blackopalbooks.com**

DEDICATION

This book is dedicated to my friend and fellow author Dan Barrett who's had difficulty seeing things lately but for whom, it seems, things are starting to look better.

It is also dedicated to all the human abductees who've had their bodies probed by alien visitors, and especially to those who've later been introduced to hybrid children who may be their own intergalactic offspring.

Prologue

For those of you who don't know me, my name is Dan Arrow. I was working as a private detective in DC when a client asked me to find her husband's killer. During my investigation, I found aliens living and working with New World Order forces in underground facilities all over the United States. The long and short of it is that I discovered that my client's husband wasn't really dead. Through alien technology, he had been moved from his body into the body of an eighty-year-old woman!

In the process of investigating the alleged murder, my ex-girlfriend Mona was kidnapped and artificially inseminated by a reptilian. Before we could abort the hybrid baby, the reptilians removed it from her and placed it into an artificial growth chamber. Disguised as NWO Interrogators, Mona and I traveled to the moon, where we found the child, and eventually brought it back to Earth.

The root of the story, however, is that the New World Order had been planning to reduce the population of the Earth and then share its habitable surface with reptilians from the planet Draco. The NWO had been using alien migration technology to keep its leader alive for almost seventy years, moving him from one short-lived body to another while alien scientists perfected the process of cloning humans so that selected individuals could live forever through migration.

But I managed to blow up the flying saucer that carried the NWO leader in his new body, thus thwarting the imminent takeover of the Earth. Later, Mona's boss, an FBI official, convinced us to move to a rural community where more than two hundred alien-human hybrids and their families were living. So we did that, and settled in to raise little Stella in the human culture. All's well that ends well, right? Well, not exactly…

Chapter 1

Mona was upstairs putting Stella into bed when her boss, Special Agent Mack Smith, called me on my cell phone. I had a feeling that it wasn't a social call.

"Dan, can we talk?" he asked.

"Yeah," I replied, "Mona is upstairs with Stella. It's been a long day. We finally finished unpacking our stuff and dragging the empty boxes out to the curb, so we're planning to turn in early."

"Then it's good that I caught you," he replied.

"What's up?"

"I'm going to send you a link to a YouTube video that has gone viral. I think you'll find it interesting."

"Can you clue me in?"

"It's a guy who is promoting being born again."

"Another fundamentalist preacher?"

"No, he claims to be a scientist who has developed a process that enables people to live forever by cloning their bodies and moving them into their clones as their own bodies age. He claims that his invention will bring about a new world where death no longer exists."

"That sounds a lot like the Draconian migration process, Mack."

"Yeah, and the New World Order," Mack replied. "But you gotta see the guy in the video, Dan."

"Why's that?"

"It's Hitler!"

"Couldn't be!" I replied. "You were there when we blew him and Commissar Nargas to Hell with Waam's latest plasma weaponry."

"That's why I want you to check out the YouTube video. I swear it looks just like him. And you can't dismiss the fact that he's promoting migration."

"Okay, send me the link and I'll take a look at it."

"I already have. It's waiting for you in your email. Give my regards to Mona." He hung up.

I knew better than to open that email, especially when I should have been slipping under the covers with Mona, but I did anyway. The link that Mack had sent me started on its own. Its title, *You CAN Be Born Again,* sounded like an info commercial for some fundamentalist church, so I paused the video, opened my browser, and searched the title on Snopes. Snopes said it wasn't a hoax. So, I tried again on Hoax Busters. Nope, it wasn't listed a hoax.

I figured that Mona could wait a couple of more minutes for me to come to bed, so I hit the play arrow on the video. As I did, I noticed that this video had already been viewed some 2,300,000 times, give or take a few hundred thousand. I put my buds into my ears and settled back to watch.

I knew I was getting into some deep shit when the first thing to appear on the screen was that all too familiar Nazi-like phoenix, gripping the globe in its talons. It was the New World Order logo. Below it were swirling letters which, one by one, fell neatly into place: *A New World Production.* "Aw fuck," I muttered.

A scene from some movie that I remembered seeing as a kid appeared on the screen. It was Jesus in a robe talking to a bunch of followers. "Verily, verily, I say unto thee, except a man be born again, he cannot see the kingdom of God."

A male narrator then said, "God wanted us all to live forever, but it was up to us to figure out how to do it. So, how *do* you become born again?" The picture switched to an elderly Catholic priest. "For two thousand years, priests have been telling us that we must die and then be born again in the Kingdom of Heaven. Frankly, that isn't what Jesus meant at all."

The picture then switched to Jimmy Swaggart, covered in sweat, with his mouth open and his finger pointed into the air.

"Fundamentalist preachers have been telling us that we must be born again in this body by receiving Jesus and being saved."

The picture changed to a woman who was dancing and singing with three snakes in her outstretched hands.

"Jesus didn't want us babbling in tongues and fainting when the spirit enters us. Jesus didn't want us dancing with snakes, either."

The picture switched to a golden statue of the Buddha. "Buddha lectured that we must be born a thousand times, each time getting closer and closer to perfection, but only a few people ever attain Buddha's status. That's not a modern image of being born again, being a different person each time, sometimes a male, sometimes a female, sometimes wealthy, and sometimes in abject poverty."

The picture changed again, this time to a Hindu meditating in the lotus position.

"The Hindus believe that only a Dvija may study

their holy scriptures. A Dvija is a young male who has been born again by studying with a guru. Do you believe that only males may be born again and that females cannot be reborn?"

The picture switched to a young man in a doctor's white lab coat. The voice of the moderator was now in sync with the young man's moving lips.

"Hello," he said into the camera, "For the purposes of this presentation, my name is Dr. Harold Flite, and I am here to tell you that through the miracle of modern science, you *can* be born again. And again, and again. In fact, you can live as long as you desire, being born each time as the male or female that you wish to be, and with full memory of every life that you have lived. Imagine what it would be like to never have to go to school again. To retain your current knowledge and skills while you add new skills each time you are reborn. To regain your youth and yet retain an adult mind. To own your property in full after a few brief years of mortgage indebtedness, knowing that it will be yours forever."

The picture on the screen changed to a white building, surrounded by flowering trees. It was too damn perfect, I thought.

The narrator continued, "At the New World Rebirth Center in Astana, Kazakhstan, men and women like you are currently being evaluated for participation in my special rebirth program." The picture showed a woman undergoing a medical examination. "Selection for the program requires a brief medical exam, including parental medical history, and a DNA analysis. Those selected will donate a few hairs and oral skin tissues that will be used to grow a cloned body, which will be ready for occupation in as few as eighteen months."

The picture switched to a fetal body floating in a tube of liquid. I had seen bodies in tanks like these before, in the alien breeding tubes about a mile beneath the runway at the Denver airport. "Prior to the cloning process, selection of gender, hair and eye color, height, and body shape, all achieved through DNA augmentation, will enable you to create the perfect you for the next sixty years of living."

The picture changed to a map of the globe, rotating on its axis. Posted in red and gold above it, glowed the message *Rebirth Centers Opening Soon Near You*. As the globe turned, yellow stars appeared, one each in London, New York City, Rio, Los Angeles, Melbourne, Tokyo, Hong Kong, Moscow, New Delhi, Cape Town, Cairo, Dubai, and Berlin. I counted thirteen, plus the one in Astana.

The screen then displayed a URL address where you could get further information, if you were interested in being born again. I found a ballpoint pen and jotted it down onto my palm. They could have made it a hyperlink, but they didn't. Go figure. I could have written on a piece of paper, but I didn't. Go figure, again.

When the video ended, I typed the URL into my browser and found the web site. It bore the same NWO symbol and displayed pictures of the interior of the New World Rebirth Center in Astana. The machine in the picture of the migration lab looked different from the unit that the NWO used at Livermore when they attempted to migrate Hitler into a new body, but technology advances, and the new unit had a more professional look. It had to be the same thing, though—an NWO electromechanical wolf in sheep's clothing. And Dr. Harold Flite certainly looked exactly like Hitler. "What the fuck are they up to?" I muttered to myself.

I shut down the computer and climbed the stairs to bed, checking on Stella before bothering Mona. Little Stella lay in her crib, breathing rhythmically with a slight snore. She gets that from Mona. I pulled her thumb out of her mouth and adjusted her pink blanket. She stopped snoring but didn't stir. Sometimes life is good, huh!

As I pulled back the covers to climb into bed with Mona, she pulled violently on the covers and complained, "Jesus H., Danny, you're letting in all the cold air!"

I don't think Mona was awake. That's just how she is. I chuckled at my predicament, laid down on the third of the mattress that was allotted to my side of the bed, and fell asleep. Sort of.

I didn't sleep too well. In fact, I tossed and turned a lot as my mind kept replaying Hitler's death in Commissar Nargas's tureen near Mars. Waam and I had actually watched that tureen explode as it fell into the sun. So, then, who the hell was this dude who looked just like the newly migrated Hitler? And, what was with this web site where he was selling people opportunities to migrate into clones of themselves? How much was he charging? Who were his customers? What did his selection process consist of? How was this program tied to the NWO's agenda? There was no doubt that Mack was wondering the same sorts of things, and he'd be bugging me about it in the morning.

Chapter 2

Mona woke me at eight. "Mack called," she told me. "He said he's coming over and will be here in an hour."

"Can't a guy catch a break?" I complained. "He called last night and his call made it hard for me to get any sleep."

"I saw the YouTube video this morning, Danny. I'm surprised that you got any sleep at all. It's clearly Hitler, and he's in that same brown-skinned body that we saw inside the Moon and on Mars."

"Yeah, but you saw him die with Nargas," I replied. "We both did."

"Maybe. But, what if we only saw a lookalike accompanying Nargas and not the real Hitler?"

My mind drifted back to the day that Nargas surprised us at Waam's Ummite outpost on Mars. I remembered thinking that Hitler seemed a little quieter than I had expected him to be. So, Mona had a good point. Many kings and queens in history have used doubles to foil would be assassins. It's very possible that a double had been accompanying Nargas that day. So, it seemed evident that the real Hitler was now selling timeshares in cloned bodies, or *containers* as the reptilians call them. That, in itself, seemed strange, because it just didn't seem like it would be his style.

"Do you think he sells them or leases them?" I asked Mona.

"What are you talking about?" Mona replied with a confused look on her face.

"Sorry, baby. I guess that I jumped ahead. What I meant to ask you is 'If Hitler is migrating people into new containers, like he claims in that video, is he selling the containers to them or is he leasing them?'"

"I never considered the lease option, Danny. That opens a shitload of possibilities, doesn't it?"

"And how much is he charging? Is there a monthly payment plan?"

"I'll bet he makes you sign the contract in blood, Danny, and the cost is your soul."

I shuddered at the thought of it. Mona nodded in agreement.

⇜⇝

Mack arrived promptly at nine o'clock. I had just fin- ished showering and already had the Death Wish coffee percolating. I had seen it advertised during the Superbowl and figured that its name was something that I could pre- tend would do the deed on Mack. Our relationship was a two-edged sword. On the plus side, Mack had saved my life in Denver, and he had found us this new home and a school in this little community where Stella's eyes and her intelligence wouldn't cause her to stand out like a freak. On the other hand, I still wasn't sure of him, but, then, nobody can ever be sure of spooks and Bureau guys. There is always a hidden agenda with them, and I hate people with hidden agendas.

"Hey, Mack, come on in," I told him when I opened the door. "Mona is upstairs dressing Stella. How about some coffee?"

Mack nodded, so I poured him a mugful. His eyes opened wide when he tasted it. "Definitely on the darker side of the roast," he told me. He took another sip. "Flavorful."

I put a little water into my mug before filling the remainder with coffee. I'm not a big fan of shit like expresso. But Mona likes it. It must be a cultural thing.

"Did you see this morning's paper?" Mack asked.

"No, I haven't subscribed yet."

"NASA just announced that they've found water on Mars!"

"You're shitting me!"

"Nope. They've analyzed photos and determined that the water rises to the surface, freezes during the evening, and then evaporates in the morning sun."

"No shit. You know, that doesn't surprise me because there was water in the Ummite facility when Mona and I were there, and I can't imagine that they'd ship it there in large quantities in some kind of interstellar tanker."

"You know," Mack said, "Waam called me this morning from Italy. He had read the article, and he says that someday NASA is going to declare that they've found e-coli on Mars."

"Why's that?" I asked.

"The spot where NASA found that water is the location of the septic leach field of the Draconian facility."

"So, the headline in today's paper should have read 'NASA finds lizard piss on Mars!'" I blurted. We both laughed.

"So, what's your take on that video, Dan? Is it Hitler?" Mack asked, getting right to the point of his visit.

"Looks like him, Mack, but something isn't right about it. Why would some guy who wants to conquer the world put himself online selling a service to people who are afraid of dying? The megalomaniac who brought us World War II wouldn't be doing that. He'd be building his army and planning to launch an invasion somewhere. For certain, he'd be running the NWO through fear and intimidation exercises and making all the top brass sweat bullets."

"I think it could be some sort of diversion, or maybe a change in strategy, Dan. Maybe the NWO has replaced him as its penultimate leader and he's been assigned to lighter duty. Maybe they've migrated him to an altogether different body to keep him hidden from those who would do him in while he's planning to implement the NWO takeover of the globe."

"So, it's a no-brainer. Put your best men on it and find out what's going on."

"That would be you, Dan."

"No, I don't think so, Mack. Mona and I have just moved in. We haven't even met the neighbors, yet. Well, Mona has talked to the family next door, but I haven't, and besides, I have an obligation to assist with security here in Villagio Ibrido. It's part of my lease agreement, if you remember: free rent in exchange for services rendered. I'm supposed to meet the CO tomorrow right after lunch."

"We need your services on this mission, Dan."

"Find somebody else. I've put my ass on the line twice for you guys, and both times I was a whisker's breadth away from being an ingredient in the soup. Besides, I've got a daughter to raise, Mack."

"It's not so dangerous this time. We need you to fly

out to California and see what you can learn about this internet version of Der Fuerher. He's the key speaker at a seminar this weekend, and your registration fee has already been paid to the Bohemian Club."

"Sounds like hippie-ville, and I'll stick out like a sore thumb," I complained, because I could see that the die had been cast. "Mona isn't gonna like this, Mack. Where the fuck is this Bramanian place, anyway?"

"Bohemian," he corrected, "Bohemian Club. It's about seventy-five miles north of San Francisco. You'll fly there and rent a car for the rest of the trip."

"A Prius for an eco-friendly image?"

"How about a Tesla? It's electric, gets great gas mileage, and you'll look like a wealthy supporter of the NWO agenda."

"That sounds better," I replied. Who wouldn't want to test drive a Tesla for a couple of days? Then I drifted back into reality. "By now, they've gotta have my face and prints on their computers as a potential saboteur. They'll pick me out of the crowd like a strawberry at a blueberry festival."

"We've hacked their system, Dan. Your face and prints are registered as a big time liberal with the Hollywood set. You'll be widely accepted as their newest member. They've even sent you an invitation."

"You're a fucker, Mack. I've got things to do here and you're sending me away from my family."

"You'll be back in four days. I promise. Besides, the village CO already has been briefed on your change in orders."

"Are you the one telling Mona, Mack?"

"That's your job. You're her husband. Besides, she probably won't mind a break from your snoring at night."

"Who told you that I snore?"

"She did."

I huffed in frustration. "When am I supposed to be there?"

"Your plane leaves DC at noon on Thursday."

"That's two days away, Mack!"

"Your tickets and flight information will arrive by courier later this morning. The package will also include info about your Tesla, a credit card, and false credentials, and some info that we've been able to put together about the Bohemian Club annual event. I think you'll find it interesting."

Mona came down the stairs, carrying Stella at her shoulder. "Hey, Mack, good to see you," she said giving him a polite kiss on his cheek. "Staying for lunch?"

"No, I've got to get to a briefing at Camp David, and Dan already gave me a cup of coffee that'll keep me awake for the entire drive." Mack walked to the front door. He opened it, turned to Mona and told her, "Dan will fill you in on what we've talked about. Good seeing you and Stella, Mona. See you both again soon."

"So what was that all about?" Mona asked me when Mack closed the door.

"Mack's ensuring that he's out of here before I tell you what he has in store for me."

"I knew it wasn't a social call. Where's he sending you?"

"Northern California. That guy in the video who looks like Hitler is giving a presentation at some kind of conference. Mack wants me to check him out."

"At least Mack's not sending you back to Mars or in- to one of the DUMB's. I couldn't bear the thought of the lizards getting their hands on you. Mack must know that you're high on their most wanted list."

I nodded. Lately, I had spent too much time tempting death in deep underground military bases. "Yeah, but I had hoped he'd give me a few months here with you and little Stella before he called in the chits and shipped me off on some clandestine operation."

"How long will you be gone, Danny?"

"Four days."

"That's not too bad. What's your cover?"

"He's got me registered as a guy in the movie industry."

"At least you can justify ordering prime rib and after dinner brandy as part of your cover. I had planned to give you hotdogs and tuna casserole this week. When do you leave?"

"Tomorrow. My plane leaves DC on Thursday. My credentials and tickets are supposed to be delivered sometime today."

"So, Mack didn't wait for you to agree to this mission before ordering that stuff."

"He knows I can't say 'no' to him, especially since he owns my ass now with this house and Stella's special school."

٤٥٤٥

The courier rang our door bell at three p.m. and made me sign for two packages, one addressed to me and one for Mona. It was the second package that raised the hackles on the back of my neck. Mack hadn't said anything about a special mission for Mona. I wondered what he was up to.

Mona opened her package. "It's a picture of a gray alien and a brief letter from Mack. He says that this guy is coming for a visit tomorrow, after you've left for the airport."

"It's a Reticulan gray, baby. He's one of the good ones. The Draconian grays have elongated faces and their eyes just look evil."

"I know all that, Danny. Don't you remember that Nargas had two Draconian grays leading me around on a leash?"

"Yeah, that's right. I just didn't want you to be afraid of that little guy in the picture."

"Mack says that he wants me to Google something called 'Remote Viewing' before this gray arrives. He says it's a good opportunity for me."

"He has a hidden agenda."

"Yeah, I know."

Chapter 3

I was fifth in the queue when I pulled my new royal blue Tesla-S to a stop at the entrance to the Bohemian Grove late on Friday afternoon. Well, it was mine for the weekend, anyway. Driving it from San Francisco was a treat, especially when I hit the winding roads that led from Santa Rosa to the Bohemian Grove near Monte Rio. It hugged the curves and accelerated briskly, but I couldn't get over the sensation of speed with virtually no engine noise, except for the soft whine from the transmission when I backed out of the parking space at the airport. I wondered if I could get Mack to buy me one of these babies for around town shopping back in Virginia. Probably not.

I had just finished a very long day of sitting on my ass. I had kissed Mona and Stella goodbye sometime around dawn and climbed into my SUV for a long drive to the airport. I put the pedal to the metal and arrived at Dulles International at nine-thirty a.m. My flight left at ten-fifteen a.m., so after parking and running through the terminal, I made it to the gate at last call. Mack had done me a favor, though, and had booked a first-class ticket. I hadn't expected that of him. Actually, it was the first time I had ever ridden in first class. The seats were soft Italian leather and they were wide, which meant that my fanny and legs weren't going to get cramped the way they did in tourist class. And the drinks were free.

The flight to San Francisco had a forty-minute layover in Chicago, which gave me just enough time to empty my tanks before getting back onto another plane. Because the next leg was overbooked, United offered a free ticket to anyone who would agree to catch a later flight. So I volunteered and got a flight voucher in first class seating compliments of good old Mack. It was good for twelve months. The next flight wouldn't leave for two hours, so I found a bar and sat down to a couple of scotches, which I charged to the credit card that Mack had provided.

The next flight dropped down into San Francisco at four p.m., West Coast time. My luggage was waiting for me at the baggage claim office, and my Tesla's fuel gauge read "fully charged" when I signed for it. I handed the guy a twenty after he showed me how to program the GPS for the Bohemian Grove, and then I peeled rubber for ten feet on my way out of the garage. The Tesla's accelerator was a little more sensitive than I had anticipated. I wondered if I should have paid for additional insurance.

⌘⌘⌘

The roads out of San Francisco were jammed with cars, which you would expect on a Friday at rush hour. But once I was north of the Golden Gate Bridge, they opened up and it was a quick trip to Monte Rio. I'll bet I didn't burn ten percent of the Tesla's batteries' charge.

Then, while I sat waiting my turn at the check point, I watched as the guards were carefully inspecting each of the cars in front of me, scanning identification papers, opening the trunks, using mirrors on extension poles to look for explosives on the undercarriages, and even opening random pieces of luggage. Security was clearly high. I wondered if they were expecting trouble from one or more of the invitees. Hell, maybe they knew that I was coming.

When it was my turn to be interrogated, the guard asked for my identification and registration. Then, he asked me usual questions:

"What is your home address, Mr. Lessle?"

"That's LaSalle," I replied, "with three Ls."

"Yes. And what is your home address, Mr. LaSalle?"

"Thirty-Five Thirty-Two Outpost Drive, Hollywood Hills." It was a good thing that I had memorized the papers that Mack had given me. The address was easy to remember because the first two numbers were my age and the second two were Mona's. I didn't know if it was a real address, but then I figured that this guy didn't know either."

"And your occupation?"

"Film producer."

"And how long have you owned this nice Tesla, Mr. LaSalle? Does it get good gas mileage?"

I knew this guy was looking to trip me up. "It's a rental. I picked it up about an hour ago. It's electric. My Ferrari is in the shop."

"Thank you, sir." He looked at his log and then handed back my registration and driver's license. "You're quartered in bungalow four-two-five. Just follow the right fork for about a mile, and you should find it on the left. Dinner will be served from six to eight-thirty. Tonight's program begins at nine. Enjoy your stay with us."

I followed his directions, and soon parked beside a Morgan +4 convertible, which had been parked perpendicular to the bungalow. The Morgan was fire engine red with a tan leather belt across its bonnet. It was sweet. The bungalow, however, was vintage 1940s with no paint on its pine exterior. Green gingham curtains were visible through the glass. It was not my idea of expensive lodgings, but this shared space was costing the FBI close to five hundred per night. I got the immediate impression that the people who came to this conference didn't mind paying a lot of money to sleep in sub-par lodgings and eat hamburger at Beef Wellington prices. I also got the impression that there might not be a bathroom inside, and I had full tanks.

As luck would have it, my roommate was in the shower when I opened the bunkhouse door, so I dropped my suitcase beside the untouched single bed, then went out back and relieved myself into the bushes. I think they were some kind of holly because they prickled my fingers when I accidentally brushed against them. It was no big deal, though.

Back inside, I unpacked my underwear and socks into the top drawer of the dresser beside my bed, and I hung my clothes on the rack that was mounted on the wall beside it. "No closets in this dump," I muttered to myself.

When the bathroom door opened, out stepped a woman who was simply buck naked and dripping wet. She was carrying a towel in her right hand, and water dripped onto her back from her short, slicked-back hair. My car caught her attention, so she pulled the curtains to the side and peered out the window at it. Then she turned, saw me, and gasped. Quickly, she pulled her towel in front of her. "Who the fuck are you?" she demanded.

"Sandy LaSalle," I replied with a smile.

"Shit, I hoped that Sandy LaSalle was a woman," she replied. "I should have known better!"

"I didn't mean to surprise you," I said. "I didn't know the name of my roommate, or I'd have asked for a change of billeting."

"Shit!" she said again. "The last thing I ever expected was to stand naked in front of a complete stranger."

"And the last thing I expected was to have a naked woman walk into my room," I replied. She laughed, so I suggested, "How about I go take a walk for half an hour. Then maybe we can enjoy formal introductions." She nodded in agreement.

Out the door I went. I didn't know her name, but I had already seen that my roommate wasn't a real blond. I hoped that she wasn't going to get all pissy and make a big deal with the management that I was inside and gawking when she came out of the shower. Hell, it wasn't my fault. Besides, I'm a married man with a wife who still threatens to cut off my identity with a dull knife if I ever think about cheating on her. I wouldn't do that, anyway. Mona and I already have been through too much for me to do something like that to her.

About a hundred yards down the ten-foot wide path of pea stones that snaked through the tall conifers, I found a map of the 2500-acre resort. If I took a path that meandered over the slight rise to my left, I would find the dining hall. Since it was already a couple of hours past my East Coast dinner bell, I caved to my hunger and hiked in that direction.

I was not alone in my hunger. The dining hall was full of conference-goers, all talking and laughing together as though they were old friends. The noise inside the single-story hall was almost deafening. Dinner was buffet style. The line was short, so I hopped on its end and grabbed a white ironstone plate when it was my turn. The fare was simple: chicken in some kind of white sauce, fried potatoes, rice, green beans with almonds, a vegetarian dish of some sort, a large bowl of mixed greens with three choices of dressing, bread, butter, and vanilla tapioca pudding for dessert.

I slopped the chicken and sauce over a spoonful of potatoes, put a few green beans beside them, and took three rolls with butter. This place was no Delmonico's, but it would fill me.

I was half finished with my meal when a thin man sat down across from me. He looked familiar, but I couldn't remember where I had seen him before. "It's nice to see you again, Mr. LaSalle," he said. "Do they have any wine?"

I looked up again. He was wearing a white blazer over a red-and-blue-striped buttoned-down shirt. His light brown hair was unkempt, about mid-ear in length. "I don't think so," I replied.

"It's okay. I have a couple of bottles back in the cottage."

Then it struck me: This guy was the woman I had seen in the cottage! "I wouldn't call it a cottage," I replied, "but I guess from a female point of view, calling it a cottage makes a shack easier to sleep in." She smiled. "You look different in clothes, Miss..." I prompted.

"Simone," she whispered. "Simone Lopez. But please call me Simon when we're around others."

So, I figured she didn't want anyone to know her secret. "You don't look Hispanic," I told her.

"It's my ex-husband's name. Sonny Lopez. He's a jockey. I'm sure you've heard of him."

"Only if he's raced at Pamlico, and only on the one day a year that I happen to find myself there. Sorry, but his name doesn't sound familiar to me."

She continued speaking in a very low voice, and I had to lean forward to be able to hear everything that she said. "So, you're not a horse-racing fan, then, Sandy?" she asked.

"No, not really. Only in the movies, and I've never produced a horse-racing movie."

"Oh, you're a producer!" Suddenly her interest in me piqued. I thought for a moment that it must be a California thing, but then I remembered Mona's tendency to pick up those junkie gossip magazines whenever she's in a waiting room. "What have you produced?" Simone asked.

"Mostly kung fu movies," I lied. "They play big with the Asians, the military, and with kids."

"Do you know Bruce Lee?"

"Not personally, but he has starred in several movies that I've produced."

"Which ones?"

"I'm not allowed to say. It's a contractual confidentiality thing. I am more of a silent partner as producers go."

"That's strange, I guess, but I've heard of many strange arrangements in the movie industry."

"Are you in the film industry, Simone?" I asked.

"I run a stable of makeover specialists, Sandy. You know, as the stars age, my people keep them looking young until they have no choice except to go under the plastic surgeon's scalpel."

"So how does that work?"

"Directors call me and describe the problem with how a star looks in a particular scene. I send the appropriate technician who saves the day and the film."

"Have you ever done work on a kung fu star?" I asked.

"Just Bruce Lee, once when his face was bruised in an accident on the set."

"The director never told me," I replied, shrugging my shoulder. "So I guess you're here to listen to Dr. Harold Flite. It sounds to me like he's going to try to run you out of business."

"Actually, I'm hoping to buy into one of his clinics. I'd like to own the franchise in Hollywood."

"That's interesting, and I guess it makes sense. You can keep the movie stars in make-up until they need a new body. Then you can sell them a new one. You'd own both ends of the spectrum and be the most popular business in town."

"Exactly."

At Simone's suggestion, we left the food court so we could continue our conversation without her being overheard. After all, the Bohemian Club is a male-only organization. That really makes it elitist. I figured that Mona would really be upset when I told her about that, and even if I wanted to join, she'd kill me if I did.

Simone and I chatted about little stuff for about half an hour as we walked back to the shack. Inside, she offered me a glass of Malbec, which wasn't too bad. I generally prefer scotch or beer, and I usually go for the merlot or the cabernet when I'm forced to drink wine, but she didn't have any of the basic wines. From my point of view, wine is for snobs, which I've never been accused of being.

At eight o'clock, she told me to put on a sweater or light jacket so we could go to the opening ceremony.

"This is my first time here," I reminded her.

"This will be your initiation, then," she said with a smile. "It'll be something you'll remember for the rest of your life."

"So, you've been here before?" I asked.

"I snuck in here two years ago, just to see what it was all about."

I grabbed a black blazer and followed Simone out the door and through the trees until we joined a line of men who were headed to the same place we were. I overheard one guy quietly mention some kind of sacrifice. I hoped they weren't planning to butcher a sheep or something.

The pathway that we were following was dimly illuminated by spotlights in yellow plastic cones. Clearly, the management had spared no expense. We walked slowly for about a quarter of a mile along the pathway until we came to a clearing with a small lake. Maybe it was a large pond. In the middle of the far side I could see that a stage had been erected. Behind it stood a large stone owl with a bonfire at its feet. Around it stood men in silver and red robes.

One man, possibly the ceremonial leader, wore a silver robe with a tall headdress, similar to the Pope's. Another wore a headdress with deer antlers. Bugs of all sorts were flying in the light that reflected from the lake. We were definitely out with the flora and fauna. And when I saw several totally naked people in the crowd, I decided that we were out with some weirdos, as well.

Simone and I had been standing at the lake's edge with more than a thousand other men for about two minutes when the lights went out without warning, leaving us all in absolute darkness. Several whoops and whistles went up from the crowd, followed by murmurs of anticipation.

As my eyes began to adjust to the darkness, stage lights came on across the lake, illuminating the large stone owl. Simone whispered, "His name is Moloch. He's a forty-foot tall Canaanite deity."

"Oh," I replied. I couldn't remember my Sunday school lessons very well, but I knew that Canaan was some place in the Holy Land.

Bagpipes began to play, signaling the start of the ceremony. Simone told me, "This is the Festival of Fire. It signals the beginning of two weeks of meetings and presentations. When the body arrives, they'll do the Cremation of Care."

"What's that?" I asked.

"Just watch, Sandy. I'll fill you in as the ceremony progresses."

Then, motion to the left side of the lake drew my attention. Behind a row of thirteen metal crosses, torches were being lighted, and as each torch burst into flame, the torch bearer joined a procession that wound along the opposite shoreline. When the procession stopped in front of the owl, in all I counted thirteen evenly separated flames. I hoped that thirteen wasn't some sort of satanic symbolism, and I hoped that this ritual was some sort of playacting and not actually real.

Then a horse drawn hearse appeared to our right. Through its glass windows, I could see what looked like a man's body. Although the darkness obscured some of what was going on, four men in red robes moved the body from the hearse and tied it to the bow of a boat. The men then used poles to push the boat across the lake, sort of like the way the keel boats were moved in Disney's old Davy Crockett series. "They're moving the dying man across the River Styx," Simone said.

I gave her a concerned look.

"It's only an effigy, Sandy. They don't really kill anybody."

I hoped that she was right about that.

Loudspeakers crackled and the high priest's voice proclaimed, "The Owl is in his leafy temple. Let all within the Grove be reverent before him." He moved some stuff on the altar and then said, "Oh, great Bohemian Owl, grant us thy counsel!"

At that, fire burst up from the feet of the stone owl.

The priest came down a stone stairway from the altar and then proclaimed, "Shake off your sorrows with the city's dust and scatter to the winds the cares of life." He turned toward the boat and said, "Our funeral pyre awaits the corpse of Care!" Pointing at the dying man, the priest then ordered, "Throw him into the flames!"

And, then a recorded voice screamed, "Fools! Fools! Wilt thou try to burn me again? Ha! Ha! Ha! Haaa!" Its volume was very loud and echoed from the surrounding hills. It continued, "Fools! When will ye learn that me ye cannot slay? Year after year ye burn me in this Grove, lifting your puny shouts of triumph to the stars. But when again ye turn your feet toward the marketplace, am I not waiting for you, as of old? Fools! Fools! To dream ye conquer Care!"

The four men in red robes removed the dying man from the bow of the boat, carried it to the top of the altar, and threw it into the fire. The priest's voice continued, "Be gone, Oh Care! The flames shall set us free from thy bonds!" Suddenly, the flames burst into a fireball that leapt almost to the height of the stone owl's nose.

The recorded voice of the dying man turned to screams of pain. At the same time, the thirteen metal crosses on the left bank burst into flames, like giant sparklers.

After a brief pause, the flames and sparklers subsided, and the priest's voice proclaimed, "Once again, midsummer sets us free! Eternal flames upon the altar burn!" At that, a loud cheer and applause rose from the all around us. Not wanting to stand out from the crowd, I put two fingers into my mouth and whistled. Simone winced and covered her ears.

As the murmur of the crowd grew into louder conversation and laughter, the strings of spotlights came on again. It was obvious that the show—make that the "ceremony"—had ended.

Simone and I followed the mass of men back toward

the cabin area. Once inside our own little shack, she handed me a glass of wine and asked, "So, what did you think, Sandy?"

The wine was pretty good. Actually, it was better than the ceremony I had just witnessed. "I'd give it three stars out of five, maybe like a B-rated movie script from the 1950s."

She laughed. "Some people really get off on it, especially those who embrace the Bohemian Club as a satanic cult. They're the ones who attend naked or who dress in Druidic costumes."

"So why did they burn the effigy?" I asked.

"Have you seen the Grove's Great Seal?"

"No, not yet."

"It is a statue of Moloch and around it are the words 'Weaving Spiders Come Not Here.'"

"So, what's that mean?"

"It's from Shakespeare, Sandy. Being in cinema, I thought you'd have known that."

"I do kung fu movies, Simone. I'm not too educated in real theater stuff."

"What it means is that people who come here are supposed to leave all their cares and worries about work at the gate when they enter the Grove. They're supposed to have a good time here and to learn new things and make new friends."

"Gotcha!" I replied. "Now it makes sense." I wished that Mona was here with me, because she is better at literature than I am. When it comes down to it, I'd rather go see a Rambo movie than go to a play or a concert. I guess that I'm just not too cultured, but then not everybody is cut out for the highbrow stuff. While other guys eat quiche, I eat my eggs over easy. Besides that, I'm cute, and as Mona says, cuteness counts for something.

Chapter 4

The doorbell rang. Looking through the peephole, Mona saw that her visitor had arrived. When she opened the door, a long, thin arm reached out to grasp her hand with its three suction-cupped fingers. She gently shook his hand, looked into the gray's friendly eyes, and heard him tell her, "My name is Fred."

"Come in, please, Fred," Mona said. "Would you care for something to eat or drink?"

"Strawberry ice cream?" he asked.

"Yes, of course." Mona knew that strawberry ice cream was a favorite of the Reticulan grays. It was also Stella's favorite. She went to the kitchen and prepared the snack for her guest.

When she handed Fred a small dish of ice cream, he asked her, "Where is the female child?"

"Stella is napping. You've picked an excellent time to drop in."

"Then let us begin," Fred replied, putting a spoonful of ice cream into his small mouth.

"Begin what?"

"Your first lesson."

"But shouldn't we discuss…"

"It is best to experience and then discuss."

Fred placed his bowl of ice cream on the coffee table and motioned for Mona to sit in a comfortable position on her carpet, using the front face of the sofa to support her back. He sat facing her on the floor, his legs in the lotus position. "We will begin by focusing upon our breathing," he told her. "Have you watched your Stella breathe as she is playing? Have you seen that she breathes with her belly and not her chest?"

"I guess I have. I never really paid attention to it until now."

"By nature, children breathe with their bellies until we culturally teach them to flatten their bellies and breathe with their chests. Breathing with the chest causes shallow breathing, stripping the container of the oxygen that is so vital to its health. It lends the body toward stress response. On the other hand, belly breathing gives life to the container and brings it peace. You cannot be successful at remote viewing unless you rid your container of stress and it is at peace."

"By belly, do you mean diaphragm?"

Fred extended his left hand and touched Mona's diaphragm with the backs of his knuckles. "Yes. Breathing with the diaphragm lends the container to relaxation response. You must learn to breathe with your diaphragm."

Mona found it contradictory to normal to breathe with her diaphragm. In general, people don't want their bellies protruding because it flies in the face of preferred body shapes. But, she followed Fred's instruction and practiced belly breathing for ten minutes. When he asked her if she felt relaxed, she admitted that she had almost fallen asleep, twice.

"See," Fred told her, "care is leaving your body. When you remote view, you must be absent of care." He extended his arms, palms facing upward. "Place your hands on mine," he told her, "palms facing downward. Focus upon your male. Where is he and what is he doing?"

Mona did as Fred directed. As her palms touched his, she could feel a slight tingling and then she began to visualize images in her mind. She saw mountains covered in evergreens and a blue car beside an old clapboard cabin. Then she saw an owl launch itself from a tall tree on a mountaintop, fly over the cabin's roof, and descend directly at her with its talons extended. "Oh!" Mona cried, pulling her hands back from Fred's.

"I saw it, too," Fred told her calmly. "Does it have meaning for you?"

"No," Mona replied. "Not yet."

"Is your male in the mountains?"

"I'm not sure. He's in northern California."

"When I have gone, write down what you remember. When you speak with him again, ask your male the meaning of these things that you saw." Mona nodded at Fred. "You have now experienced assisted remote viewing. Do you wish to continue your lessons?"

"Yes. I'd like to learn more about it. Is it always so vivid?"

"For humans, working unassisted, you tend to see shapes and forms, hear sounds, and obtain scents. Such detailed experiences are rare. But when you practice assisted remote viewing, vivid, detailed experiences are commonplace."

"When do I start?" Mona asked.

"You have already begun. Practice belly breathing three times per day. It must become more natural to you. Your hybrid baby may be with you when you practice. Your group classes are held in the recreation center twice per week, Tuesdays and Thursdays at nine a.m. and then again at noon."

"May I bring Stella?"

"Daycare is available for you at the center during class times. It will be good for her to interact with other hybrids, and it will be good for you to interact with other humans who are learning to view things remotely."

When Fred left, Mona jotted down the images she had seen while touching Fred's palms. She wondered if Danny would know what they meant. The owl diving at her was particularly perplexing. She couldn't wait for him to call.

Stella was stirring, so Mona quickly changed clothes and then entered Stella's room to greet her.

"Mommy!" Stella exclaimed when she saw Mona at the door. It was still strange to Mona that so young a child should already be speaking.

"Are you ready to go play with Rachelle? She's expecting you soon," Mona said. Stella nodded. "Before we go, you need to get into your play clothes, brush your teeth, and comb your hair."

Mona lifted Stella from her crib, kissed her three times, and placed her on the floor. Stella rolled onto her knees and pushed herself to her feet. Then, she walked unsteadily to her dresser and pulled open the bottom drawer. She looked for a moment and then pulled out a pair of light blue pants and a white tee shirt with a sunflower printed on its chest. "These!" she told Mona.

Mona noted that Stella had never crawled but had simply begun walking. And now, she was making choices on her own. How long would it be before Stella didn't want to wear something that Mona wanted her to wear? Mona could remember arguments with her own mother over such things when she was in elementary school.

Such thoughts caused her to dread, at least a little, similar possibilities in the very near future.

Mona opened the top drawer and pulled out a set of big girl underwear and white socks that were appropriate for blue slacks. She handed them to Stella and asked, "Want help?"

Stella nodded. She was already out of diapers and using the potty on her own, but she still lacked the coordination to put on her own socks or to tie her own shoes. But it wouldn't be long before these skills would be no big deal.

Hybrids do develop quickly, Mona thought.

Chapter 5

When I woke up at eight o'clock, the sun was beaming through the Grove's canopy of leaves, casting a golden light into the windows of our cabin. Simone was already in the shower, so I went outside and emptied my tanks into the bushes again. As I was standing there, two guys smiled and waved as they walked by in jogging outfits. Other than Simone and maybe a couple of other possibly transgender females, the Grove was full of men, so I guess my watering the plants was no big deal.

Back inside the shack, I re-checked the schedule of events and saw that Dr. Harold Flite's presentation on his migration process was scheduled for ten o'clock at the East Fork Amphitheater. It looked like a fifteen-minute walk from the food court, so I planned to catch a quick shower and then go get some coffee before heading to hear His Excellency, as the reptilians called him.

When Simone came out of the bathroom, she was fully dressed, which was better than the first time we met. She was wearing a tight-fitting long-sleeved tee shirt which exposed the fact that she had wrapped an Ace bandage around her chest to flatten the natural bulge of her breasts. But when she put on her dark blue blazer, her disguise hid her gender pretty well. She told me that she had scheduled a breakfast meeting with one of Dr. Flite's staff this morning, so I wished her good luck on her quest to purchase the Hollywood migration franchise.

After she left, I took a shower and then called Mona. I had forgotten that it was going on noon Back East, so she only had a few minutes to chat before she took Stella for lunch and a play date with another little hybrid, the daughter of a military family that lived about six doors down from us at Villagio Ibrido. The father had been deployed to Afghanistan again—his third trip in five years—so the mother, a woman of Cuban extraction named Milagros, was struggling to meet all her daughter's needs by herself. From my own experience, I knew that was a monumental task, especially since hybrid kids grow up so fast, both physically and intellectually.

Millie, as her friends called her, and Mona both had experienced being abducted and impregnated artificially, and then suddenly being without a child in the womb. In Millie's case, she was abducted a third time, during which she was introduced to her child and told that she would be taking her back home. When she woke up in her own bed after what seemed like a weird dream, her baby was lying beside her. That morning, Black Ops came to her home and told her that she was being relocated to the Villagio. She had no choice. Her husband was brought to her in the Villagio at the end of his second deployment to Afghanistan. At the time, he didn't know that she had been pregnant for a brief period of time or that he was a father. Or that his daughter had the eyes of a reptilian.

I told Mona that I might be delayed getting home by a couple of days. "That's no surprise, Danny," she said.

"Every time we get involved with something Mack has going on, we wind up being gone for much longer than anticipated. Just keep in touch, and I'll see you in a couple of weeks."

"Give my love to Stella," I replied. "I miss you both."

"Gotta go, Danny. Call me when you can."

Mona hung up abruptly. I'm never sure what drives her to do things like that, but I'm never jealous or suspicious. I just figure that something's out of her control and if she doesn't take care of whatever it is, she'll have a mess on her hands.

So I shut the door to the shack and walked to the amphitheater. I was a little early, but the crowd was already beginning to form. There was sitting room for maybe four hundred people and standing room for another two or three hundred around the perimeter. The seats were already two-thirds full. It looked to me that Dr. Flite was going to draw a big crowd.

I found a seat near the rear of the amphitheater. A few minutes later, Simone sat beside me. "You don't mind, do you?" she asked. Her face was beaming, so I knew that she had something to tell me.

"I was saving this seat for you," I lied. "You're beaming like a Cheshire cat, so I guess things went well with Dr. Flite's associate?"

"Better than I had hoped. Dr. Flite joined us about fifteen minutes into our meeting. He is very interested in establishing a Hollywood franchise, and since I'm the first person to approach him about it, he's giving me the right to first refusal."

"Why would you refuse?"

"I'm guessing he's going to want a large outlay of cash so we can construct a world-class facility."

"Is that going to be a problem?"

"I may not have enough. We'll see what he expects when he meets with me on Wednesday in Hollywood."

"I'm sure you'll be able to pull it all together."

"Well, I may need to bring in a partner. Someone with some ready cash."

I nodded. "Yeah."

"Would you be interested, Sandy? It probably wouldn't be more than a few million."

I swallowed hard at the thought of it and then continued to lie. "Sure. If you need it, I think I can shake a few million loose, but no more than ten until after my next film is released in December."

She squeezed my arm affectionately. "Then I guess we're partners!" she whispered with a smile.

"Can I come to the meeting with Dr. Flite on Wednesday?" I asked. "I need to be in Hollywood on Tuesday, anyway, and you can introduce me as an associate, so he doesn't realize that we're business partners."

Two obese guys worked their way through the row of seats and sat down beside Simone. "Sorry, fella," the one closest to Simone said as his body mass pushed against her shoulder, causing her to scoot an inch or two closer to me. "I'm Angelo from Brooklyn."

I reached over and shook his hand. "I'm Sandy and this is Simon. We're both from around LA."

Simone twisted her body awkwardly to shake Angelo's hand. "Oh, I remember you!" she said. "You were at the Links meeting last month. In Manhattan."

"Yeah, we were," Angelo replied, "me and Tony."

Simone and I took turns shaking Tony's hand. Then it struck me. I had seen these two guys on an episode of *Mob Wives*. Yeah, it's something that glues Mona to the television. And, I'm either sitting with her or I'm out in another room. Frankly, it's easier to be with her than to hear her complain later that I never want to spend time with her, even if all we're doing together is watching a show about a bunch of arguing women. It's a girl thing, and I love Mona, so I sit there and hold her hand, even though I'd rather change the channel. You know what I mean.

A crackling sound from the loudspeakers let us know that the presentation was about to begin. The entire crowd turned its attention toward the podium. "What's the Links?" I whispered into Simone's ear.

"Officially, it's a social club in Manhattan. It's something like the Bohemian Club, except that it's more formal and it's indoors," she told me. "Its members include people from business, military, politics, entertainment, and education. They have monthly social events and educational programs. Members are not supposed to discuss business inside the club building, but everyone does. About ten percent of the members attend the Bilderberg's every year."

I nodded. I already knew about the Bilderberg Group. They supposedly decided what countries would go to war, and when, and what leaders would be assassinated and who would replace them. They were all about brokering power and money-making. They were the original covert world governing organization until the New World Order came along and made them look like a bunch of junior leaguers. With alien allies and alien technology at their fingertips, the NWO immediately seized power and put the Bilderbergers into the back seat. In fact, a few of the most influential Bilderbergers joined forces with the NWO to maintain positions of power in the event that it is successful in achieving ultimate world domination.

The moderator welcomed everyone and then introduced Dr. Flite. Flite was tan-skinned and probably too young in appearance to be old enough to have graduated from medical school. As he adjusted the microphone, I noticed that standing on each side of the dais was a tall man dressed in a hooded monk's robe. One scanned the crowd and, as his head turned, I realized that both men were bodyguards and that they actually were Draconian guards. Either nobody else in the crowd seemed to notice, or nobody cared.

"Good morning," Dr. Flite began. "I am happy to be here with you this morning representing the New World Order." The crowd broke into a round of applause. "How many of you are already in the migration queue?" About twenty hands rose into the air. "Good," he said. "Would you all mind standing so that the others here can recognize you in case they have additional questions about our processes." The twenty people rose to their feet, one about five yards to Simone's left. "Thank you."

The twenty sat back down.

"What I am here to discuss today is an alien technology, given to us by our brothers from the Draconian system, and perfected by NWO scientists over the past ten years so that it is perfectly harmless to the human essence." Flite cleared his throat. "For those of you who are new to the distinction between the essence and the body, let me explain that our bodies are only containers. Our true selves—our personalities, our memories, our knowledge, and even our souls—are a form of electrical energy that inhabits our containers. When our containers age, our true essence leaves the body—traditionally what we call death—and, as our eastern friends have known for centuries, our true essence inhabits a new body, or container. The eastern philosophies call it 'reincarnation.' We call it 'migration.' I like to think of migration as a form of controlled reincarnation."

A man wielding a metal cross in his right hand leaped from the front row and raised the cross as if the strike Flite with it. "This is blasphemy!" he screamed as he rushed the dais. Flite stepped backward from the podium. As he did, the Draconian guard to the left side of the podium sent a volley of plasma from his helmet, severing the dissident in half. Droplets of blood and small pieces of meat peppered the crowd in the front two rows. The peak of the Draconian's cloth hood, which had covered his forehead, burst into flames. He patted it out with his huge right hand. It was obvious, now, to everyone that he was a Draconian, especially since his helmet was now visible and the hand that had put out his hood was green, scaly, and bore three claws.

As Dr. Flite returned to the podium, several ushers put a tarp over the body parts that lay smoldering on the ground in front of the first row. "I apologize for the interruption. My bodyguards have little tolerance for those who threaten my safety." He opened a clear plastic bottle and took a sip of water. Then he began again. "I refer to migration as controlled reincarnation because during regular reincarnation your true essence leaves one container and then enters the first available container that it finds. There is no discrimination as to the new container it inhabits. And, in the process, most memory of the previous life and previous container is erased from consciousness. Thus, education must begin anew. Under controlled reincarnation, or migration, we select the best possible container for the true essence to inhabit, and then we control the process of exiting one container and entering the other container. During our process, no memories of the previous life or container are lost. Hence, life simply continues in the new container with no need for re-education. Thanks to advances of our Draconian friends, we also are able to manipulate DNA such that intelligence, physical characteristics, and good health can be ensured, especially if we grow the new container ourselves, a process which takes a brief eighteen months from a single cell to a mature adult container." A round of applause erupted again from the crowd.

Simone leaned toward me and said, "Dr. Flight is building my potential customer list as he speaks. Already, you can hear murmurs of excitement going through the crowd!"

"So, what about Wednesday?" I asked her again. "Can I join you?"

"Yes, Sandy. I think it'll be all right. But it'll be necessary for you to remain as a silent partner."

"Just like in the movie business," I replied.

"Yes, just like in the movies."

Dr. Flite then described in detail the steps in the migration process and instructed that any Bohemian Grove members who wanted to undertake the migration certification examination needed to sign up by noon Monday at a special desk that had been set up outside the Grove Visitor's Office. To me, it sounded like the same medical history exploration that he described in his YouTube video: any hint that an individual had family members with a chronic condition would eliminate that individual from eligibility for migration. The same exclusion went for those with any hint of minority heritage, mental illness, or an entire list of undesirable conditions or genetics. It was Mein Kompf all over again.

When he completed the migration portion of the presentation, Dr. Flite began speaking about the need for all governments and elite organizations to support United Nations Agenda 21. He spoke about global climate change as a threat to all mankind, including in his list of evidence, including the encroachment of the deserts, the lack of clean water, and the melting of the polar ice caps and glaciers. In that moment, he sounded like Al Gore championing green footprints. Flite also preached that the salvation of mankind is the purification of humanity. He proclaimed, "Only perfect human specimens should be permitted to live after the coming pandemic and emergence of the NWO as the principal global power."

I wanted to barf at the image that he painted of the value of ethnic cleansing, but the suckers who were listening to him in the amphitheater seemed to be engrossed in what he had to say.

Flite pressed on, saying, "Those who wish to ensure the future of humanity on the planet but who are not perfect must be sterilized." He suggested that a new religion be created, combining the best of humanity's current religions with new concepts "that will be shared with us by our Draconian brothers." He said, "Blessed are those who give up their lives for their brothers by voluntarily dying to save humankind." He proclaimed that "those who elect to die are assured of salvation in the next life, a 4th dimension world of perfection."

This is Hitler at his finest, I thought, *sounding somewhat like a prophet and somewhat like an Imam converting young men into jihadist suicide bombers.* The crowd applauded enthusiastically. I got up and walked out during the cheers. I couldn't wait to meet with Flite on Wednesday in Hollywood.

Chapter 6

Group Remote Viewing was completely different from the private lesson that Fred had given to Mona. The group consisted of seven people, including Mona. Each individual was seated in a learning carrel with high sides which prevented him from seeing what others were doing. To Mona, it was almost as if she were alone. On the desk in front of her was a tablet of unlined paper and a sharpened pencil.

Fred was not the instructor. Instead, an army staff sergeant taught the class. Standing in front so that he could be seen by all, he first led his students through a belly breathing exercise. After five minutes, he simply told them that a target had been assigned for the day's work. Each student was to sit quietly with eyes closed and then to use the pad of paper to draw any shapes that came to mind. If important, students could write words that explained what they saw, heard, or smelled.

From her internet exploration of remote viewing, Mona had learned that viewers sit quietly and wait for their subconscious minds to find the unknown target and begin to send images and impressions into their conscious minds. Some claimed that skilled viewers were able to tap into universal consciousness, a place where time does not exist and where all things happen in the same instant. All knowledge of the past, present, and future is accessible, as if turning a DVD to a specific moment in a movie and watching what happens. When Mona read about this concept, she remembered that Shakespeare had said that the whole world is a stage and that every person is simply an actor. What had he known and how had he discovered it?

When the students went to work, the room became deathly quiet. Mona tried to free her mind from care, but Stella kept creeping into her thoughts. And then so did Danny, especially since she was still very interested in learning the meaning of the owl that dived at her in her vision with Fred.

Eventually, however, Mona felt herself almost drifting into sleep, but not quite. In that state, she saw shapes and images that made no sense. They seemed to flow like puffs of smoke from behind her, around her head and take shape as she watched them drift away from her. Following instructions, she began to draw what she saw. Her lines were squiggly, somewhat parallel. Along the bottom were a few small circles. She wrote the word "wet." When she opened her eyes, Mona thought that her drawings resembled the scribbles made by a monkey. Did they have meaning? *Maybe it's meatballs and spaghetti*, she quietly snickered to herself.

When the staff sergeant called, "Time," Mona dropped her pencil onto the desktop.

The sergeant asked the students to come forward one at a time to display what they had seen during the session. The first man showed three pages with various sized letter Vs. After seeing his drawings, Mona felt that this first group session clearly had been a failure for her. But two others showed that they had drawn squiggly lines similar to Mona's and one had drawn little circles and had written the word "cold." Two students had drawn nothing discernibly similar.

Then the staff sergeant turned on a computer and projected an image onto the whiteboard at the head of the classroom. "Our target for today was the western coast of Wales, near the town of Cardigan," he told them. As the image came into focus, Mona could see that it was a coastline of high craggy bluffs overlooking the vast ocean. Lines of surf touched the narrow sand beach below, where many large rocks lay silently at the foot of the bluffs. "Most of you had direct hits on the environment, but nobody felt where it was on the globe. We'll have to work on that aspect of RV. However, those of you who saw the lines of surf and the rocks and birds were definitely on target." The sergeant's words made Mona feel better about her drawings, but she was unclear about how she had done it. As she was congratulating herself for hitting the surf, rocks, and the term "wet," the sergeant's voice interrupted her thoughts. "Mrs. Arrow, may I see you after class?" he asked. Mona nodded.

The staff sergeant then reviewed various techniques for relaxing the mind and helping the images and sensations to come forward from the unconscious to the conscious. Mona took a few notes as reminders. Once he had urged the class of seven to continue deep breathing and relaxation exercises, he dismissed the students. Mona remained behind.

"Mrs. Arrow," the staff sergeant began.

"Please call me Mona."

"Thank you, Mona. You may call me Bill or, as the guys do, Sarge."

"Sarge, it is," Mona said with a smile.

"Mona, I just wanted to learn more about you. This

is your first visit to our remote viewing course, but obviously you have been engaged in remote viewing for a while. I would say that you are at level four. Would that be accurate?"

Mona smiled and said, "Thank you, but this is actually my first day of remote viewing. I had never heard of it until five days ago. I've had one assisted session with Fred, and that's it."

"Fred?"

"Yes. Fred, the Reticulan gray. You know Fred, don't you?"

"No, I don't know anybody named Fred. You say that he's a Reticulan?"

"Yes. He's about four feet tall and looks like he weighs no more than sixty pounds. He's the one who gave me my first lesson, and he's the one who told me about these group sessions."

The staff sergeant shook his head. "What did he do during this assisted session?"

"He taught me about belly breathing and he placed his hands beneath mine to give me my first remote viewing experience." Mona showed Sarge how she and Fred had touched hands. "But he told me that assisted remote viewing would be different from what I would experience here, and he was right about that."

"What do you mean by different?"

"When our hands were touching, I saw vivid images, as though I were actually there. I saw mountains, a blue car, a wooden cabin, and an owl that dived at me. It was all very real. But today, I'm not sure I saw anything other than indistinct shapes that formed out of gray fog."

"You're definitely level four, Mona. It took me almost a year to get to level four, and here you are a beginner and you were at the top of the class today." Mona smiled in pride, still unclear about what she had achieved.

"By the way," he continued, "I've never heard of assisted remote viewing. Maybe it's some new development in the practice." The sergeant rubbed the back of his neck with his right hand. "I don't suppose that you'd introduce me to Fred sometime, would you?"

"I've met him only once myself," Mona replied. "If he ever wants to meet with me again, I'll ask him if I can invite you to join us, Sarge."

"That would be great, Mona."

Sarge opened the classroom door and walked into the hallway with Mona. "Well, this has been an interesting day," she said. "But I have to get Stella and take her shopping for some new clothes. It seems like my little girl goes through a pair of shoes every couple of weeks."

"Can I meet Stella?" Sarge asked.

"Sure, come on. She's in daycare."

They walked down the hallway to the daycare center and entered. Mona's eyes panned the room until she saw Stella, sitting with two little boys on a cream-colored shag carpet. As she approached the children, a daycare worker took her arm. "They're T-Playing, Mrs. Arrow," she said when Mona turned to look at her. "You should observe her for a little while."

Mona stopped and stepped backward. Sarge joined her. "Is everything okay?" he asked.

"Is this Mr. Arrow?" the daycare lady asked.

"No, this is Sarge," Mona replied. "He's teaching a course here. He came to meet Stella."

"Staff Sergeant William Molandowski," Sarge said, taking the lady's hand.

"Mrs. Arrow, Stella is T-Playing with the two boys. Is this the first time she's done it?"

"T-playing?" Mona asked.

"It stands for 'telepathic interplay.' Many hybrids can do it. Some can't. This is the first time we've seen

Stella doing it. Usually this skill develops around age two. Stella is way ahead of the curve."

"She seems ahead of the curve on so many things," Mona replied. "I was hoping that she wouldn't grow up too fast. I want her to enjoy her childhood."

"She is enjoying her childhood, Mrs. Arrow. But her enjoyment comes from learning and expanding her intellectual capabilities. See how she's interacting with the boys?"

Mona and Sarge watched as Stella and the two boys exchanged toys and played together without saying a word. When Stella looked up and saw Mona, both boys instantaneously did the same.

"When Stella saw you, she told the boys that you were her mom," the lady told her. "That's when they both looked up."

"Can you hear what they are saying to each other telepathically?" Sarge asked.

"No. I've just worked with enough hybrid children to know what's going on when I see it. I'm just a pure human, the way you are, stuck with our five basic senses."

The daycare lady hurried over to the other side of the room to pull two quarreling students apart. As she did, Stella stood up, said goodbye to her two news friends, and walked over the Mona, plopping to her bottom and getting back up once along the way. When she reached her mom, Mona hoisted her into her arms and asked, "Did you have a nice time today, sweetheart?" Stella nodded and pointed to the two boys, who were still playing on the carpeted area. "Are those your new friends?"

"Yes, Mommy."

"I'd like you to meet my new friend, honey." She turned Stella toward Sarge and said, "This is Sergeant Mo."

Stella just stared at Sarge, as though she was exploring him, first externally and then internally. Then her eyes blinked from the sides.

Sarge extended his hand and said, "It's a pleasure to meet you Miss Stella."

"Go ahead, honey. It's okay. Say hi to Sergeant Mo," Mona coaxed.

Stella extended her hand and touched Sarge's. "Oh," he said.

"What happened?" Mona asked.

"She doesn't trust me," Sarge replied. "I'm not her father."

"How do you know what she's feeling?"

"She just told me so. When she touched my hand, I heard it in my head as clearly as if she had said it aloud to me."

"So, she was T-Playing with you."

"I wouldn't call it playing, Mona. She doesn't trust me because I'm a strange man and I'm with her mother. She warned me to stay away."

"Sorry, Sarge. She'll learn to accept you after a while."

He took a step backward from Mona. "So, I'm hoping I'll see you in class next time?"

"Sure thing, Sarge. I have a lot to learn. I'll do the belly breathing and keep practicing how to focus upon targets until then."

"Good. I'll look forward to seeing what you can do with our next target." He turned to Stella. "Bye, little lady. Keep up the good work." Then Sergeant Mo headed out of the daycare center.

Mona touched Stella's nose with her index finger. "Good girl. Never trust a man you don't know."

She said goodbye to the daycare lady and then drove Stella home. It had been a good day, not only for Stella, whose hybrid communication skills were certainly developing, but also for herself. Knowing that Stella could now use telepathic interplay, Mona felt that it was important that she, too, develop her own skills so that Stella would not see her mom as too much of an intellectual blockhead—although Mona knew from simple observation that Stella's intellect far surpassed her own. And Danny's.

Chapter 7

I left Simone at Dr. Flite's presentation and walked back to the shack that I was sharing with her. I got into my Tesla and drove to the main gate of the Bohemian Grove, where I told the guard that I needed some medicine and that I would be back in about an hour. He gave me a re-entry pass and told me to enjoy my drive. As I exited the gate, a bunch of protesters shouted at me and waved signs that screamed *Down with the Elite* and *Fuck the Bohemians*. One even had a drawing of the Grove owl with the no-smoking circle superimposed over it. I flipped them off and drove through them, thinking that anything I could do to piss people off about the Bohemians was probably a good thing.

When I found a small picnic area at an overlook, I pulled off the road and shut my engine. It was time to call Mack. "What's new in Washington?" I asked.

"Are you back already?" he asked. "I thought you'd be gone for at least five days."

"No, I'm still out having fun in the warm California sun," I replied. "I just finished listening the His Excellency's presentation."

"So what do you think?"

"It's him. At least this guy Flite seems to be pushing the Nazi agenda. He's into migration, but only for people who have no black marks on their family tree."

"Do you mean no Africans?"

"Yeah, but also no minorities of any type, and no history of mental illness or deformity in the family. He's a whack-o, but the people attending this conference seem to dig what he has to say."

"They're Hollywood types, Dan. They don't ever think about repercussions. It's all image."

"Yeah," I replied. "So, you didn't answer my question. What's new in Washington?"

"I'm not in Washington. I'm in Astana. We've just finished dinner."

"No shit! What are you doing there?"

"NWO meeting. I'm representing the president."

"Can you talk?"

"Yeah. I've got maybe five minutes." Mack took a long breath and then said, "Let me quickly brief you on what I've learned."

"Shoot!" I replied.

"Have you heard the speakers or anyone at the Bohemian Grove use the term 'the Hive'? It's what this meeting in Astana is all about."

"No, not yet. But I've got a couple of days yet. I'm also staying over a few days."

"You'll have to tell me about that later. Any extra days are going to cost me money."

"Yeah, but it'll be worth it."

"Sure. Now listen, remember the term 'the Hive,' okay?"

I felt like I was a third grader being lectured to by his mother. "Yeah, you already told me."

"It all started at Duke University," Mack said, "where researchers created the first organic computer by connecting the brains of several rats and chimpanzees together."

"Rat brains joined to rat brains, or rat brains and chimp brains joined together?" I asked.

"Rats and chimpanzees all connected together. They were all alive and their brains were linked, creating greater intelligence and computational power than any single brain in any individual experimental animal."

"No shit?"

"It gets better. Go now to the University of Washington where researchers first linked human brains together. Using electroencephalographs and transcranial magnetic stimulation, they actually had subjects communicating telepathically over a distance of two miles."

"Did they connect the human brains like they did with the rats at Duke?"

"No, US scientists can't experiment on human subjects like that. It's against the law," Mack replied.

"So they did they do it outside of the US or did they do it underground?"

"I'm getting there. The University of Washington experiment showed that humans can communicate over long distance with just their brains, if the brains are enhanced by technology. They call that MMI, or mind-machine interface."

I nodded my head. Mack was using some ten-penny words, but I was still following him.

"Now let me take you to Switzerland, where their Institute of Technology has developed a method of storing data in silicon. The kicker is that they use DNA molecules! They store the data in DNA molecules that they embed in silica—you know, like, in glass!"

"I don't get the significance," I told him.

"So, Dan, how long can we store data on a computer disk?"

"I don't know. Maybe two hundred years?"

"Try only fifty! But we can store DNA molecules in glass for a million years! And we can use the four nucleotides of DNA, the A, C, T, and G, to make programming simpler than the ones and zeros of our current computer programming"

"Now you're getting way beyond me, and I still don't get the connection, Mack."

"So, consider this: both of the research labs in the US are conducting experiments in linking brains. In Switzerland, they're using alien technology to upgrade the chips that they implant in human brains from simple locator devices to computer communication devices. And each of the projects is fully funded by the NWO!"

"So, what you're telling me is that those bastards are developing communication devices that will let their NWO troops communicate with each other by telepathy. If so, their commanders will be able to instantly send orders to their troops on the battlefield and make instantaneous mass troop movements. That will definitely increase their capability of winning almost any battle!"

"Oh, it's worse than that, Dan. The NWO has launched plans to implant every selected human with a wireless chip that links all of their brains together, harnessing their collective knowledge and intelligence to solve the greatest problems faced by mankind. At least that's how they're selling the concept."

"Actually, that doesn't sound like too bad of an idea, Mack. Think how we might find cures to cancer and other diseases if we could link all of the brains of the best research scientists and focus them on solving the problem."

"They won't be selecting the best research scientists.

Think about the migration process that Hitler has been marketing across the globe. He's continuing his efforts to create a pure Aryan race. He'll put silicon-based computer control chips into the brains of all the new containers before he migrates people into them. Because they're silicon-based, they won't set off metal detectors and will be difficult to find, except maybe by ultrasound devices."

"Did they tell you this at your NWO meeting?"

"Not directly. They said that the purpose of the chip is to keep track of the new container, so that if anything goes wrong with it, migration into an alternate can occur immediately. But, I'm pretty sure that they also plan to create an army of robots who will, like a hive of ants and bees, do whatever is necessary to protect the hive, even in the face of imminent death to the individual."

"Did they update you about anything else?" I asked.

"Yeah, and it's all connected. They also have been experimenting with control software, sending lone gunmen to kill innocent people and then to commit suicide. Their biggest success has been using random religious radicals who blow themselves up in public places. People always wonder why someone would do that. Well, nobody would do that unless a computer chip that was embedded in their brain told them to do it. Almost all the mass killings have been an experiment—an NWO software beta test! The controls appear to be working well, and nobody has connected the rash of bombings and killings to anything other than lone gunmen and religious martyrs."

"Shit, Mack," I said. "I don't even want to think about it, but it all makes sense, doesn't it? Our press and our leaders point their fingers at the lone-wolf gunmen and the religious radicals, but they never pin the blame at anything other than loonies and religion, when the real root cause is the NWO!"

"That's how I see it, Dan. They'll give people excellent reasons to be migrated into new containers—you know, age, health, beauty, strength. And simultaneously, they'll secretly create a hive of worker bees who will do anything they want. It's a real life zombie apocalypse!"

Mack and I agreed that he would come to Villagio Ibrido for a weekend once we both got back on the East Coast. It would give us a chance to relax and to fully debrief each other about what we had learned. I asked Mack to invite Waam to come, too. Between the three of us, and Mona, too, maybe we could develop a strategy to destroy the Hive before the NWO used it to do anything bad.

Once we hung up, I called Mona. It was about two-thirty p.m. in Virginia, so I knew I wouldn't catch her sleeping. After the usual greetings, I asked her, "Hey, whatcha been doing while I've been gone?"

"It's neat stuff, Danny. It's called Remote Viewing." She told me about meeting Fred the gray alien and how he had helped her to have visions. *Great*, I thought, *don't they put people who "see things" into the looney bin?* Then she told me that while Remote Viewing she had seen mountains and a blue car. "Does that mean anything to you?" she asked.

"Well, this retreat is in the mountains, and Mack let me lease a blue Tesla."

"See! It *is* true, Danny. Through assisted Remote Viewing I can see where you are and what you're doing!"

"Slow down, baby. Those are just coincidences."

"No, they're real. But there's more. I also saw a large owl fly down from the mountains and dive at my head like he was trying to hurt me. Does that mean anything to you?"

"Well, there is a giant statue of an owl here, but it isn't going to fly. It's solid granite."

"See!" she squealed. "Promise me something, Danny. Please, promise me!"

"Okay, okay, what is it?"

"Keep your eyes on the sky. Don't let that owl fly down and hurt you."

"It can't fly, Mona. It's a forty-ton rock."

"Well, don't walk near it. It might fall over on you!"

"Okay, I promise that I won't walk near it!"

Mona can sometimes take things too literally, but I got the drift of what she was saying. The Bohemian Grove could somehow jump up and bite me, maybe not the Grove itself, but those who are members, or somebody else who is here. You know what I mean. It was like Caesar's wife warning him about a dream she had. Even though I don't believe too much in things like psychics and mind readers, I figured that it would be smart to pay attention to what Mona had to say about what she had seen. Just in case.

Chapter 8

After a couple of more days of Bohemian grooving, I said goodbye to the nuts who camp out there for the full two weeks and drove my Tesla back through Monterey and down the coastal highway to Big Sur and then on to Los Angeles. Along the way, I stopped to look at elephant seals that were basking in the sun on the beaches, and I realized how much Mona would have enjoyed the trip. It was her kind of place, except maybe for the lack of barriers that would keep you from falling over the cliff into the cold waters of the Pacific if you took your eyes off the road.

It was Tuesday, and I had an appointment in Hollywood with Simone and His Excellency der Fuehrer on Wednesday at ten a.m. Simone had left the Grove on Monday in order to prepare her facility and staff for Dr. Flite's visit. She was both excited and nervous about the opportunity of owning a migration studio in Hollywood, the only one scheduled for California and one of only two to be franchised on the west coast.

When I hit LA, I stopped at a street corner in the porn flick district and asked a hooker where I could buy a gun. She looked disappointed that I didn't want to party, but I offered her a Benjamin Franklin if she'd connect me with the right person. "Be back here in twenty minutes, John," she told me. "Be any later and he be gone." I nodded and drove away. She'd be easy to remember, a tall red head in a leopard skin dress. Her Adam's apple gave away her gender, but I didn't let on that I knew.

About a mile down the road, I stopped at a Taco Bell and used the john. A quick burrito later, I was back in the Tesla. I pulled to a stop at the same corner where I had spoken with sweet cheeks. I was two minutes early, but she was waiting for me. "He say go around the corner and park behind a pink Econoline. He be with you shortly." I blew her a kiss and followed her directions.

The pink Econoline was easy to find. I mean, how many are painted any color other than white? I pulled to a stop but left ten feet between my Tesla and the rear end of the pink flower truck. Just in case I needed to make a quick exit, I left my ignition in the "on" position, but the Tesla's electric motor made absolutely no noise. Two Mexicans got out of the van and approached me, one on each side of my car. "Are you the dude looking for flowers?" the one on my side asked.

"Yeah. I want a semiautomatic in nine-millimeter, and maybe a bouquet of lilies for the widow."

He smiled. "Nice ride," he said, rubbing his hand along the side of the Tesla. "Yours?"

"Naw, I just rented it," I replied. "You got the lilies that I want in the right caliber?"

"Nickel or blue?"

"Blue."

"With a fully loaded clip, it'll cost you five hundred dollars."

"That's retail for a used semi," I replied. "You can do better than that, can't you?"

"It'll cost five hundred twenty-five with the lilies."

I opened my wallet and emptied three Franklins into his hand. "You'll get the other two when I get the gun," I told him.

"That's what I like," he said, "a man who knows how to do business." He walked to the back of the Econoline, opened the rear door, and was back in about a minute with a bouquet of carnations. "Inside the wrapper is what you're looking for."

I tilted the bouquet toward the floor mat and a new looking Sig Sauer 9mm fell into my left hand. Keeping my business in my lap, I popped the clip and saw that it was full. The primers had not been fired, so the bullets looked good. I slapped the clip back into the grip, pulled back the slide, and sent a bullet into the chamber. "Looks good," I said, and I handed him the $200 I owed him.

"That will be another $100 for shipping," the guy told me.

I pointed the new pistol at his partner, who was still standing to my right. "Leave your weapon in your belt," I said to him, "and come over to this side of my car." He put his palms up and quickly walked around the front of my car to join his partner. "Now look," I said when they were standing together, "you got twice as much as you should have for this piece. I'm okay with that, but you aren't getting another fucking dime. Shipping is free." They just stared at me. "Now back off," I ordered, flicking the Sig at them.

As they started backing up, the guy who sold me the Sig dropped his right hand and pulled a pocket pistol out of his rear pants pocket. But before he could point it at me, I pulled the trigger on my new acquisition. It was a lucky shot, or else it surprised him, because he fell backward and his little semiautomatic bounced about ten feet down the street. I didn't wait for him to get up. I just pointed my pistol at his partner, who dived to the ground as I hit the accelerator on the Tesla. Four seconds later I was two blocks away, doing sixty in a thirty-mile-per-hour zone. I made a left hand turn and slowed to thirty-five. I didn't need to draw any more attention than a Tesla already would in this neighborhood. In a Tesla, everyone would think that I was either a pimp or a rich guy looking for some coke.

I found my way back to Highway 101 and headed north. It was a three-minute drive to the Vine Street exit. I dropped south on Vine until I saw the marquis of the Redbury Hotel. It looked expensive, but my room was being paid for by credit card, so I pulled in. Knowing Mack, I couldn't be sure if my mission was being underwritten by the FBI or maybe the NWO. Valet parking took my car and a bellhop took my luggage. The tab was $350 per night, plus tax. Hey, but what's money when you're in Hollywood, right?

In my room, I called the airport in San Francisco. I had already missed my return flight to Dulles, and I was informed that there would be no refund. Oh well. So, I booked a ticket on a flight home that was leaving Thursday afternoon. That meant that I would return to the Villagio sometime in the early morning on Friday. I couldn't wait to walk into our bedroom and give Mona a passionate kiss. Of course, with my luck, she would have eaten garlic for dinner.

I also called Mona, just to let her know where I was and when I planned to arrive back home. There wasn't much news, except that her next Remote Viewing class would be on Thursday and that Stella's new skills continued to amaze her.

I couldn't wait to get home to see some of that myself. But Mona had additional information for me. "Listen," she said, "I was playing around with an anagram

program on the internet and discovered something interesting."

"What's that?" I asked.

"Well, the letters in your name can be rearranged to
say, 'warn road,' which sort of describes you, doesn't it?"

"You're so funny, sweetheart."

"Well, the letters in my name can be rearranged to
say, 'woman roar.' You have to admit that that's funny,
especially when I'm mad at you."

I chuckled.

"But the best of all is this one: Harold Flite can be
rearranged to say 'Adolf Hitler'!"

"No shit?" I asked.

"Big shit!" Mona replied. Adolf Hitler is Harold
Flite, the doctor you're going to meet with tomorrow.
That sort of puts everything into a neat package, doesn't
it? Wait until I tell Mack!"

જીજી

I arrived at Simone's place at nine-thirty a.m. and
parked my Tesla beside her red Morgan +4 convertible.
As I stood up on the asphalt, I noticed that her keys were
still in the ignition, and an empty Dunkin Donuts bag was
crumpled on the floor on the passenger's side. I tucked
the Sig into my belt at the small of my back, safety off.
Then I put on my Blazer and walked inside. Simone was
busy talking to two young women when I saw her. "Nice
digs," I said loudly.

She turned abruptly. "Oh, Sandy! Good to see you!
How was your trip back home?"

She wasn't as flat chested as I remembered her being. Maybe it was the tight-fitting pullover top that she
was wearing, or maybe it was the lack of the ace bandage
that she had wrapped around her chest in Monte Rio.

"Great," I replied. "I came down through Big Sur and was welcomed home by a Mexican florist. Did you send the flowers?"

"No, but I should have. Maybe after today's meeting!"

"I brought a bottle of champagne," I replied, holding up a bottle of Armand de Brignac, compliments of Mack's credit card. It cost fifty dollars more than Dom Perignon, so I figured it should be good.

Simone pointed to a young woman. "Margarita will put it in the refrigerator, Sandy."

Margarita took the bottle of brut from me and whisked it away.

"Have you heard from Dr. Flite?" I asked.

"Yes. His staff assistant confirmed our meeting by telephone yesterday afternoon. I expect him shortly."

"Good. I look forward to learning more about the franchise requirements and to how long it will be before we can conduct our first migration."

"Remember, Sandy," she reminded me, "that you are a silent partner. I will be introducing you as an associate, not as a possible partner."

"Yeah, I'm on board with that," I replied. I reminded myself to keep my mouth shut and not to speak unless asked a question by someone. That was going to be tough for me to do, but I already had had some practice in self-restraint when Mona's parents visited us before our move to the Villagio. Believe me, I bit my tongue several times over that weekend, and Mona rewarded me gratefully once they had gone home.

I drifted around the inside of Simone's building while she continued prepping for Dr. Flite's visit. She and her team were make-up specialists, keeping movie and recording stars looking young and unblemished until they had no choice except to undergo plastic surgery.

Most interesting to me was that each of her artists was a subcontractor who was given an individual workspace behind a closed door. I figured that confidentiality was especially important among the Hollywood elite. Simone also had a large undeveloped second floor, maybe four thousand square feet, where I figured that she would hope to locate the migration equipment, the clone growth chambers, and the necessary magnetic storage devices.

At precisely ten a.m., four black H1 Hummers pulled into the parking lot, stopping in a line that was perpendicular to the painted parking spaces and blocking any opportunity for Simone or me to drive away. It was a strategy of intimidation. Two seven-foot-tall lizards climbed out of the back seat of the first Hummer in full combat gear. They opened the door to Simone's salon, looked inside, and then nodded that everything appeared to be okay. Four NWO guards in flak jackets exited the second Hummer and created a saber arch, but instead of raising sabers, they raised AK-47s. From the fourth Hummer, four of those tall dudes with blond hair emerged. Also about seven feet tall, they were dressed in their usual black suits with black fedoras and matching sunglasses. They surrounded the third Hummer in protective fashion. The door closest to the wedding arch opened, and out stepped Dr. Harold Flite and a young female assistant. Flite appeared to be maybe twenty-six years old, but I knew that the true conscious man in that container was over one hundred. Flite's medium brown skin blended well with the Carolina blue jumpsuit and pink sunglasses that he was wearing. His assistant, about his same age, wore a woman's gray pinstriped business suit, and her peroxide blond hair was slicked back with some sort of shiny mousse. Flite had arrived like an international movie star, but his entourage wasn't pulling any punches about how deadly they could be if necessary.

I excused myself from Simone long enough to go to the unisex bathroom and drop my Sig in the toilet tank. No sense being caught with a weapon at this meeting.

When I returned, I saw that Simone had escorted Dr. Flite into a small conference room. Two of the men-in-black and one Draconian guard stood in three corners of the room, while two men-in-black stood just outside of the conference room door.

The second lizard and two of the NWO guards had disappeared from view, but I suspected that they were checking out the entire building. The four vehicles were protected by their drivers and the two remaining NWO guards. Clearly, Flite's safety was of ultimate concern to his team.

After introductions, Flite's assistant began the conversation. "A franchise will cost you a fee of four million up front. You'll need another two million for the migration equipment and one point five million for the computer controlled cloning tanks. We'll throw in the magnetic storage units if you pay cash up front; otherwise, they are another quarter million. We will provide a staff of one doctor and four fully-trained technicians to operate the equipment. The first six weeks are on us. After that, you'll have to pay the doctor twenty-five thousand per month and the technicians ten thousand per month each. Twenty percent of net profit will be paid in cash to the NWO on a quarterly basis. We will send a courier to collect on the first day of each quarter, and we will audit your books on a monthly basis. If you miss one payment, you will forfeit your franchise, and we will license it to someone else. The waiting list is already ten deep." She took a sip of water from the bottle that Simone had provided. "Do you have any questions?"

"Yes. Would you like to see our second floor, where I plan to create the migration salon?" Simone asked.

"We prefer the term 'Rebirth Center,'" Dr. Flite told her. "You will use that term in your literature and advertising,"

"Yes, of course," Simone replied.

"We have already examined your facility," Flite's assistant said, "and we believe that it will be perfect for your first two years of operation. By the third year, we expect that you will be under construction. Our architectural office will forward the plans that you are to use. It will be a facility of one million square feet and will mirror the facility in Astana. Upon receipt of your franchise fee, we will fly you to Astana to see the facility for yourself, and you will see why we insist upon it. We are creating a new world, as you know."

"When can we expect the franchise fee, Mrs. Lopez?" Flite asked.

"I can give you the full franchise fee this morning, if you'd like. I will have to pull the remaining three point five million from several accounts. That may take as many as ten business days. Would that be okay?"

"Yes," Flite said. "My assistant will make arrangements with you for the receipt of that cash. It has been a pleasure doing business with you." He stood up, helped his assistant to her feet, and marched out the front door. His assistant waited in the foyer with a lizard until Simone handed her a briefcase containing four million dollars. The assistant provided her with a signed receipt and a digital photograph of the open briefcase, displaying the banded cash. When Simone's cell phone beeped the receipt of the photo, the assistant climbed into the third Hummer, where Flite was waiting, and the parade left Hollywood. The entire meeting had taken less than fifteen minutes.

"What was Dr. Flite's assistant's name?" I asked.

"I don't know," Simone replied. "He just said, 'This is my assistant,' and I was too nervous to ask."

"When will the equipment arrive? Will they install it? How much power will we need?"

"I don't know. I was too nervous to ask."

Jesus! With Simone at the helm, I figured this place would be belly up before the end of the first year.

"Sandy, I'm going to need three million in cash within the next ten days. Can you deliver?"

"Yeah, sure," I lied. "I'll bring it to you on Tuesday." I was going to be nowhere around Hollywood on Tuesday, so I figured that Simone would be forfeiting her four million sooner than later. Too bad.

I went to the bathroom and retrieved my free-diving Sig semiautomatic. I used paper towels to give it a basic drying, blew droplets of water out of the magazine and barrel, and then I tucked it back into my belt. A trickle of water ran down my butt from the barrel that was resting against the small of my back. It looked like I was going to have to give my Sig a thorough cleaning and lube job. Meanwhile, now that I knew how he traveled, I was going to have to figure out a way to capture Dr. Flite alive, and that was going to be difficult.

Chapter 9

My trip from LA to San Francisco was uneventful. Once I crossed the city line, I used the dashboard computer to find the nearest police department, where I showed my ID and turned in the Sig. It was my lucky day, because the city's annual firearm buy-back program was going on all week, and the desk sergeant handed me twenty-five dollars in exchange for the weapon, no questions asked. I wouldn't call it a fair trade, but I knew I couldn't take a weapon onto an airplane and I didn't want to throw it into a trashcan where some bum or a kid might find it.

I arrived at the airport about ninety minutes before my flight was supposed to board, so there was ample time to return the Tesla. Its battery pack was down to ten percent charge, so I had to pay a refill fee, just as if it had been a gas guzzler. No problem, though, because it all went onto Mack's credit card. Then it was a ten-minute hike through the terminal to check my luggage and then a twenty-minute single-file process at the TSA frisking station before I was cleared to approach Gate G22. Along the way, I stopped at a watering hole to buy a beer, which

I poured into a paper cup so I could drink it in the waiting area. Once all passengers had boarded and we were in the air, I used the remainder of my gun buy-back reward to purchase a couple of scotches, and then I settled in for a four-hour nap. Life can be good sometimes.

It was two in the morning on Friday when I walked in the door at home. Mona was waiting up for me. "You've gotta be beat, Danny," she said as she hugged and kissed me. "Go brush your teeth."

I guess my breath must have been pretty bad, so I climbed the stairs and did as directed. When I came out of the bathroom, Mona was already in her nightgown.

She stopped me from unbuttoning my shirt. "My job," she told me.

She began at the bottom button and worked her way up. Then she pushed my shirt off my shoulders, so it clung to my elbows and restricted my arm motion. Mona kissed my chest and then licked the side of my face as she unbuckled my belt. I could see where this was going, and I didn't mind at all. When we fell onto the bed together, it was pleasure city until she rolled off me in exhaustion and we both drifted into sleep. After a road trip, it's nice to have a small welcome home party because you realize that maybe you've actually been missed.

છબછ

Mack and I had been talking for half an hour before we both felt static electricity lift the hairs on our arms and heads.

"Waam has arrived!" Mack told me.

We went to the back door and peered into my yard. Four areas of grass, flattened by the landing struts, gave away the location of Waam's tureen. Obviously, his cloaking device was on, and the only way anybody would know that a tureen was parked there would be if they accidentally walked into a strut. It was a Saturday morning, and the Villagio's mowing crew wasn't on duty, so that type of incident was unlikely. I just hoped that some kid wouldn't run through my back yard and unexpectedly coldcock himself on an invisible strut, but that was unlikely, too, because, like most of America, the kids in Villagio Ibrido were engaged in structured sports and activities on the weekends. Free-play games like kick-the-can, capture-the-flag, and hide-and-seek were a thing of the distant past.

"There he is," Mack said, pointing to a spot of bright light on the grass. "His boarding ramp is pointing away from your house."

Mack was right about that. From our perspective, nobody could see Waam descending the ramp until he miraculously appeared in the morning sunlight. And who would be looking, anyway?

I had forgotten how tall Waam really is, but watching him stoop over to enter through my back door refreshed my memory quickly.

"Ah, you have vaulted ceilings!" he said with delight once he was inside the door. When he stretched back into standing position, Waam's head was less than a foot from the ceiling, and the only thing he had to worry about was bumping into the ceiling fan which was hanging in the middle of the kitchen. "I love vaulted ceilings!" he reiterated.

"Can I get you something to drink, Waam?" I asked.

"I brought my own," he replied, holding up a gallon-sized aluminum mug. "Want some? It's jybwat juice from Ummo."

"Thanks, Waam, but we have coffee," Mack said.

Waam walked into the living room and sat in the middle of the white leather sofa that Mona had bought before we moved to the Villagio. Mack took a side chair, and I took the recliner.

Waam wasted no time in getting down to business. "I've already discussed the Astana meeting with Mack," he said. "So, how was your trip to California?"

I told him about the goings on at the Bohemian Grove retreat. The large owl interested him. "You know," he remarked, "that many humans who have been abducted don't remember the incident; however, they will often recall having seen an owl someplace. I wouldn't be surprised if the genesis of the owl god wasn't an abduction experience."

I sat quietly for a moment. Sometimes Waam can be too intellectually reflective for me, so I changed the subject. "Mona discovered something interesting while I was in California. Flite's name is an anagram."

"Really?" Mack asked.

"Yeah," the letters in the name Harold Flite can be rearranged to spell…"

"Adolf Hitler!" Waam exclaimed. "I should have realized that the first time I heard the name!"

"Interesting," Mack said. "I wonder why nobody else, especially the media, has discovered this."

"They probably have," Waam replied. "Your media are complicit in pushing the NWO's agenda. Why would they expose Hitler until it is the pre-determined time?"

"You've got a point, Waam" I said. Then I told him about the brief meeting at Simone's in Hollywood. "Back to my trip…I had hoped that I could capture His Excellency Harold Flite after the meeting, but that sort of thinking was really naïve," I told him. "His security was way too tight. Flite travels with a young woman, probably his CFO, and with an entourage of eight armed guards, including two Draconian soldiers. They swept the area before he ever exited the Hummer, which I assume was fully armored. "

"Then we aren't getting to him without a fight and possible casualties," Mack noted.

"Yeah, that's how I see it," I replied.

"We will have better opportunity if we surprise him in unfamiliar territory, somewhere outside of Astana," Waam said.

"Then we may be in luck, gentlemen," Mack replied. "At the meeting in Astana, it was announced that Dr. Flite would be attending the grand opening of the new Rebirth Center in Dubai on Tuesday. It will be the only migration center in the Middle East, and all those oil-rich bastards will want to be first in line for a new container."

Mona's voice interrupted us. "Send in the navy SEALs, Mack. Nobody knows the Middle East like the SEALs."

"Oh, hi, baby," I said. "We didn't hear you come in."

"I parked outside behind Mack." With Stella still in her arms, Mona gave Mack a peck on the cheek and then did the same to Waam. "It's good to see you again, Waam," she said.

"Mona's right, Dan. The SEALs would be a good option," Mack said.

"Can your SEALs plan and carry out an operation in three days?" Waam asked.

"SEALs can do just about anything," Mona replied. It was obvious that she could have been captain of the navy SEALs' cheerleading team.

"I'll have to get Pentagon approval for a mission into friendly territory," Mack said. "The United Arab Emirates isn't exactly ISIS territory, so if we have any collateral damage, there will be hell to pay in the media."

He got up and went outside where, through the front windows, I could see him on the cell phone. His left hand was waving in the air as he spoke, so I knew he was in a heavy discussion.'

While Mack was outside, Mona opened a box of mixed Italian cookies and offered some to Waam and me. "Danny's not the best host," she said to Waam as he took a large handful. "Next time you come, I'll make sure that he cooks you breakfast."

Waam laughed and nodded.

After a few minutes, Mack came back inside. "I'll hear back from Naval Command in a few minutes." When Mack spotted the plate of cookies, he dived in and helped himself.

I guess I should have cooked breakfast. I made a mental note to do that the next time we meet.

We batted around ideas for a few minutes, and then Mack's cell phone rang. This time he didn't go outside, but simply answered it with, "Smith here." He said, "Yup" a couple of times and then finished with, "What time should he be there?…Okay." When he finished with his call, Mack turned to Mona and said, "I'm going to need your boy for a couple of more days. Is that okay with you?"

"Where are you sending him this time?" Mona asked.

"He's going to the Middle East for a capture and re-trieve mission."

"I guess it's okay, as long as he's got a flak jacket and he can carry an AK-Forty-Seven," Mona replied. "He's better when he's been away for a few days."

She winked at me when she said that. I hoped that she didn't mean it as a critique of my bedroom perfor-mance.

Mack looked at Waam and me. "You two have to be in the Middle East by six this evening, East Coast time."

"Where are we going?" I asked.

"You're going to land on the *USS Ponce*. It's a forward operations vessel with a huge, flat, rear deck and it's equipped with the navy's only operational laser weapon system. Waam's going to have to fly you there in his cloaked tureen, or else you'll never make it. There's a big military operation going on right now. It's called the International Mine Countermeasures Exercise, the largest maritime exercise in the world, and it includes international maritime forces from more than thirty nations. They're training together across the Middle East, so it's a great cover for a covert operation into Dubai, where you'll retrieve Dr. Flite from navy SEALs who'll extricate him from his hotel room before dawn on Tuesday morning."

"The day of the grand opening of his Rebirth Center," Waam mused. "He won't be expecting this, and his guard should be down."

"Why are we leaving tonight? It's only Saturday," I complained. "Isn't there a national basketball final on tonight?"

"That was last week, Danny, when you were in California," Mona told me. "Villanova won." I could see whose side she was on.

"It's already Sunday morning in Dubai," Mack reminded me. "You'll have to meet with the SEALs team to brief them about our target and to prep them for the resistance that they'll encounter. I doubt that they have ever encountered lizards with plasma weapons before. We'll need them to be ready and not to be taken by surprise."

Stella wobbled over to me. "Daddy going bye-bye?" she asked.

Mack seemed surprised that she could understand what was going on and that she could already speak in short sentences. Heck, what was the big deal? She was almost seven months old!

"Yes, sweetheart, Daddy is going on a short trip," I said, lifting Stella onto my lap. "I'll be back in a few days, and I'll miss you while I'm away."

Stella hugged me as though I was already going out the door, and then she climbed off my lap and wobbled back toward the dining room where a couple of her toys were waiting for her on the rug.

Mona asked Waam, "What time will you have to leave if you're going to make Dubai by six this evening?"

"I can circle the Garden planet in less than an hour at twenty thousand feet," Waam replied. "I think we should lift off by four-thirty, just in case we encounter unanticipated obstacles."

"Good," Mona replied. "What would you like for an early afternoon dinner?"

"Something Italian," Mack replied.

"I was asking Waam, Mack," Mona said with a snarl and one eye closed. She was kidding, of course.

"Italian is always good," Waam said, "but you Americans don't know how to cook real Italian. How about…"

"Italian it is!" Mona replied before Waam could suggest an alternative. I chuckled at Waam's challenging her to cook a real Italian meal. I think he did that for Mack's sake, because Mack really likes Mona's cooking.

Mona cooked eggplant parmesan and chicken marsala for a midday supper. The main courses were embellished with a medley of olives, a basic Caesar salad, and garlic bread. Mack and Waam were deeply appreciative, Mack belching as a compliment, and Waam telling Mona that her sauce was among the best he had ever tasted. That was good enough for Mona and left her smiling.

Before Waam and I walked out the back door to

board his tureen, Mona packed us eggplant parm sand-wiches. I reminded her that the trip would be less than an hour, and we'd be visiting a US Navy vessel, where the food is usually incredible. Of course, I wasn't sure if Waam would show himself to our nation's finest, so hav-ing access to a snack might be welcomed.

When Waam and I left, Mona stood at the back door, holding Stella in her arms. She showed Stella how to blow a kiss, so Stella blew me two of them as I stood at the base of the ramp into Waam's tureen. I returned her kisses and wished that I could skip this trip to the Middle East. There was no doubt that Stella's awareness and skills were changing every day as she absorbed and learned from everything that she encountered. And Mona was doing an excellent job as her mom. I felt great love for them both.

Inside the tureen, Waam had me sit in the co-pilot's seat, in case he needed my assistance with some small technical issue during the flight. He touched a screen and the ramp closed. He touched another, and I felt slight movement.

We were in the air. Waam told me that he had pre-programmed the coordinates into the tureen's computer, and the computer would actually control the flight until the last few seconds, when Waam would assume manual control.

Within three minutes, we slowed to one thousand miles per hour near Andrews Airforce Base, just east of DC, where the radar operators scrambled three jets to in-tercept us.

Waam smiled as they approached. "Watch how the computer handles their approach."

I watched through the transparent skin of the tureen as the jets gained on us and then suddenly appeared to fall miles behind, as though they had stopped in mid-air. I felt no sensation of acceleration, but Waam told me, "We just jumped to ten thousand miles per hour."

"Why did you do that?" I asked.

"Just teasing them," he said. "I guess it wasn't fair, was it?"

It was a side to Waam that I had never seen. He had a touch of mischief in him. I liked that. He had taken a vow never to harm a human, not even an evil one, but that didn't mean that he couldn't play around with one. I heard once that the Greek and Roman gods played around with mankind. I wondered if Ummites like Waam were the gods of those early civilizations. I made a mental note to ask him about that.

Chapter 10

A t two-forty-five a.m. Dubai time, Waam hovered our tureen over the stern of the *USS Ponce*, while I used his communication system to request permission to land on the ship's helicopter pad. The navy had been expecting our arrival, but not in a tureen.

"When do you anticipate arrival?" the *Ponce*'s radioman asked.

"We are already here," I told him.

Their radar systems had not picked up our arrival, so when Waam uncloaked the tureen, sailors who had been scanning the skies, looking for us with binoculars, suddenly went scrambling in all directions on the rear deck. It was like a scene from *The Day the Earth Stood Still*, except that, when the ramp descended, I walked down it wearing a flak jacket with my hands held high in the air in the surrender posture. Waam closed the hatch and stayed inside.

"I'm Dan Arrow, here representing the FBI," I shouted at the men holding weapons pointed in my direction. "I'm here to meet with the navy SEALs about a special mission."

A young officer held his hand in the air and walked forward. "Who is your commander?" he asked.

"FBI Special Agent Mack Smith set up this mission. I have the particulars on the target and his defenses."

"Follow me, sir. Warrant Officer Harding has been expecting you." I dropped my hands and followed the officer through an iron hatchway and into the narrow corridors of the ship's interior. As we walked, he said, "Sir, I hope you don't mind my asking, but that vehicle that you arrived in…is it US Navy Experimental?"

"No, its old technology, but it's been enhanced with advanced laser technology, like they've done to your ship."

"Never seen anything like it, except in the movies."

"Yeah, I know," I replied. "But it's been in service since before you were born."

"Any chance I can go aboard?"

"Only if its owner gives the okay. Otherwise, go see the new *Star Wars* movie."

"Is it a movie prop?"

I didn't answer him because I had already said too much. Besides, we had arrived at the briefing room. As I entered, the six men who were seated all rose to their feet.

"Dan Arrow," I said.

"Warrant Officer Tom Harding," a buff guy at the far end of the table said. "These are your team leaders, Johnson, Styles, Negron, Baez, and Weinstein."

Weinstein was a female, which surprised me, but in today's armed forces women often played key roles previously held only by men. Years ago, she never would have been permitted aboard a ship because of the disruption that women caused among the men. I could understand that. But as a SEAL, this woman could kill a man six different ways in less than ten seconds.

"I'm glad to meet all of you," I said. "Our target is Dr. Harold Flite. He is to be captured, not injured in any manner, if possible." I showed them a picture that had been published in *Time Magazine* in an article entitled *Body Broker for the New World.*

"Piece of cake. So what's the catch?" the female asked.

"He's wanted for international terrorism. He doesn't look like much, but he runs a covert international operation intent on overthrowing all world governments," I replied. "It's not going to be a piece of cake. You can anticipate resistance the likes of which you have never experienced before."

"So what can we expect?" Tom Harding asked.

"Our intel says that he's staying the night in a three-story hotel in Al Haba, on the outskirts of Dubai. He could be on any floor, but we think that the third floor will be the most likely location, and we think he will have leased the entire floor."

"So, an air assault by choppers might be best approach. We'll rappel to the roof and enter through the usual stairwell."

"You may want to attack from several directions" I proposed, "because it will disperse his bodyguards and small military entourage."

"Al Qaeda?" the female asked.

"New World Order, men-in-black, and lizards," I told them.

"You're shitting me, man," Harding replied. "You've been watching too many sci-fi movies. What kind of make-believe operation is this? Who sent you here to put us on?"

"Request permission to introduce this meeting to the pilot who flew me here," I asked.

"This is bullshit, Arrow," Harding said.

"You have to meet my pilot. Then you might take me seriously."

Warrant Officer Harding led the group down the narrow corridors to the rear deck. As we exited the interior, the SEALs stood in amazement. There in the lights of the aft deck was Waam's tureen, its dull silver finish reflecting the beams of the flashlights held by several SEALs.

"What the fuck?" Harding remarked, not believing his eyes. "Is that a flying saucer, Arrow? Did you come here in a fucking flying saucer?"

"A picture is worth a thousand words, isn't it, Harding?" I said. "Let's go meet the pilot."

"Goddam, wait until the fleet hears about this!" Baez remarked.

I stopped the group. "This is 'above top secret.' In fact, this above 'above top secret.' You can never tell anyone about this mission, and you can never tell anyone about the tureen that you are looking at right now. No photos, please."

They mumbled in agreement, and then I escorted them to the side of the tureen, where I knocked on a landing strut. A moment later, the ramp lowered. "Lady and gentlemen, I would like to introduce you to my friend and pilot, Waam from the planet Ummo."

Several gasps came from the SEALs as all ten feet of Waam descended the ramp.

"Holy shit, Arrow," Harding exclaimed. "You were on the level."

"Can we move to a larger meeting room, Harding? I don't think that Waam can negotiate the corridors in the interior of your ship."

Harding moved us to a three-sided open-air room that had been formed by three shipping containers which had been strapped to the deck near midships. Then Baez and Styles brought folding chairs, assisted by a seaman who dropped his chairs in surprise when he saw Waam. "You didn't see nothing, did you, Marshall?" Baez said.

Marshall shook his head and left the area in a hurry.

When everyone had a seat, Waam said, "Gentlemen, Mr. Arrow and I are sending you on a mission to save the world, not just the free world, but the entire Garden Planet. There exists a covert alliance between individuals from several planets and certain governments on Earth. This alliance plans to eliminate ninety percent of the Earth's population and then install a one-world government. The individual that you are to extract from Dubai is one of the masterminds of this plan."

Then I spoke. "Once this New World Order has become established, Dr. Flite intends to rule it in collaboration with a reptilian race which currently inhabits subterranean bases here on Earth and on several neighboring planets."

"Then the tabloids aren't entirely wrong," Weinstein remarked.

"There is more truth than fiction in the stuff that seems preposterous," I replied. "Now, as I was saying earlier, Dr. Flite will be staying overnight in a three-story hotel in Al Haba. He will be heavily guarded by a minimum of eight individuals. Four will be humans who have undertaken training similar to your own. Two will be tall men, probably between seven and eight feet tall, whom you have heard referred to as Men-in-Black. And two will be reptilian guards from the planet Draco. They will stand approximately eight feet tall and will be carrying plasma weapons."

"What is a plasma weapon?" asked Harding.

Waam replied, "It is liquid light, as hot as the fireball in an atomic bomb, that will sever an enemy in half and cauterize the wound at the same time."

"Sounds as painful as having sex with a man who's

been eating habanera sauce," Weinstein snickered.

A couple of seals chuckled.

"It's instant death," I replied. "If you see a lizard touch his breastplate, take him out immediately. If you don't, plasma will launch from his helmet and strike whatever he's looking at."

This turn in the discussion brought a serious tone to the meeting because the SEALs realized that they would face a new and intimidating enemy with dangerous, unknown assault weaponry. However, as the meeting ensued, it was decided that three stealth-modified Blackhawk helicopters would be used in the raid. One would drop a squad onto the roof of the Al Habasha Hotel, and the others would drop squads at the front and rear of the hotel. The squad on the roof would monitor possible assaults from outside of the hotel by setting men up on all four sides.

The squad at the front would disable the switchboard, take out security, prevent use of the elevator, and create a diversion to draw some of Flite's personal protection down from the third floor. They would also monitor evacuees to ensure that Flite was not among them. The squad at the rear would ascend the stairway to the third floor, take out the remaining guards, and take Dr. Flite captive. They would then usher him to the roof, where he would be loaded into a chopper and whisked back to the *USS Ponce*. The second and third choppers would follow in quick pursuit. The entire operation was to take no more than ten minutes.

When the meeting broke up, the SEALs left to prepare their gear and to be sure that the chopper pilots and operations command personnel who would remain in radio contact on the *USS Ponce* would know what to expect and when. Departure time was "oh-dark-thirty," or four-thirty a.m. Dubai time. The squads were estimated to arrive at the Al Habasha Hotel at five-thirty a.m. and to depart for the return flight at five-forty a.m.

At four-fifteen a.m., Warrant Officer Harding found me talking to Waam on the aft deck. "Mr. Arrow, sir," he said, "we respectfully request that you accompany us on this operation."

"That wasn't part of the deal with the FBI," I replied.

"Sir, we need you to give positive ID of the target. You've actually seen him in person. All we have is a picture, and if he disguises himself, he might slip through our fingers unnoticed."

"They have a good point, Dan," Waam said. "It may be wise for you to go with them."

I reluctantly agreed. Mona wouldn't like what I was planning to do, so I turned my cell phone off. I wouldn't be calling her until after the raid was over, anyway.

Warrant Officer Harding gave me a flak jacket and a helmet, and then he offered me a Colt 45. "Ever use one of these?" he asked.

I gave him perturbed look, popped out the clip, and then slammed it home. "It's like my Sig, only heavier," I replied.

The deafening sound of a helicopter's motor springing to life drowned out all other noises.

"Let's go!" Harding shouted.

I blew Waam a kiss. He waved goodbye.

Chapter 11

I rode in the chopper with the back door squad. Weinstein was the squad leader, and Johnson was her second in command.

"You're the last one in," she told me. "I want you out of the line of fire."

That was okay with me.

We arrived at the Al Habasha Hotel at five-twenty a.m., a good ten minutes ahead of schedule. I guessed that we were traveling ahead of rush hour and remarked that nobody had fired a shot at us on our way in. Johnson reminded me that this wasn't Syria. We were actually in friendly territory and those in the know would assume that we were part of the International Mine Countermeasures Exercise. He was right about that.

Our three Blackhawks descended simultaneously, dust flying everywhere. Before we exited our chopper, we waited for a signal that the men on the roof were in position. Once we got the go-ahead, Weinstein slammed the sliding door open and five SEALs jumped to the ground. I followed, hunched over and pistol in hand. The lead SEAL kicked in the back door, perused the inside, and gave the signal for the others to follow.

Suddenly three quick shots rang out in the front of the building. They were followed by a single shot. Then everything went quiet—well, for maybe a second, and then the sound of panicked voices could be heard, screaming and shouting in some kind of Arabic language. Then footsteps could be heard coming down the stairs in our direction. Five people appeared, a man, three women, and a child, all Middle Easterners in pajamas. They were afraid at first when they saw us, but we waved them on and let them pass. Weintein radioed, "Civilians are exiting through the rear door."

We continued our climb to the second floor. As we reached the landing, a burst of plasma hit the wall and splattered as it carved a hole into the room beyond. "Holy shit!" Johnson cried, jumping backward. One of the other SEALs pulled a pin on a grenade, held the grenade to the count of five, and then tossed it into the air toward the third floor. It went off, showering us with tiny bits of plaster and cement. A lizard suddenly tumbled down the stairs on his back.

"That's one!" I shouted. "Don't touch his breast plate!"

Weinstein put two rounds into the reptilian's face, just in case. "They stink!" she shouted to the rest of us.

Johnson extended his arms and fired a burst of five rounds from his AR-15 into the stairwell above us. Nothing was returned, so we climbed over the dead lizard and made our way to the third floor. As the lead SEAL reached the top, more shots rang out, but I wasn't sure who fired first. I just heard a heavy thud, and I hoped that it was the other lizard. Word was passed down, "Tall dude, blond hair." It was one of the men-in-black.

Before I reached the third floor, I heard the distinct whine of another burst of plasma. Sparks blew into the hallway. They were followed by several bursts of rapid fire from the SEALs. I also heard bursts of fire from the floors below, probably from the ground floor, I thought. We were definitely encountering resistance.

A noise behind and below me caught my attention. I spun around just in time to see the blond head of a man-in-black as he turned to ascend the last flight of steps to the third floor, pistol-like weapon gripped in his left hand.

I popped three quick rounds from my Colt model 1911 into the giant, hitting him once in the head and twice in the neck.

Blood splattered onto the concrete walls behind him. As his body slid to the floor, I wondered if he was one of the bastards who had harassed Mona and Hal last year. I hoped so, but I'd never know, and it didn't make much difference because his harassing days were over. Then I noticed that his dark sunglasses were canted at an angle, exposing one of his eyes. It was solid black, with no whites at all. I wondered if they were really his eyes, or some sort of alien contact lens. I made a mental note to ask somebody that question when I had the chance.

Given what had just happened, I covered the back stairway just in case somebody else decided to come from behind while the SEALs were finishing their work of ferreting out His Excellency. After a couple of seconds, movement caught my eye. This time it was one of ours. He stopped for a moment to look at the man-in-black and then looked up. I waved. "All's clear below, Arrow," he said. "Got your guy? Choppers are waiting for us."

A voice shouted, "Arrow!" It was Weinstein, who had come from the corridor behind me. "We took out the other lizard and two humans in some sort of military garb. I think we've got your guy. Johnson has him."

I shrugged my shoulders at the guy in the stairwell, followed Weinstein into the corridor, and then into a small suite. On the floor was a dead Draconian gray and a dead guy in an NWO uniform. Johnson was holding his pistol against the head of a young dark-skinned man in light blue pajamas. "Is this the dude?" Johnson asked.

"Yeah, that's Flite!" I replied. "He travels with a woman."

"She's dead" Weinstein replied. "She hit one of our guys in the arm with a round from a small caliber pistol. He didn't mean to kill her. It was just instinct."

"You're from Hollywood!" Flite blurted, recognizing me.

I was going to say something witty, but Weinstein tapped my arm with the butt of her assault weapon. "Let's get to the choppers," she said. "We've been here too long already, and we don't want trouble from the local cops or military."

Johnson pulled Flite from his covers and ushered him out of the room. I followed behind Flite, jabbing him in the back from time to time with the nose of my pistol, just to let him know that he shouldn't try anything funny. I figured that he knew that anyway, but an old teacher of mine once told me that repetition is good for the memory.

Four of us and Flite hurried up the stairs to the roof. The others went back down the stairway to the rear courtyard. When the SEALs on the roof saw us emerge from the stairwell, one of them signaled and a chopper descended to the roof so we could climb in. Johnson lifted Flite and tossed him to the first SEAL who already had climbed in.

"Ladies first," I shouted to Weinstein, so she could hear me over the roar of the chopper's spinning rotors.

"Eat shit, Arrow!" she shouted back at me.

I guess that meant that she wanted me to climb in, and that she didn't want me to offer her a hand, either. She reminded me a bit of Mona that way. So, I climbed in. Weinstein came in behind me and waved some kind of signal out of the hatch with her right arm. Two of the SEALs who had been guarding the perimeter from the roof then left their posts and jumped aboard.

As our chopper lifted off the roof, I watched two other SEALs rappel from the roof to the ground, where another chopper was waiting for them. As the two SEALs were releasing their ropes, a small explosion went off about forty feet from the chopper on the ground. It might have been a hand grenade that really missed its mark. A SEAL in the chopper sent a volley of bullets in the direction of two men who had ducked behind the short concrete wall that enclosed the courtyard. When the volley of lead ended, the two men ran away, hunching over to keep their heads low. When the men exposed themselves, the SEAL sent another volley, and one of the men fell to the ground. I figured that he was down for the count.

I watched the two SEALs who had rappelled from the rooftop climb into the waiting chopper. Then our Blackhawk leaned to the right and headed west toward our destination. The other two choppers lifted off the ground and quickly joined us.

"Mission accomplished!" I shouted to Weinstein.

She gave me the thumbs-up sign and then spoke into her helmet's mike. She nodded.

Weinstein then scooted over to me. "One wounded, no dead on our side," she told me. "It's only a flesh wound!" I smiled and nodded. She continued, "Two dead lizards, two dead men-in-black, two dead grays, two dead unknown military, and three civilian casualties on their side. We captured our target and are on our way home. It's been a hell of a good day!"

Within ten minutes, we were joined by four jet fighters, who escorted us back to the *USS Ponce*. All three choppers set down on the mid deck. When the rotors stopped spinning, I waited for the SEALs to exit before I helped Dr. Flite to his feet. The SEALs had bound his wrists behind him with a plastic zip tie, making his movements awkward.

"Why are you doing this?" he asked with a slight German accent. "These bonds are hurting my hands, and I need them to be perfect because I am a surgeon."

"Come on, Flite, you have an appointment with destiny," I said as I pushed him out the hatch to a seaman who had come to help us exit the Blackhawk.

"I'm not Dr. Flite!" he insisted, stumbling to retain his balance on the steel deck of the *Ponce*.

I jumped down to the deck. "Sure. And I guess you didn't recognize me back at the hotel, either!"

"My name is Cassini," he insisted. "I *am* a surgeon. I was an assistant to Dr. Laskey, who perfected the migration process. Dr. Flite migrated me into this container so that I could continue the work of expanding the Rebirth Centers around the globe."

"So how did you escape death when your tureen fell into the sun?" I asked

"I don't know what you're talking about."

"Sure." I pushed him in the direction of Waam's tureen. He got the idea and began walking toward the stern of the ship.

"What's your name?" he asked.

"You don't get to ask questions, Flite. You get to answer them. Keep moving."

"Where to...the brig?" the seaman asked.

"Nope, to the craft at the aft," I replied, trying not to snicker at my own poetry.

"It isn't there. The captain thinks that it must have left sometime after your mission took off."

I knew that Waam wouldn't desert me unless something important had come up. "Let's go see about that," I replied.

I walked ahead of Flite, who was followed by the seaman who held Flite's wrists and kept a cudgel pressed into his back. As we reached the aft deck, the ocean and sky that formed our panorama began to blur and then Waam's tureen appeared out of thin air.

"What the fuck!" the seaman cried in astonishment.

"High tech camo," I told him. "Someday you'll see entire aircraft carriers concealed by it."

"And they'll be completely invisible?" he asked.

"Only to the eye. They'll still be visible through infrared goggles."

Waam must have been watching the arrival of our choppers, because he opened the ramp before I could knock on the side of his tureen to let him know that I wanted to come in.

At the sound of the ramp descending, Flite backed up, unsure of what awaited him, but the seaman pressed him back into position.

"You were successful!" Waam said when our eyes met as he descended the ramp. "Any casualties?"

"Just one flesh wound."

Waam smiled.

I motioned to Dr. Flite and said, "Do you recall His Excellency?"

Waam nodded. "The last time I saw you, you were a passenger on Commissar Nargas's starship. How did you escape?"

"I don't know what you're talking about," Flite told

him. "My name is Cassini. Like I told him," he said, nodding in my direction, "I'm a surgeon."

"He's been claiming to be a 'Dr. Cassini' for the last few minutes," I told Waam. "He must have used the flight from Dubai to dream up a whopper."

"We'll know the truth soon enough," Waam replied, reaching for Flite's sleeve. I could see the panic in Flite's eyes as Waam's large hand approached him. To me, it felt nice to have the biggest dog on my side, because nobody would screw with a guy Waam's size. Not even a man-in-black.

Before I could walk up the ramp, a voice called out, "Arrow!" I stopped and turned. It was Warrant Officer Harding, who had led the first meeting with the SEALs. "Are you off without saying 'farewell' and without returning my piece?"

I removed the Colt from the small of my back and handed it to Harding. "Your SEALs did a great job, Harding, especially Weinstein. For a woman, she's quite a guy!"

Harding's head sank quickly into his shoulders, and he looked behind him. "Don't ever say anything like that around her, Arrow. She'll kick your ass!"

"That's what I like about her, Harding. She doesn't take shit off anybody, does she? Someday I'd like her to meet FBI Agent Mona Casola. They have a lot in common."

"So what do I write in my report, Arrow?"

"I think you can write that your teams went on a special classified training mission for the Department of Homeland Security as part of the International Mine Countermeasures Exercise. They were accompanied by a civilian observer. One small injury occurred during the training. All records are sealed and all participants have been ordered to maintain above top secret silence about their mission."

"That sounds about right. Will I ever see you or that giant you're traveling with again? I have a lot of questions."

"You never know, Harding. You may see us next week and then again, maybe never."

"Is he human?"

"He's from the planet Ummo, Harding. He looks like us, eats, and shits like us, bleeds like us, and has all our emotions. But I think he'd consider it an insult to be called a human."

"So where are you taking your captive?"

"You know that answer is top secret. Follow us on your radar if you can." I think he really thought I'd tell him where we were going, like we were some kind of buddies or something. "Listen," I said, "we've been here too long already. It's possible that reconnaissance drones may have spotted Waam's tureen on your ship and wondered what it is. I'm surprised that you haven't already gotten inquiries about our mission. It's in your best interest to let us go quickly."

"You're probably right, Arrow. Sorry for the questions. Maybe if we meet again, you can tell me a little bit more. This is the craziest thing I've ever been involved in."

"Yeah, I know how you feel. It blows everything you thought you knew right out of the water, doesn't it?"

"Oh yeah, I nearly forgot." Harding handed me a small device that looked a little like a cell phone but was clearly something else. "Weinstein asked me to give you this thing. She found it on the nightstand beside your target's bed. She was going to keep it as a souvenir, but she couldn't figure out how it works."

"Tell Weinstein, 'Thanks,'" I replied, saluting him.

Then I turned and followed Waam and Flite into the tureen.

Waam closed the ramp, while I buckled Dr. Flite into a seat. Flite complained that sitting with his hands tied behind him was uncomfortable. Too bad. Waam set a few controls and our tureen rose and hovered silently a few feet off of the deck. Then, just for effect, Waam cloaked his tureen, making it vanish into thin air before everyone's eyes. He waited a few seconds and then accelerated, heading west, which wasn't where we were going at all, but if Harding's radar men were watching us, they saw our blip head west on their screens for a few seconds and then simply disappear off the edge and out of their range. Inside, we were almost oblivious to the effects of motion, especially to inertia, which, in a human-made vehicle, would have slammed our brains against the insides of our skulls when Waam accelerated. I don't have enough understanding of physics to be able to explain how Waam's technology works, but I can vouch that it does, and our flight from the *USS Ponce* was comfortable, even if Flite, himself, wasn't.

In case we were being tracked, Waam directed our tureen west to the middle of the Atlantic Ocean, and then he turned south. At the South Pole, he shot straight into the stratosphere, following the arc of the earth's magnetic field to the North Pole. Then he turned southeast and took us to Italy where his subterranean base was hidden deep within the mountains, a few blips from the remote village of Montano Antilia. He settled our tureen onto a small plateau between two snow-capped peaks and then flipped a switch that caused the ground beneath us to shimmer, such that we submerged directly through it and into the otherwise solid rock beneath. We passed through the darkness of the earth and rock until we emerged into a well-lighted hangar, hidden from view deep within the mountain. It was like revisiting the Sandia facility, except that there was no visible entrance at the surface that could be discovered accidentally by a hiker, hunter, or shepherd. To me, it was a no-brainer that Ummite technology was certainly more advanced than the technology used by the NWO, at least in the deep underground bunkers that they had constructed in the United States.

Once our tureen was secured, Waam took His Excellency Dr. Flite to an interrogation center, while I was escorted by a Reticulan gray to a wireless center in the Ummite underground facility where I could Skype with Mona. She tends to worry, and I had been away for a day without contacting her. I wanted her to know that our mission had been accomplished and that I was safe.

Before the gray left, I asked, "How long have you guys been working with the Ummites?"

"Guys? We are not males, Mr. Arrow."

"Oh. All of you?"

"Yes."

"Do the men stay home to watch the kids?" I asked with a smile. I hoped she knew that I was kidding.

"We are different from your many Earth species, Mr. Arrow. Long ago we decided that males were too selfish and brought only hostility and aggression to our race, so we became polyploids."

"I thought that your race was developed as a hybrid by another species. And what exactly is a polyploid? Is it like an Amazon?"

"Originally, our race was developed to serve mankind, much like you humans. And, like you, we have always had control of our own reproduction. But about six million years ago, we decided to eliminate the males."

"So how do you reproduce without us guys?"

"We clone ourselves. To keep our gene pool strong, we milk the sperm from the males of certain species, including you humans, and extract the genetic material we need to construct female clones with just the right mix of ingredients for the roles that they are cloned to perform. As an asexual species, we polyploids mature very quickly, up to six times faster than if we depended upon traditional male/female reproduction. And, there is a positive side benefit of being polyploid: if we lose a limb, we are able to regenerate that limb in a few weeks."

"So, abductions of humans by occupants of UFO's is essentially to assist your species in reproduction?"

"Oh, no, Mr. Arrow! Only about one percent of human abductions are for our reproductive needs. If we abducted more humans, the Ummites would not approve. The remainder of your human abductions by UFOs are related to hybridization programs of half a dozen galactic races, as well as for scientific experimentation by your own species. I would estimate that forty percent of all human abductions are conducted by human governments."

"No shit?" I asked.

"No shit, Mr. Arrow."

Chapter 12

I was going to use one of the generic computers in Waam's wireless center to Skype with Mona, but then I decided to try out Facetime for the first time. I like this new technology stuff, but so much of it is beyond me.

However, Facetime looked pretty easy to use. It wasn't too bad. Somehow I cut Mona off almost immediately after she answered my call, but when I tried again, I proved that the second time is the charm. Isn't it always?

"Hey, baby," I said.

"Jesus, Danny, it's like two o'clock in the morning. Is everything okay?"

Mona's hair was a mess, her eyes were baggy, and her face bore several lines from her sheets or her pillow. Maybe Facetime isn't such a good thing. "Yeah, sorry about the time," I said. "I forgot about the eight-hour difference."

"Where are you?"

"I'm in a DUMB in Italy. Well, I guess it isn't really a DUMB because it isn't military. It's Waam's Ummite facility on Earth, in the mountains."

"So you got him?"

"Yeah, how did you know?"

"Remote viewing. I'm getting better at it, Danny. I saw a three-story building and a couple of helicopters. I actually saw myself in combat gear taking out a lizard."

"That wasn't you, baby. That was Weinstein. She has a personality a lot like yours."

"Interesting. I'll have to ask Sergeant Mo about that. I thought that I might be seeing something from the future, like maybe I will be on a case with you instead of playing mom. I think that I may be missing working in the field a little. Funny, huh?"

"I know, baby. We can talk to Mack about that. Maybe he has some case work that's local to Little Devils Stairs." I paused for a moment and then added, "You know, Mona, I can be a capable dad. Maybe I can watch Stella while you're out doing some FBI thing."

"Maybe. Let me think about that."

I could tell from the tone in her voice that Mona was a little conflicted about staying at home as her FBI assignment rather than being in the field. She's really good in the field.

"But there's something else, Danny," she said.

"What's that?"

"You have the wrong guy."

"We got him, baby. I'm certain that he's Hitler. He even recognized me from our meeting in Hollywood."

"Yeah, you got the guy from Hollywood, but he isn't Hitler. He didn't recognize you from your encounter on Mars, did he? I think that the real Hitler is in a large stone villa with Queen Igua from Draco. I think he's somewhere in Europe."

"Don't tell me…you saw this through remote viewing again?"

"I'm telling you that I'm getting good at it. I'm not

certain about everything, and I don't understand everything that I see, but I'm spot on target more than I'm not. Sergeant Mo says I'm one of the best he's ever seen, even better than he is. I just need more time on task to get better at interpreting what I'm seeing."

"So, maybe you're just picking up what this guy's been telling us. He's been spinning a tale that he's some Doctor named Cassini. He says that he was an assistant of Dr. Laskey's. I think Waam's checking that out now."

"I'm telling you that he isn't Hitler, Danny. You got the guy that you were going after, but he's not the right guy."

"I guess that we've got to figure out who this guy is. How many possible Hitlers could there be? Do you think they cloned a bunch of them to keep us confused?"

"If so, it was a good strategy, wasn't it? Think about it: They cloned one that fell into the sun with Nargas, and you just captured one who is actually somebody else in a clone's container. Somewhere there is a third and possibly a fourth and a fifth, and one of them is the real Hitler. I think if you can find Queen Igua, you'll find your target."

Mona heard me sigh a puff of frustration into the phone. "I thought I'd try to find my way home tomorrow, but I might be a couple of more days, especially if we don't have Hitler."

"Then I'll see you in a few days because you don't have him."

"I love you, baby."

"Good night, Danny. I love you, too. Bye."

When I stepped outside of the wireless center, the gray who had escorted me there was patiently waiting. "I trust all is well," he said.

"Yeah, but things could be better. Can you take me to Waam?"

"He is waiting for you with news of importance."

The gray led me through a few corridors and sealed doors before we finally found Waam's conference room. It had to be Waam's, because the door was twelve feet high and six feet wide, and it opened in that same fuzzy disappearing manner that seems to be the Ummite preference. When I walked through the door, Waam was busy talking to somebody on a large screen behind his desk. I didn't pay attention at first, but then I saw that it was Dr. Laskey, the guy who had perfected the Draconian migration process and was now working with the Ummites.

"Yes, I am certain of it!" Laskey said to Waam.

My entrance caused Waam to turn around. Then he quickly spun back to face the screen. "Dr. Laskey, I trust you will remember Mr. Arrow from Livermore."

"You're the man who rescued me from service to His Excellency! I never did thank you. I think, at first, I wasn't sure if it was a good thing. But now I know that I owe you a great debt of gratitude."

"How've you been, Doctor?" I asked. "I hope they're treating you well on Ummo."

"I'm not on Ummo, Mr. Arrow, but I can't tell you where I am because these communication devices can be monitored by the Draconians and, as you know, I have a price on my head."

"Oh, yeah, sorry." I replied.

"Suffice it to say that my experiments have led to a second and third generation of migration devices that would never have been accepted by His Excellency. Great things are happening here, and you shall soon learn of them."

"That's great." I turned to Waam. "I heard that you have some news of importance for me. Can we talk now, or do you want to meet later?"

"Now is fine," Waam replied. "Actually, it is Dr.

Laskey who bears the news of interest."

"Yes, Mr. Arrow," Laskey said. "Commander Waam asked me to interrogate your captive. I am afraid that you have been duped. Instead of His Excellency, you have in your possession my former assistant, Dr. Cassini. He is a good man, and I believe that with some soothing of his ruffled feathers, he will come around to recognizing that he is better off working for your coalition than for the New World Order."

"Are you positive about this ID?" I asked.

"Absolutely. I asked him technical questions about our migration process and its developmental mishaps that only he would know. He told me that his primary goal in continuing our work is to introduce migration to his fellow humans as a viable alternative to death from insidious and virulent diseases. The more Rebirth Centers that he can open, the more people that he can help. It is as simple as that. He does not share the NWO's goals of world domination, and certainly not the political and military aspects of their agenda."

"Then we thank you, Dr. Laskey," Waam said. "I believe that we owe Dr. Cassini an apology."

"Well, don't be too conciliatory, Commander. Until early this morning, he was still working with the NWO so he will have to earn your trust, as you will his."

"Good point, Doctor," Waam replied. "Perhaps you can help us to win his trust."

"I have already begun the conversation by relating my experience to him during our discussion this morning. With your permission, I will continue to talk with him."

"We've got nothing to lose," I offered.

After brief cordial farewells, Waam shut down the video link and said, "We have to let Mack know what we've learned."

I agreed.

Chapter 13

Yes, Your Excellency, the raid was conducted in pre-dawn darkness. According to Arab witnesses, the raiding party arrived in unmarked Blackhawk helicopters. We lost two grays, two hybrid bodyguards, two reptilian guards, two of our NWO soldiers, and three civilians, including Cassini's assistant."

"The woman?" Hitler asked.

"Yes, the woman, Your Excellency."

"And what of Cassini?"

"He was taken captive."

"Thank you for this unfortunate information. Tell the Facility Commander to move to Security Status Two immediately."

The messenger snapped into a traditional Nazi salute. "Yes, Your Excellency!" He turned and marched briskly out of the Queen's dining area.

Queen Igua was the first to speak. "Plans by the Resistance to assassinate you are continuing, Your Excellency."

"Yes, Your Majesty, it appears so. I must remain in hiding until the pandemic has been unleashed. By then, the Resistance will be too weak to interfere with our initiative any longer."

"Will the loss of Dr. Cassini alter your plans to open more migration facilities?"

"Obviously, I will have to reschedule the opening of the Dubai Rebirthing Center. This will be only a temporary setback"

"Clearly, the raid on Dubai was intended only to capture you. You cannot go there yourself."

"No, I will have to send an ombudsman, but someone in a position of authority, someone who has full knowledge of both our business plan and the necessary technology. I will have to think on it."

"The attackers were not Ummites, because they killed humans," the queen mused.

"And they may not have been Americans, because they killed a woman," Hitler added.

"Ah, yes, Dr. Cassini's assistant." The queen scratched her brow. "They used American helicopters. Perhaps the Americans have changed their policies on the rules of engagement."

"Yes, possibly. They now permit women to perform combat roles, and I know of no woman whose female DNA would cause her to hesitate to take out another female in jealousy or combat…present company excluded, of course, Your Majesty."

"Don't underestimate my feminine side, Your Excellency. I have been known to exercise my claws with the best."

Hitler smiled. "I'm certain that you have, Your Majesty."

The queen sipped wine from her goblet. A small stream of red fluid ran down her chin and spotted her white taffeta collar. As she wiped her chin with a cocktail napkin, she added, "It is interesting to me that the Resistance did not wait to attack at a time when they could destroy the Dubai facility and all of its equipment. It is also interesting that they did not kill Dr. Cassini. Perhaps they are interested in obtaining his knowledge, as they did when they captured your nuclear physicists at the end of your last great war.

Hitler nodded, "Perhaps they see benefit in the migration process and its promise for humankind. This is perhaps good, and something that we can use to our advantage."

The door to the queen's kitchen opened. Three women in NWO chef's uniforms entered, carrying trays with serving dishes. With the light clatter of china upon the dining table, dinner was served.

"And what delicacy are we dining upon this evening, Your Excellency?" Queen Igua asked.

"It is called barbecued pork loin, Your Majesty. Swine is an American favorite."

Queen Igua speared one of the three slices on her plate and shoved the entire portion into her mouth. After three chews, she swallowed. "Yes, this is tasty," she told Hitler, "but I much prefer the flavor and texture of long pork."

Chapter 14

A litalia flight AZ 4000 touched down at Dulles International Airport at four p.m. Eastern Standard Time. Also known as "volo papale," or the "papal flight," this plane carried the pontiff and an entourage of thirty Vatican officials. In addition, it carried seventy reporters from around the globe whose daily stories about the pope's activities fed the news-hungry Roman Catholics in every nation.

Upon landing, the pope disembarked from the plane only after the reporters had found positions in the press section beside the gate to the airport, where they could snap photographs and jot hurried notes to draft their stories. As the pope appeared at the hatch, the US President stood on the tarmac at the base of the stairs, accompanied by clergy representing American Roman Catholics, the Jewish Synagogue from Georgetown, and the Southern Baptist Convention.

When the US President extended his hand in greeting, the pope shook it and briefly hugged the president. As he did, he said into the president's ear, "I am pleased to have been greeted in this manner, as opposed to the manner in which you were so rudely stood up on your recent trip to Cuba. I had hoped that the Cubans weren't establishing a new international paradigm for greeting foreign dignitaries."

In his usual fashion, the president, patted the pope's right shoulder with his left hand, laughed, and nodded his head for the cameras, seemingly unaware of the insult which had just been hurled in his direction.

Moments later both leaders were whisked away in a black governmental limo. As they hurried toward the White House, the president asked, "Why do you fly in commercial jets instead of one of your own? Surely, the Vatican can afford a private jet."

"The papacy is a positon in service to impoverished peoples around the globe," the pontiff explained. "The expense of such vainglory would be difficult to explain to those who live on less than a dollar per day. Besides, my trips actually earn the Vatican money. My travel costs are borne by the reporters who travel with me, to the tune of fifty-five hundred dollars each, roundtrip. It is the business class fare, although they must travel in the economy seats."

"Wow! That's about a quarter of a million dollars"

"Three hundred eighty-five thousand dollars to be exact. After all expenses, the Vatican sees more than one hundred thousand dollars in profit for each roundtrip flight I make. All to the glory of God and the support of the international air travel industry. I read somewhere, Mr. President, that your last trip to Hawaii cost your citizens more than a million dollars. You are lucky that they do not call for your head!"

❧❧❧

When the formalities of the official state dinner had

been completed, the pope and his entourage were escorted to a local hotel, where security was maintained at the highest level. In the morning, he returned to be greeted again by the press outside the White House, where a closed-door meeting had been scheduled for ten o'clock. Before entering the special room where the conversation was to take place, Vatican security swept the room for listening devices and cameras. They removed three, much to the embarrassment of the American officials.

Once inside the newly secured room with the president, the pontiff removed his zucchetto, or skull cap, and settled down to business. "The purpose of my visit is to discuss, in private, our efforts to keep the masses in line during the transition to NWO governance."

"Is it still your intention to remain forever as pontiff?" the president asked.

"I am seventh in line to be migrated to a younger body by Dr. Flite, after yourself, Putin, and a few other world political and business leaders. My clone is almost fully grown and awaits me in Astana."

"Then what are your concerns?"

"For myself in my role, I worry that so many Catholics continue to leave the Church, especially here in the United States, where you lead the world in abortions and where you have become so lax as to permit and promote same sex marriages. Both are tenets that the Church has steadfastly opposed."

"Put your mind at ease. Although I publicly support abortion clinics and same sex marriage, such support is only a political ploy to remain in power until the pandemic. At that time, all those who practice such abominations will be terminated and in the soup."

The pontiff sighed.

"Your biggest concern," the president continued, "should be in ensuring that there is a mechanism for Ro-

man Catholicism to continue to be practiced after the an-
nihilation of the masses. The religion that I practice
seems better able to control its people to do the will of its
leaders. It may well erase any future the Catholic Church
once had."

The pope rose to his feet. "And your biggest concern
should be removing the firearms from the homes of your
citizens. Those weapons are the biggest deterrent to our
takeover. The small militias that will form in every
American community will cause many deaths and casualties to NWO forces and to our Draconian allies."

"It is already in hand. We have the names of over
ninety-seven percent of gun owners in the United States.
They will be among the first to be infected with the virus.
It will be impregnated into a paper they will receive in
the mail from a shill group, The Sons of Second Amendment Liberty, calling for gun owner support in preventing
the government from confiscating their guns, as was done
in Australia. Those who open the envelopes and touch
that letter will be dead within three days, and they will
infect others with whom they come into contact."

"When will this happen? Has the date already been
established?"

"Soon is all I know. We only await orders from His
Excellency to implement the plan of action in the United
States. As you know, the interruption of His Excellency's
migration at Livermore, followed by the destruction of
the lunar facilities, have delayed our plans and strained
our relationship with the Draconians."

"Surely, the release of the pandemic should occur before your next election cycle. How far away is it, four
months?"

"Given recent events, nothing is certain anymore.
But, if need be, my successor has been selected by the
Bohemian Group, and she has already announced plans to

eliminate the Second Amendment by Executive Order, if she is elected."

"Then her election is not guaranteed."

"No, but it is almost certain. Our elections are conducted by sophisticated computer systems, into which algorithms have been entered which virtually guarantee her the popular vote. The people never doubt the results."

"I wish my people followed me with such devotion."

"Focus your efforts on utilizing the Hive, mon signor. The chips are continuing to be implanted internationally at the rate of ten thousand per day, and soon the Hive members will outnumber those who do not carry the chip. I suggest that you negotiate with the Draconians the development of an algorithm that keeps Roman Catholics faithful to the tenets of your religion, although I am not certain that the Draconians or the NWO will see any value in it. What do you possess that they might want?"

"That is the penultimate question, isn't it, Mr. President?"

Chapter 15

I had been discussing the Cassini situation with Waam and Mack, when I decided to share Mona's vision with them. Mack was in Washington, DC, and was meeting with us via teleconference, scrambled for security purposes by Waam's technicians. "I haven't told you this," I said, "but I was forewarned that we had not captured His Excellency."

"Who forewarned you?" Waam asked.

"I know you're going to think I'm crazy, but it was Mona."

"Mona?" Mack replied in disbelief.

"It's your fault, Mack," I told him. "You got her into that Remote Viewing stuff and she's been getting good at it. She claims to be better than her instructor." I turned to Waam and asked, "Are you familiar with Remote Viewing?"

Waam nodded his head. "We call it by a different name, but it is a skill that some of our females have been able to develop. Females are more sensitive to receiving such insight."

"So, when I went to the Bohemian Grove, Mona saw

the forty-foot owl that they have erected there. And when I called her after the mission to capture His Excellency, she told me that we got the wrong guy. Those were her words, 'You got the wrong guy!' She says that the real Hitler is hiding in Europe somewhere with Queen Igua."

"If she's correct," Waam replied, "it would probably be in Astana."

"Mona isn't good enough yet to be able to pinpoint where she sees things. But she sees them and, apparently, she's pretty accurate."

Mack cleared his throat. "This is interesting, Dan, but it simply may be coincidence. In the meantime, we have to refocus on Cassini and decide what we'll do with him."

"Do you have a suggestion?" Waam asked.

"Although the Hollywood Rebirth Center may be delayed for a while because of a lack of funding, I suggest that migration be permitted to continue at other centers and that the NWO continue opening more centers around the world," Mack said. "It will be an invaluable service for all of humanity, especially for those who have contracted a deadly or debilitating disease."

"I'm not so sure," I replied. "Everybody who is migrated by the NWO is going to have one of those microchips implanted in them. The NWO would simply be creating more soldiers to help carry out their agenda. Besides, I'm not sure that I agree with cloning, and I'm not so sure that everyone should be given the opportunity to live forever."

"Certainly," Waam added, "humanity must develop policies to regulate migration. And as policies are developed, you should anticipate that some among you will find ways to profit from corruption of the policies and the systems that are developed to manage migration."

"How might the world have changed if Steven Hawking had been given a new, fully functioning body?" Mack asked. "How about if we could extend the lives and the work of great medical and scientific researchers?"

"It's a lot to think about," I replied. Actually, I wasn't really sure who Steve Hawking was. Was he some kind of scientist?

"What about Mona, Dan?" Mack continued. "What if Mona were to contract something unwanted, like some terminal form of cancer? Wouldn't you want to give her the option of being migrated into a cancer-free container?"

"But doesn't that also mean that those who plot the implementation of Agenda Twenty-One will have the same option?" Waam asked.

"They already have that option, Waam," Mack said. "It's the rest of us who don't." Mack looked at me for support. "I agree with you that we need to decide who it is who will be empowered to decide which of us should be permitted to migrate. But until that decision is made, we need to ensure that every major hospital has a working migration lab, so every parent of a kid with cancer has the opportunity to move that kid into a body that is cancer-free."

That did me in. "I guess I can't argue with you, Mack."

Waam summarized what we had been discussing. "If we are all still on the same page, then, we are going to offer Dr. Cassini the opportunity to continue his work, but here with us in Italy and under a pseudonym. He will get to meet weekly with Dr. Laskey via secure teleconference to compare notes and procedures. Also, we will provide him with an unending line of clients who are ready for migration; however, he will no longer implant his patients with the Hive chips. In fact, he will be asked to tell us everything he knows about the Hive so we can try to render it inoperative. Anything else?"

"His cell phone, Waam" I replied. "He cannot be allowed to use a cell phone or any form of communication device that will enable him to undercut our plans."

"Agreed," Mack said.

Waam directed one of his junior officers to bring Cassini to us. A few minutes later, the door opened with its peculiar whooshing sound, and two tall Ummite guards led Cassini, wearing handcuffs and leg shackles, into Waam's office.

"Remove his bonds," Waam directed.

Cassini rubbed his wrists. "I hope that you have learned that I am who I said I am."

"Yes. Dr. Laskey and a remote viewer have convinced us that you are Dr. Cassini, trained surgeon and migration process expert," Mack replied from the screen on the wall.

"Am I able to go now?" he asked.

"No, not yet. We cannot have you continuing your work for the NWO. Their agenda is not one that is good for the majority of human kind," Mack said. "We will agree to permit you to continue your work here in Italy, provided that you no longer implant your clones with the microcomputer chips that enable them to be controlled. We also want you to tell us everything that you know about the network of human clones called 'the Hive,' how it works, what plans exist for it, and where the control mainframe is located."

"And what do I get in return?"

That was easy, so I responded. "You get three squares, the opportunity to confer with Dr. Laskey on a weekly basis, you get to continue your work of helping humans who have no better option than migration, and I don't chop you into small pieces and feed you into my garbage disposal—"

Waam cut me off. "Listen, Dr. Cassini, we think that what you are doing holds great promise for human beings, especially those with cancer and similarly debilitating diseases. However, we would like you to consider continuing your work with us rather than with His Excellency and the New World Order because their agenda leads to the destruction of the very people whom you hope to serve. You can come out of this as a hero rather than as an accomplice in the destruction of ninety percent of humanity."

"This is what Dr. Laskey related to me this morning. I don't care about the New World Order or its plans. I only want to continue my work. If you are offering me that opportunity, gentlemen, I am willing to give it a try."

"Excellent," Mack replied. "Then I will have the equipment intended for Hollywood moved here instead. You should be ready to begin work within a few days." I assumed that Mack saw the disbelief in my eyes because he paused for a moment and then added, "We apprehended the cargo ship near the straits of Gibraltar yesterday. The equipment was removed and is already on its way to Italy."

"So tell me, Doctor," I asked, "how many of you are there?" Cassini looked a little confused by my question, so I continued for clarification. "I watched a guy who looks just like you ride a one-way flight into the sun. And, I saw a guy who looks just like you give rousing speech on the Moon. Now, I see a guy who looks just like you...well, you get the picture. How many guys look just like you, if you know what I mean?"

"There are three of us, Mr..."

"Arrow. Dan Arrow."

"There are three of us, Mr. Arrow. The Draconians

made three versions of the clone into which I have been migrated. When His Excellency's primary clone was destroyed at Livermore, he was moved into one of the three remaining clones until such time as a more suitable clone could be made from the last few hairs and body tissues that remain of Der Fuhrer. My own body developed a palsy that made it nearly impossible for me to conduct surgery, so I willingly migrated into this young container. The third was one of His Excellency's bodyguards, who migrated as a means of being a double in case of an assassination attempt upon Der Fuhrer. There are no more of us than that."

"So, the body double flew into the sun and you are here. Where is Hitler?" I asked.

"He is with the reptilian queen. Find her and you shall find him."

"Thus, the third head of the Ophidian is the head that we need to sever," Waam said.

"What the hell is an 'oaf idiot'?" I asked.

"Ophidian," Waam replied. "It means snake…or serpent…perhaps the Devil himself. What we have been dealing with is a three-headed ophidian."

Chapter 16

I wasn't sleeping well. It had been a long day and I think I was over tired. But something just wasn't sitting right within me. When I decided to get up and try to shake whatever it was that was bothering me, I realized that I couldn't move. My muscles seemed paralyzed and wouldn't respond to my commands.

Then I noticed motion in my room and realized that I wasn't alone. To my left I saw three Reticulan grays approach my bed. Then three others appeared on the right side of my bed. This was some crazy dream, I thought. Wasn't I still in the guest quarters deep underground in Waam's facility in Italy? I looked about the room by moving my eyes. Yes, I was definitely at Waam's. But I was being targeted by Reticulan grays for some unknown purpose. Perhaps the queen or someone else had finally figured out that I was the one who had cracked the moon. I hoped that that was not the case.

I felt my body rise from the bed and move toward the guest room door. I don't know what technology they were using, but the grays carried me directly through the door without opening it. It was an interesting sensation, especially since the door felt cooler than the air temperature as I passed through it. It was also denser, like passing through water.

The six grays did not appear to be walking, but, rather, to be floating as they maneuvered me through several corridors and then into a large hangar where a black tureen was waiting. I was lifted onto the ramp and then upward through the hatch and into the vehicle. Inside, everything was bright white, as brilliant light emanated from all the walls, the floor, and even the ceiling. I had to squint to try to see where I was being taken, and fear began to take over my body.

I was deposited abruptly in the middle of a room of some kind by the grays. As my eyes adjusted to the light, I could see various panels in the ceiling above me and in the walls to my left, but otherwise, all surfaces appeared to be smooth and white. And there I lay, unable to move and alone. I didn't like the uncertainty of what awaited me.

I don't know how long I laid there, maybe twenty minutes, when several figures appeared beside me. Three were small, like dwarfs, with large heads, shortened arms, and stubby fingers. They all wore mint green robes with hoods. Behind them stood a very tall and thin figure, dressed in a similar robe. I couldn't tell if it was male or female, but its face shocked me. It was an insect of some sort, maybe a grasshopper or a praying mantis.

The insect seemed to be the leader, giving instructions to the others as to what to do. The dwarfs undressed me and sprayed my privates with a warm liquid. Then a thin transparent tube descended from a panel in the ceiling. One of the dwarfs snapped a plastic receptacle onto the end of the tube and inserted my penis into the receptacle. Suddenly I could sense that a gentle vacuum had been turned on as my penis was pulled upward into the interior of the receptacle. I felt embarrassment that I was naked in front of these creatures whom I did not know, and anger that they were manipulating my private parts against my will. If I could have pissed into the receptacle, I would have, but I was no longer in control of my body.

Then one of the dwarfs retrieved a small device from the wall beside me. He lifted the receptacle and pushed it to the side. Then he placed the device under my balls. Instantly, I could feel a small electrical impulse tickle my sack and before I knew it, I was erect and ejaculating into the receptacle! Those bastards were milking me, the way a veterinarian milks the sperm out of a bull before performing an artificial insemination procedure. There was no pleasure involved. The sperm just ran out of me like someone had opened a spigot and emptied it onto the ground. Except, in this case, my sperm was running up a tube into the ceiling of what I could only assume was a medical tureen.

When the insect nodded, the dwarf removed the electrical device and the tube from the end of the receptacle, and then pulled the receptacle from my penis. He placed it into a panel in the wall. The tube was retracted into the ceiling. The insect and the dwarfs left the room, and there I lay, naked, alone, and sticky. I felt used and victimized.

A subtle sensation in my stomach told me that the tureen was in the air. It was the same sensation that I had felt in Waam's tureen when he had taken Mona and me to Mars, and when Commissar Nargas had forced me to fly in his tureen to the dark side of the moon. I am no psychic or sensitive, but I have learned to trust my stomach when it comes to interstellar flight. I wondered where we were going and what other procedures awaited me.

I didn't have to wait long. Within a few minutes, I could see motion to my right. Another person was being brought into the room with me, carried in the same manner by Reticulan grays. I strained my eyes to see what was happening, but I couldn't turn my head and the next victim was simply too far away for me to see. One of the dwarfs noticed that I was straining to see what was happening, and he pointed out my interest to the insect. The insect gave him an instruction and the dwarf ambled over to me, grasped my head in his two hands, and turned it toward the new victim.

The insect and two dwarfs were busily preparing the person beside me for some sort of procedure. I hoped that the poor bastard wasn't going to be milked like I was. I didn't want to know that someone else was going to suffer through that indignity, and I certainly didn't want to watch. When the dwarfs removed the clothing on the guy next to me, I realized that he was a woman. As I watched, a very long needle descended from the ceiling. The insect grasped it and turned it to a forty-five degree angle and inserted it into the female's navel. Her back arched slightly at the pain and she cried out, "Danny!"

It was Mona! It was Mona and I hadn't even realized it until she called out my name in pain. And there was absolutely nothing I could do to help her. I fought against the unseen bonds that held me to the table, but my efforts were fruitless. What was that son-of-a-bitch doing to her? I was ashamed that I couldn't rush to her side, squash that bug, and remove the needle that had caused Mona to cry out.

As I was thinking those thoughts, the insect touched her temples with his right hand, and Mona stopped evidencing pain. If anything, she appeared asleep, maybe like she was in an operating room having an appendectomy or something. At that moment, I knew that she would not feel or remember the brief pain of the needle. She would likely not remember this encounter with aliens in a tureen in the middle of the night somewhere in time and space.

There was motion to my left side again. Somebody tapped my left arm, but I couldn't turn to see who it was. Then I saw the top of a brunette head bobbing along at the foot of the table I was lying on. As the head turned to come to my right side, I heard a tiny voice say, "Hi, Daddy!" It was Stella! She was there with Mona and me. I wanted to pick her up and hide her from the insect and his dwarf servants. I wanted to hold her, to tell her not to worry and that everything would be okay. I also wanted to tell her that I loved her.

"I love you, too, Daddy," she said in response to my thoughts.

'*How is Mommy?*' I thought.

"Mommy with doctor," Stella replied.

'*Is Mommy feeling pain?*' I thought.

"Mommy sleeping. Doctor let Mommy sleep."

'Good,' I sighed inside my head. '*Thank you, Stella.*'

"Doctor nice man."

The insect walked over to me. As he put his fingertips over my forehead, I heard Stella say, "Good night, Daddy."

⁊⁊⁊

Mona shook me in the morning. "Hey, why didn't you wake me up when you came home last night, Danny? I wasn't expecting you, or else I'd have waited up."

"Huh?" I asked, confused. I had gone to sleep in Waam's underground headquarters but had awakened in my own house in Villagio Ibrido. It was a strange reality, and I pinched myself to be sure I wasn't dreaming.

"Stella is going to be so happy to see you."

I pulled Mona down onto me and planted a passionate kiss on her lips. Then I rolled her over and ran my hand under her pajama top. I pushed it up, pulled her pajama bottoms down to her hips, and ran my tongue around her navel. As I did, I looked for a needle mark. There was a very small red spot near the bottom of her navel, but I couldn't be certain that it had been made by a needle.

"How's my girl?" I asked.

"I had a really great night's sleep last night, Danny. It must have been that I sensed that you were home. I feel absolutely great this morning!"

"I want to make love to you, Mona."

"Stella will be waking up any minute now. You'll have to save your appetite for tonight. I'll be all yours after she goes to bed at eight."

Mona jumped out of bed and went into the bathroom to brush her teeth. Regardless of how I got there, it was good to be home and back in the routine. But I was going to have to contact Waam to let him know what had happened. Maybe he could clue me in on what I had just experienced.

Chapter 17

After breakfast, I sent a scrambled text to Waam, apologizing that I wasn't in his facility in the morning.

He Facetimed me on my cell phone. "So how did you manage to get home?" he asked. "I was planning to fly you home after lunch today."

I told Waam about being abducted and being milked, and about Mona and Stella both being in the tureen with me. "I know that abductions are relatively commonplace among humans today," I replied, "but I thought it would be the reptilians or the NWO that would do it. It wasn't either of them. The leader was an insect."

"Was her head like a praying mantis?" Waam asked.

"Yes! Exactly!"

"They are the ones that we call 'the Watchers.' They are interdimensional time travelers, and they have full authority to intervene in the lives of humans."

"Why me? And why Mona?" I asked.

"We have no way of knowing what their purpose is in abducting you, and we do not have the capability of stopping them. Like all of us across the Galaxy, you'll just have to accept what they did to you and the consequences that it brings into your life."

"Mona doesn't remember the incident or the procedure that they conducted on her. Why did they let me watch? Why did they let me remember?"

"We have no way of knowing—"

"I think that that they wanted me to see that it's futile to fight them because their technology is too advanced. They can do anything they want to a human, and all humans are helpless to prevent them from doing it."

"That may be one scenario, Dan, but unless they reveal the real reason, you will never know what it truly is."

A buzzing sound on his end caused Waam to put me on hold for a moment. When his face reappeared on my cell phone, he said, "I will call you later. I have received some important news from Ummo. You, Mack, and I may need to talk." He hung up.

∽৩∾

Following a text message from Waam, Mack and I met with him via teleconference after lunch. I was in the Villagio, and Mack was in DC.

"I bring special greetings from Ummo," Waam said when he got us both connected. "I have news that will interest both of you."

"Are you on Ummo?" Mack asked.

"No, but this news from Ummo merits special greetings."

"So, what's up?" I asked.

"Mona was correct, Dan. His Excellency has been residing with Queen Igua in a European castle."

"Where? Do you have a strategy to get to him?" I asked.

"I am unsure of the European location. It doesn't matter anyway. But, 'yes' to the strategy. The two of you will go to the South Pole!"

"You're playing games with us, Waam," Mack replied.

"The news from Ummo is this: our confidants indicate that both Queen Igua and Hitler have relocated to an underground facility that is a mile beneath the South Pole. Crude maps of the facility and its entrance are being developed, with input from several sources. We've been able to confirm that the entrance to the facility exists and that it can be seen on Google Earth."

Waam split the screen and showed us a picture of the rocky entrance, taken from a satellite in orbit around the globe. "The entrance is about thirty meters high and ninety meters across. We have been able to verify aerial activity coming and going from that location."

"Can you give us the coordinates?" Mack asked. "I'd like to have some of our FBI tech specialists check it out."

Waam texted the coordinates to us while we were still in teleconference: Google Earth coordinates—minus sixty-six degrees, thirty-six minutes, twelve-point-fifty-eight seconds, plus ninety-nine degrees, forty-three minutes, twelve-point-seventy-two seconds.

Mack was ready to go. "Dan, I think I can get us on an air force hop to the South Pole, if you believe it would be worth our while. It's going to be cold."

"I think it's worth a shot. We have to take out Hitler and put a stop to this coming pandemic. I'd go just about anywhere to get that bastard."

"Because of the danger involved," Waam told us, "I think you both should receive NWO identification chips. I would suggest that you insert them beneath the skin, directly below the globe on the NWO tattoo on your fore-arms."

"I don't have a tattoo on my forearm, Waam." I re-plied.

"That's my second suggestion," Waam said.

❧❦❧

Mack sent an FBI chopper to pick me up in my back yard. Mona had been out all day, shopping and remote viewing, and she had accidentally left her cell phone on the kitchen counter, still plugged into its charger. So, I left her a hand-scrawled note that basically said that I was out with Mack and that I wouldn't be home for dinner. I'd text her later. Any possibility of sex tonight just blew out the window. Thanks, Waam.

The chopper dropped me off at Andrews Air Force Base at three o'clock. I was greeted by two MPs in a jeep, who transported me to the base hospital where Mack was waiting for me in the plastic surgery unit. The male nurse at the desk told me, "Go to room six, Mr. Arrow. Agent Smith wants to talk to you while he is engaged in the pro-cedure."

The procedure?

I knocked twice and entered room six. Mack was sit-ting in a hard-backed chair with his forearm on a table. A woman with purple hair and a full set of multi-colored shoulder tattoos was leaning over him, using a portable tattoo machine to inscribe a permanent NWO logo onto Mack's forearm. The Nazi-like phoenix was already complete, and she was now working on the globe.

"This is Nadine Maslow, tattoo artist on special as-signment to the FBI today," Mack said.

"I'm a dermographic artist," Nadine said, correcting Mack's obvious improper use of nomenclature.

"You're next," Mack said. "This takes about an hour."

"I'm not sure how Mona is going to respond when she sees that damn tattoo on my arm. She hates the NWO."

"You can get it surgically removed later."

"Yeah, you can," Nadine said, looking up at me. "I do dermo-restitutions all the time."

I was pretty sure that no matter what Nadine did to my forearm, it was never going to look the same after she was finished.

"Besides that," Nadine continued, "I'm using a new kind of ink. It's still in beta-testing, but the ink breaks down in about a year. There is also a solution that I can inject into your tattoo that completely erases it. It's gonna change the long term effects of tattooing, and I think everybody is gonna want one now."

"You mean you can give me a shot and the tattoo will be erased?" I asked.

"Not quite. I have to redo your tattoo but I use the erasure fluid in my needle."

"So it hurts going on and it hurts coming off, but it does come off."

"You sound like such a baby," Nadine said. "Suck it up!"

"How long has the beta testing been going on?" Mack asked.

"You two are the first."

Great, I thought.

Mack got down to business while Nadine colored the oceans blue on the NWO logo on his forearm. "We will be flying from Andrews to McMurdo Station this evening. My staff is working with navy outfitters to put together the stuff that we're going to need to survive the cold. Is there anything special that you can think of?"

"Scotch," I replied. "Make it a couple of bottles."

"It sounds like a great idea, but our guys tell me that it will make you colder. No alcohol permitted."

Mack was beginning to sound like a party pooper. "How about electric blankets?" I asked.

"You're funny, Dan! No power, except from generators, and we can't waste precious weight restrictions on a generator and gasoline. Besides, it would tire the dogs quickly."

"Dogs? Aren't we using snow machines?"

"Dog sleds are better. The dogs can sense hidden crevasses under the snow and won't cross them. A snow machine is a recipe for instant death in an icy crevasse. Besides, if an unexpected blizzard pops up, the dogs can help keep us warm."

I had no idea how to drive a dog team, much less where to find the ignition on the sled. This looked like it was going to be a cluster fuck. Without a heater and a functioning GPS, I was pretty sure we'd be lost in no time. Well, at least the dogs would be able to survive by taking turns snacking on my remains until help arrived.

When Nadine finished with Mack, she had me sit in the same chair while she focused on my forearm. Jesus, that little needle hurt as she moved it across my skin to outline the phoenix and the globe before filling them in with bright colors. I'm not really into tattoos, mostly because of how permanent they are. I dated a redhead once who tattooed *Danny* onto her neck and then added *Oh* and *Boy* before and after it when we broke up, but I've told you about that before. However, before feeling what Nadine could do with a needle, I'd never given any thought to the pain that young women go through when they have those little butterflies tattooed onto their thighs and ankles. They are better men than I am because a couple of times I winced and my eyes even watered twice during the procedure. Actually, I don't give a shit about the new kind of ink, because going on and coming off, I'd be putting strange chemicals into my body, and I always worry about the long term effects. Except, of course, for scotch.

When Nadine was finished, I thanked her and rubbed my forearm to get the blood circulating again. Mack told her to see the male nurse out front for her paycheck. Mack then led me to room nine, where a corpsman was ready to insert NWO identification chips beneath the globes on our tattoos. Thank god that the corpsman gave me a shot of lidocaine before cutting my skin to insert the chip. I had been poked too much already, and my forearm was very sore from Nadine's work. When he had finished tucking the chip in, the corpsman used a spray adhesive to suture the wound. That's a piece of new technology that I really like because there's no need to return to the clinic after five days to have the sutures removed.

Chapter 18

Staff Sergeant William Molandowski looked quietly at Mona's notes and scribbles. During this morning's Remote Viewing class, Mona had seen Danny in a very cold environment, and she was very concerned for his well-being. Her notes indicated that the predominant color was white, with the exception of a gray-cast sky. She saw dogs. She sensed danger.

"Your notes are plausible," Sarge told her, "but probably nonsense. Take a short break and then try again. Be sure to open your mind to whatever impressions come through. Feel the force, so to speak."

Mona nodded. She was convinced that the impressions she had received during this morning's session were accurate, but, as usual, she needed Sarge's help to interpret them. This morning, Sarge had been no help at all. She took her break outside, sitting on a bench beside a small garden. Her thoughts returned to Danny. She had no idea where he was and, although his note said that he would text later, he had not done so. That was uncharacteristic of him, especially of the new man he had become since they had married.

Below the south polar ice cap, Queen Igua and Hitler were meeting with representatives of the Draconian Gato and Modo. On the planet Draco, the Gato functioned as the voice of the commoners and the Modo as the voice of the elite.

"Your Majesty," Modon Flome asked, "is the lunar artifact now completely uninhabitable?"

Queen Igua chuckled, "If you are Chinese, it is."

"Then, are we expected to return the gold to the Chinese? That would be unfortunate."

"Our laborers assisted the Chinese at every phase of the mining and extraction processes, my queen," Gaton Phid warned. "They will not be happy if their work is not rewarded at its perceived value."

"Gentlemen, we have all the gold we were promised, and I have no intention of returning it. All reptilian factions will be compensated according their contributions to our plan. Our agreement with the Chinese did not stipulate that the artifact would be habitable when they took ownership. We sent word to the Chinese that the lunar artifact was theirs almost immediately after the nuclear devices were detonated."

Hitler chose this moment to speak. "Friends, it is understandable that the Chinese are upset. They were greedy and they made a bad deal. As partners in the New World Order, you should not take offense at their childish actions."

"Sir," Modon Flome protested, "we have learned that the Chinese have been injecting your Earth lizards with chemicals that turn their skins a variety of vivid colors. They sell them as pets, and almost every Chinese child owns one.

"Yes," Hitler replied, "and they are selling like hotcakes in Europe and in South America, as well. But this is simply a childish reaction to their deal gone bad with you."

Queen Igua raised her hand. "Your Excellency, we Draconians are very angry at the symbolism of the newly popular Chinese custom, but we also laugh at the stupidity of human kind for embracing this act of violence against reptiles, especially the defenseless reptiles of your planet who have not yet evolved to their ultimate galactic potential. It is only appropriate that we retaliate against the Chinese for their offensive actions."

"Sir," Gaton Phib said, looking directly at Hitler, "in retaliation, we have hacked into the NWO computer system and have instructed only the Chinese who have been implanted with control chips to begin coloring themselves in the same vivid colors that they have colored our Earthly cousins."

Hitler laughed at the thought of the Chinese with multicolored skin. "Your retaliation is less damaging than I had feared. It bears a touch of class!"

"Your Excellency, when the NWO realizes that we Draconians have done this to human kind," Queen Igua said, "they will comprehend the power that Draconians can exert over their agenda at any time that we choose."

Hitler's face turned deadly serious. "I *am* the NWO, Your Majesty!"

Modon Flome pounded his fist on the table. "We can crush you and your NWO at our whim. You need to recognize that bending to our wishes is the only way that you can retain the illusion of power and authority."

Chapter 19

Mack and I were flown in an old C-130 transport plane from Andrews Air Base to McMurdo Station, the US military research facility in Antarctica, Along with us in the cargo hold were twenty dogs, and none were housebroken. They took turns barking, three or four at a time, for most of the trip, and, to burn off pent up energy, they pulled incessantly at the leashes that bound them to metal tie downs on the deck. I loved their excitement at the thought of a road trip. Until I married Mona, I had felt much the same way.

From McMurdo Station, we were transported in large military tracked vehicles to our drop-off point, about thirty miles from the coordinates of the entrance to the Draconian sub-polar facility. Mack and I both realized how remote it was when we watched the trucks heading back to McMurdo, while we were left standing in the middle of nowhere with two sled dog teams, a small arsenal of combat weapons, and enough survival supplies to last one week. And no scotch.

"So, I still don't understand why we aren't using snow machines," I said to Mack.

"The idea is to fly under the Draconian radar. We don't want to appear military or governmental in any way, but more like a scientific research team. Besides, as I told you, hidden crevasses may be an issue between here and the entrance to the cavern."

Mack took an AR-15 from his sled and slung it over his shoulder. "Just in case," he said.

I did the same. "We've got to get going. I'm getting cold just standing here. What's the temp anyway?"

"It's a mild ten below. We're lucky that there's no wind today."

"So remind me again...how do I start this sled?"

"Like I told you on the plane, the dogs know what to do. Just tell them Gee and Haw for right and left, and the lead dog will take over. Just stand on the rear runners and pretend this is a ride at a winter carnival."

Mack shouted a command, which caused his dogs to lurch and pull at his sled. In a matter of seconds he was fifty yards ahead of me. My dogs were jumping and pulling, but my sled wouldn't move. Then I remembered that the snow brake was on. I kicked it free with my foot, and off we went, my dogs in hot pursuit of Mack's. At the onset, I almost lost my balance, but managed to pull myself upright. I had felt a brief instant of panic when I almost fell, but for the moment, as I watched ten tails and forty legs moving rapidly in front of me, I felt like Sergeant Preston of the Yukon. Or maybe Susan Butcher!

Mack had a battery-operated GPS and used it to guide our progress. For the most part, we stayed on the flat ice that lay between two ridges of black, craggy mountains which rose on either side of us. Every fifty yards or so, there would be a small gully or ridge of ice that had been carved by the new wind that had risen unannounced and whipped, fortunately, from behind us. If it had been in our faces, the going would have been really tough.

About three hours into our cross country run, Mack's dogs stopped abruptly and refused his commands to keep moving forward. At his command, "Mush," his lead dog whined and lay down on the ice. The others followed suit. My dogs stopped behind his sled and did the same. I pushed my sled brake into the hard-packed snow and walked up to Mack.

"What's wrong? Are your dogs tired?" I asked as I reached him.

"Something's not right. Maybe a crevasse."

"What do you suggest?"

"Probably we should circle around. We could loop into those rocks," he said, pointing at a cluster of large black rocks that broke through the snow at the base of the mountain ridge to our left, "and weave our way through them for a few hundred yards before trying to bring our dogs back to the flat stuff. What do you think?"

"I bow to your expertise, Mack. Until this mission, I had no idea that you knew how to operate a sled dog team. Color me impressed."

"This is only my third time guiding a team. The first was a standard training exercise while I was at Quantico. The second was a mission that took me to the back woods of Russia in the late 1990s."

"How did you get into Russia back then?"

"It was covert. I had to rescue one of our counterintelligence officers who had been outed by his lover. It was messy, but I managed to get him out through Finland."

"You'll have to tell me about it when we get to our hotel tonight," I said.

Mack just smiled and replied, "Let's get going."

I walked back to my sled and shouted "Haw!" to my dog team. My lead dog turned the team to the left and we began trekking uphill into the black rocks. Mack did the same, and soon he regained the leadership position, which was good because I didn't have a clue as to how to get to where we were going. My dogs fell in behind Mack's tracks, which seemed to pack the snow and make their going easier.

We made it to the rocks and turned right, passing through them on the snow which lay between. At about forty feet wide, the gaps between the rocks were larger than they had looked from the flat area that we had been using as our highway. We were now on neighborhood streets, so to speak. The wind in this section seemed to come from all directions, probably tumbling as it met with the immovable objects. I felt distinctly colder, especially my fingers, which weren't getting much blood, anyway, while gripping the handle on the sled.

Suddenly, out of nowhere, a ball of liquid light splattered on a rock in front of Mack. It had to be fucking lizards! The question was whether it was a warning shot or an attack. The next shot came with a whining sound and took out the first three dogs on Mack's team. Mack dived to the snow and rolled behind a small rock. His sled overturned, and his dogs panicked, pulling in opposite directions and going nowhere fast. A third ball of light ended their struggles. Coming from in front of us, it sliced through the remaining dogs, leaving them in smoldering pieces on the white snow.

Mack began firing his AR-15 in the direction of one of the rocks. A reptilian guard stood, touched his breastplate, and fired another bolt of light in Mack's direction. It hit the rock that shielded Mack, sending sparks in all directions.

I pulled my dog team to a halt behind a larger rock

that rose about fifteen feet into the air. I rummaged through the stuff in my sled until I found a box that contained hand grenades. Just about the time that I did, a bolt of light came from over my shoulder, splattering on the rock beside me. The sparks surprised my dogs, and they bolted away, taking the sled with them and knocking me to the ground. I picked up the box of hand grenades and hurried around the rock to safety.

Lying on the snow, I saw movement and watched a reptilian cross the gap between two rocks. At least I had a location for him. I pushed myself backward to be out of his line of sight.

Looking over my shoulder, I could see Mack and the reptilian that was firing at him. I took my AR-15 from my shoulder, clicked off the safety, and waited until Mack's attacker rose to fire again. When he did, I took him out with a short burst of five rounds. It was an easy shot at only fifty yards. Mack waved and pointed. I knew that he was grateful.

I waved back at him. Mack pointed again. That's when I heard the sound of crunching snow near my rock. That bastard lizard that had shot at me was now on the other side of my rock, and I wasn't sure from which direction he'd come. I pulled a hand grenade from the box that was still beside me, pulled the pin, and threw it over the rock. As luck would have it, I heard it hit the top of the rock and then I heard the distinctive sound of its tumbling back down to me. I looked up and there it was, falling downward. Fortunately, I was able to grab it in my right hand and chuck it to the right side of the rock before it exploded. When it went off, I heard a distinctive reptilian roar of pain. That lizard had been coming around the rock from my right side!

I ran around the rock in the opposite direction. He was sitting in the snow, bleeding profusely from his legs.

When he heard me coming, he turned his head and roared at me. I set the sights of my AR on his head and pulled the trigger. Three rounds burst from the muzzle and ended his pain. At least it was quick.

A whine and explosion let me know that another lizard was still engaged with Mack. I shouldered my AR, grabbed three grenades, and circled around to the left, where I could see Mack's position. The lizard had come from behind Mack and was hiding behind a rock to Mack's right. Mack had shifted his position so that his small rock shielded him from the lizard's bursts of light.

I saw the lizard stand to fire again, so I took a shot at him with a burst of five rounds from my AR. They fell short, kicking up snow. The lizard turned in my direction and touched his breastplate. A ball of light sped at me. I dived to the ground behind my rock and was showered with sparks when the light hit it.

I heard Mack fire again. Then everything went silent. A moment later, I heard the crunching sound of footsteps coming in my direction. I lifted my AR to greet whomever it was. I tightened my finger on the trigger and was ready to pull it if I saw snake eyes, but to my joy, I heard Mack's voice cry out, "Dan! Dan! Are you okay?" I lowered my gun and stood as he rounded the rock. We hugged each other in joy.

"Those sons of bitches killed my dogs, Dan!"

"I know. I saw. And they sent mine running all the way across Antarctica. We're on foot now!"

"But we're close to the entrance! The ones who attacked us were either a sentry outpost or a patrol. Either way, the reptilians know that we're out here. We'll have more company soon."

We walked over to the last lizard that Mack had taken out. Mack rifled through the reptilian's uniform and retrieved some sort of communication device. "This may be of some use to us," he said, putting it into his own pocket. "Maybe if they trace its location, they'll think we're lizards and not humans, at least until we get inside."

I wasn't so sure, but in spite of all the encounters that I had had with reptilians over the past year, Mack still knew more about them than I did. Hell, he had been in meetings with them for the past ten years and maybe more.

Going forward, we decided to stay in the rocks, where at least we'd have minimal protection if we were attacked again. We'd use Mack's pocket GPS to guide us the rest of the way to the entrance, which Mack estimated was less than a mile away. I put the two remaining grenades into the jumbo pockets of my parka, reloaded my AR-15, and asked Mack to point in the general direction of where we needed to go. "Just in case we get split up or something," I told him.

Mack pointed at the tallest mountain ahead of us. "We're headed up there, just about where the snow line ends. You've seen the pics of it from the satellite. The main entrance looks like it has an umbrella over it."

"Yeah, I remember," I replied.

In the Google Earth pics, it clearly looked like something that had been manufactured and bolted together, rather than something that had occurred naturally.

Mack checked his GPS one more time and then we set off in the direction of the entrance. The snow wasn't deep, which meant that it was mostly hard-packed ice. If we had had to tramp through knee deep snow, Mack and I would have died from exhaustion before we got to our destination. What slowed us down was constantly checking all sides of us for more attackers. Like a cowboy in the old black and white westerns, we moved from rock to rock, and made sure that nothing was moving before going to the next rock. So, it took us over an hour to hike the mile that we needed to travel. But, on the plus side, I wasn't cold anymore. Between the adrenalin from being under attack and the effort to keep moving without being a target, warm blood was pumping into all my extremities. If I say that my fingers felt hot in my gloves, it wouldn't be an exaggeration.

We reached the base of the mountain with no further interference from reptilian attackers. I was surprised about that. From where we stood, the terrain rose dramatically uphill. After resting for five minutes, we climbed for about an hour. Suddenly Mack shouted, "Duck!" I hit the ground. As I did, a sixty-foot wide tureen passed overhead, slowing and then disappearing behind a rock outcropping above us. We were almost there!

Then, as we inched our way upward, a smaller tureen, maybe thirty feet wide, appeared above us, moving slowly and then suddenly accelerating straight up until it was out of sight. Mack checked his GPS and said, "We're here! The lip has to be within fifty feet."

I climbed up the last few yards ahead of Mack. The rocks were hard and cold. When I hit a patch of obsidian, I knew I was at the lip. The rock had been melted away by some sort of laser device and had reformed into a glass-like material as it cooled. I turned and gave Mack the thumbs up sign. When he joined me, we peered into the cavern. Embedded into the constructed awning that served to protect the mouth of the entrance from snow accumulation were entry lights that were probably turned on at dark to guide pilots safely to their docking stations. You would have thought that alien technology would be so advanced as to not need a pilot to negotiate the narrow entrance, but I guessed that wasn't the case.

Mack and I crawled over the lip and slipped inside the entrance. When we were ten feet below the lip, a shadow caused the entrance to grow dark. Another tureen passed over us, gliding silently into the depths ahead of us. As it passed, I could feel the hair on my arms and the back of my neck stand on end from the static electricity that the craft generated.

We picked our way carefully down the gradual slope of the entrance. We weren't worried about tripping over a jagged floor, like in most caverns. Instead, we were worried about slipping on the floor's glass-like surface. As we made our way deeper and deeper, tureens of all sizes caused us to duck as they passed over us like bees, coming and going from the facility below. If they were conducting commerce, business was definitely good.

About a hundred yards from the main facility itself, we were greeted by two lizards pointing weapons in our direction. I was surprised to see them using AK-47s and AR-15s instead of their usual plasma weaponry. But I wasn't surprised that we were met by a guard detail. In fact, Mack and I had been expecting it since defeating our attackers out in the snow.

We both raised out hands, ensuring that our tattooed forearms were exposed. One of the lizards made guttural sounds into a communicator. Mack looked him in the eyes and asked permission to show his credentials. The reptilian nodded at him. Mack pulled out his FBI badge and an NWO credential of some kind. I had never seen it before.

While the reptilian examined the credentials, he was joined by three armed humans in NWO uniforms who came from behind him. One was clearly a junior grade officer, who took the credentials from the lizard.

"Show me your forearm," the officer said to Mack. He held Mack's wrist in his left hand and passed a small device over Mack's tattoo. The screen on the device lit up, showing Mack's face and brief information about him. Waam's suggestion about getting implants had just paid off.

"Welcome, Agent Smith," the officer said, handing Mack's credentials back to him. "And, who have you brought with you?"

"This is Sandy LaSalle. Mr. LaSalle is a wealthy NWO financier from Hollywood. He is part owner of the Hollywood Rebirth Center."

The officer asked me to show my tattoo. "Yours is new," he said as he passed the device over my forearm. "It's still seeping."

His device lit up and I was surprised to see my face appear as an NWO member.

"And what brings you to Center Earth, Mr. LaSalle?"

Mack responded before I could. "We received instructions from His Excellency to meet with Him here."

"And why did you not travel in a military tureen?"

"I know it sounds bizarre, but His Excellency's instructions were to come here via dog sled. We flew to McMurdo station and came by dog sled the last leg of our journey."

"We know. We watched the vehicles drop you off before returning to McMurdo. Your progress was monitored the entire way."

"Then was it you who gave the orders to have us killed?"

"Yes. I should have ordered your capture instead. It's fortunate for you that you both survived. It's less fortunate for my small reconnaissance squad that they did not."

The young officer told his men to take our weapons. "You won't be needing them while you're here," he told us. We handed over our ARs and the two grenades. "Anything else?" the officer asked. I unzipped my parka and pulled a pistol from the small of my back. "Financier?" the officer asked when he saw that it was a Model 1911. One of the lizards took it from me.

"Be careful," I told him, "it's loaded."

"Why would you carry an anti-personnel weapon to Center Earth?" the officer asked.

"Polar bears," I replied.

"They are found at the North Pole, Mr. LaSalle." The young officer turned to Mack again. "Because of the manner in which you arrived, I'm certain that you will face interrogation. Nobody in the outside world knows that His Excellency is here."

"Well, I know it," Mack replied. "I received a personal email invitation from His Excellency to meet with him here. He asked me to come via dog sled and to bring Mr. LaSalle with me."

"I don't believe that His Excellency sends invitations by email."

"Then your computer email systems have been hacked and we were sent here by the same person who assumed that your squad of Draconian soldiers would kill us when we came this way. I demand to see your commander."

Chapter 20

The young officer who had intercepted us in the entry tunnel motioned toward a van-like vehicle and told us to get in. Mack and I complied. As we walked toward it, I could see that the vehicle had no tires. Instead, it hovered like a tureen does. It was painted in non-reflective military green, and it bore the standard NWO logo of a phoenix gripping the globe in its talons. The officer and two lizards joined us. I assumed they were his protection from us, in case we tried to pull something. I decided not to.

The vehicle began to move, and soon we were passing over fields of grass and across streams and between trees, as through we were on the surface of the Earth. Above, a sun shone brightly, only it was some kind of glass or crystal orb in which a chemical or nuclear reaction was occurring. Like our sun, it was hard to look at directly, and it gave off both heat and light for this huge underworld. In the distance was a small city, consisting of crystalline structures.

"I saw buildings like those on the dark side of the moon," I told Mack.

"You've been to the lunar artifact?" the young officer asked.

"Yes, and I visited a deserted city that was constructed of the same crystalline material as the city that we're approaching."

"When was this?"

"I was escorted to the city by Commissar Nargas in his private tureen, perhaps three months ago," I said, stretching the truth a bit. I guess I wasn't really escorted. It was more like I was kidnapped and forced to go there against my will.

"Before the crack?"

"Yes."

My response seemed to raise my status in the young officer's eyes because he began to open up to us. "The original inhabitants of Center Earth were a silicon-based species," he told us, "not carbon-based like us."

"Same with the lunar artifact," I replied.

He nodded and then he said, "The Draconians drove them out of this subterranean resort about five thousand years ago and turned it into their primary facility for strategic planning and operations. This is where Queen Igua and her royal entourage often reside when on Earth. NWO officials come here regularly to meet with the queen."

"The air traffic was pretty intense as we came through the tunnel," Mack said.

"The frequency of those meetings has increased substantially since the lunar artifact was rendered unsafe for the human species. Its interior is currently undergoing a ten-year repair cycle."

I wanted to snicker, but I held it in. "Why ten years?" I asked. I knew the answer but wanted to see if junior did. As it was, he was right on target.

"Because the Draconians are one of the only species that can tolerate the radiation, and they aren't really interested in anyone else having access to the artifact's facilities."

c̃ɔc̃ɔ

We entered the crystalline city, which was busy with commerce, although mostly military commerce. I noted that the lack of litter, graffiti, street musicians, and pan handlers kept this place from being a real city, but I kept that thought to myself. Our vehicle stopped in front of a medium sized building that did not appear as auspicious as I would have anticipated for the location of a commander's office. Mack must have recognized the same disparity because he asked, "Where are we? I want to speak directly with your commander."

"We've stopped at the central communications office. If you've received some sort of bogus email from His Excellency, it needs to be tracked and its source identified before it can cause any more damage."

"Oh, that probably makes sense," Mack replied.

He looked at me, and all I could do was shrug my shoulders in a way that said, "Well, why not?"

Inside, we took a glass elevator to the third floor, where we could see through the floors above us and below us, as well as through the walls to the outside. I felt like Superman must have felt the first time that he realized that he could see through everything. Well, in his case, everything except lead. It was hard to focus on what was going on in front of me, when there was motion all around.

"You'll get used to it in a few minutes," the young officer told me. "Just focus on the person that you're talk-

ing to and watch his lips. Try not to pay attention to anything going on around you."

"Easier said than done," I replied.

He led us through a doorway and into an office,
where we were introduced to the Head of Digital Communications, a guy who insisted that we call him only by
his first name, Michael. "We're all brothers here," he
said.

Mack started the conversation. "I was at my desk in
DC when I got an email from his Excellency, asking me
to come to the Center Earth for a meeting tomorrow. I
was to bring Mr. LaSalle and we were to come by dog
sleds so as to avoid any perception of its being an official
visit."

"Official?" Michael asked.

"Yeah. I'm with the FBI and I sit on one of Queen
Igua's inner councils for the NWO."

"Let me see your cell phone."

"Sure," Mack replied, handing Michael his iPhone,
"but the message didn't come on this one. It was sent to
my secure number, on my FBI cell phone. I didn't bring
it on this trip because it contains too many restricted
numbers to risk having it fall into the wrong hands."

"So we have a problem," Michael said.

"Not from where I sit. All you have to do is trace all
of your outgoing calls from four days ago to the FBI. It
was an encrypted message, so it shouldn't be too hard to
identify."

"Everything going out of here is encrypted."

"So you just have to focus on one day to find it. That
shouldn't be too hard. How many emails go out of here in
a single day? And how many of those are directed to the
FBI? And, of those, how many are sent to Washington,
DC?"

Michael let out a sigh. "I'll get my people on it right away. I don't suppose you could get your people to send your FBI phone down here? If they put it on a hop to Gitmo, we could fly it to Vieques and then shuttle it here in a tureen. It could be here in two days."

"I'll call my office and see what I can do about that. What time is it in DC right now anyway?"

⌀⌀

When we finished our meeting with Michael, Mack and I were then escorted to the building where Queen Igua resided. The top floor, walls, and ceiling of the structure had been painted a moss green and it was no longer transparent. I figured that that must be where she resided and the reason for the paint job was obvious.

We were greeted at the door by a huge—and I mean huge—lizard, who passed a wand over us to ensure that we weren't carrying any explosives, strange chemicals, or sharps. He didn't find any. Then a thin lizard in an aqua-marine jumpsuit led us to the Queen's chamber. He knocked twice and then opened the door. She was seated on a throne. To her left was Hitler, seated and ready to observe and overhear whatever it was that we had to say. If I had had my 1911, I would have taken him out right then, but I looked downward and repressed that thought so the queen could not read my mind.

"Agent Smith," she said through a digital translation device, "it is good to see you again!"

"Thank you, Your Majesty," Mack replied. "It is my pleasure to be in your august presence."

"And whom have you brought with you?"

"Your Majesty, this is Mr. Sandy LaSalle. He is one of two people who financed the Rebirth Center in Holly-wood."

"Have we met before, Mr. LaSalle?"

"Only in my dreams, Your Majesty. It is indeed an honor to bask in your aura. I watched your speech at Livermore, but only from the closed circuit system in Las Vegas. Your words were well chosen and very appropriate for the occasion."

Agitated, Hitler couldn't stand himself. "And what do you know of Livermore, Mr. LaSalle? Do you know who it was who destroyed my new container? You look very familiar to me!"

"Your Excellency," Mack replied, "Mr. LaSalle is a new member of the New World Order, and he has dedicated millions of dollars to the construction of the Rebirth Center in Hollywood. He is also interested in establishing one in Las Vegas."

"Is that so?" the Queen interjected.

"Yes, Your Majesty," I replied. "I attended the Bohemian Grove retreat in July, where I saw and heard His Excellency's address to the attendees. It was there that I decided to contribute to the realization of Rebirth Centers as a partner with the New World Order."

"Your Excellency," the Queen said to Hitler, "Don't be too critical or suspicious of our new friend. If Agent Smith has vetted him, I am certain that he is of the highest caliber."

"Thank you, Your Majesty," Mack said, bowing slightly.

"So what brings you to this audience, Agent Smith?" the Queen asked.

"It was an email from His Excellency that brought us here."

"Balderdash!" Hitler exclaimed. It must have been an expression from his youth, because nobody younger than fifty would ever have heard that word before. Well, except for me, and I only heard it from my grandmother.

"Permit me to explain," Mack pleaded. "Four days ago I received an email under NWO logo supposedly from Your Excellency, asking me to come to Center Earth to meet with you. In the email you asked me to bring Mr. LaSalle. You also asked me to arrive by dog sled so as not to draw attention as an official visit. I did as you wished. About one mile from the entrance to Center Earth, Mr. LaSalle and I were attacked by three individuals. Fortunately, we escaped unharmed. Our sled dogs, however, were not so fortunate."

"I sent no such email!"

"So I have ascertained, Your Excellency. Immediately upon arrival, I reported the incident to the director of digital communications. He is attempting to identify the source of the email. Once he does, we will know who brought me here under false pretenses and who tried to kill both Mr. LaSalle and me."

The queen spoke again. "Speaking both for His Excellency and myself, I regret that this incident occurred and that you were attacked on friendly soil. Were they NWO soldiers who attacked you?"

"Unfortunately, Your Majesty, they were reptilian guard."

The queen fidgeted in her seat and cleared her throat. "That will be all, Agent Smith. Keep me apprised of your situation through my secretary. Enjoy your stay with us, as my guests. Shuttles leave here daily. My secretary will see to it that your fares are covered from my personal expense account."

"Thank you for your gracious gesture and generosity, Your Majesty," Mack said.

We both backed out of the room, so as not to turn our backs to the queen, which Mack once had told me was proper etiquette. As we left, I could see that Hitler remained upset.

Chapter 21

I really think that if we could destroy the Central Sun, the Draconians would lose both their heat and their source of power, and they wouldn't be able to live in this underground resort," I said. "Maybe if we could figure out a way to nuke it, they'd have to evacuate for the Moon or for Draco."

"I understand your idea, Dan, but I worry that a nuke might crack the Earth, the way the Moon was cracked," Mack replied. "If the Earth cracks, will we all still be able to live on it, or will it doom mankind to extinction?"

"Listen, Mack, the Moon was only a few miles thick. The Earth is thousands of miles thick. The blast might cause a big sink hole, but I doubt it would do anything else. Maybe a couple of surface to air missiles with nuclear warheads might do the trick"

"And how are we going to sneak something like that into this fortress?"

Mack had a point. Maybe some sort of plasma weapon would do it. I'd have to think on it.

☙❧☙

Mack and I had been discussing our situation and had been hatching a plan of sorts. But in order to launch it, we were going to have to go outside, where he could send a message to the FBI without its being monitored or intercepted.

When we met with Queen Igua's secretary at the start of the workday, Mack asked her if the Draconians had a pharmacy where he could get some statins to replace those that he had lost when we were attacked outside.

"We Draconians don't suffer from fatty blood problems," the secretary replied.

"May I request permission to leave the facility to recover some medication that I need for my heart. The pill bottle is somewhere in the snow where Mr. LaSalle and I were attacked just before our arrival at Center Earth."

The secretary didn't seem receptive to the idea.

Mack's voice turned to a tone of plea. "It should take only a few minutes once I am outside and reach the place where we were attacked."

"I suppose it would be okay, especially if it is a personal health issue," the secretary finally conceded.

"May I go along to help Agent Smith sift through the snow?" I asked.

The secretary ordered three Draconian grays to pilot Mack and me to the site and to help Mack find the medication. We flew in a small state-of-the-art tureen, piloted by thought. While we were in flight, Mack told the pilot, "We humans could never fly these newer models."

"From the Draconian point of view, this is a safety measure, especially since that whack-o destroyed the lunar artifact and escaped in a tureen that humans could fly. Those older tureens are quickly being phased out.

"Good," Mack said. "We've had enough interference with the implementation of the grand plan."

The grays all nodded at his words.

Our trip to the scene of our brief firefight with the three reptilians took less than a minute. We arrived just in time, because a team of reptilian garbage men were picking up the carcasses of our dead sled dogs and the one damaged sled to take them to the dump.

The pilot landed our craft. One of the other Draconian grays asked the reptilians if they would mind taking a ten-minute break while a human looked for something to extend his life until the pandemic. The garbage men laughed and agreed to do it.

"And where would your medication be?" one of the grays asked Mack.

"It could be anywhere. Hell, when we were being attacked, I did a lot of diving and rolling in the snow. Look for a brown plastic bottle with a white cap."

"The cleanup crew has already moved a bunch of things, so they could have stepped on it," I said. "We'll have to spread out."

I watched as Mack kicked snow to the left and right with his foot while moving toward a large rock. As he moved, he drifted behind the rock. I knew that Mack would shortly be sending a satellite reflected message to FBI headquarters, so I suggested to the grays that we ought to look near the dog sled and also around the other rock, where Mack had given me the big hug.

After a few minutes, one of the grays asked me where Mack was. "Over there somewhere," I replied. "Are you afraid that he's taken off? Maybe he's looking for a convenience store."

The gray headed over toward the rock where we had last seen Mack. On his way, I saw him stoop down, pick something up from the snow, and brush it off. A gray near me touched my arm, looked me in the eyes, and said, "The medicine has been found."

I immediately turned and shouted, "Mack! Mack! They found it!"

Mack's voice came from behind the rock where he was last seen. "Who found it? Where was it?" he shouted.

I saw him come from behind the rock and approach the gray who was holding his medicine bottle. The gray handed it to him. Mack inspected the bottle and then patted the gray on the shoulder. "Thanks," he said. "You're a life saver!" Then he turned to the rest of us and shouted, "Let's go! I'm getting cold."

We all piled back into the small tureen and quickly flew back to Center Earth. On our way, one gray asked Mack, "What this does this medicine do?"

"It regulates the level of the cholesterol in my blood. Too much cholesterol is bad because it clogs the arteries and stops the flow of blood."

"We don't have that problem with our circulatory systems," the gray told him. "We don't eat fatty foods. We simply absorb nutrients through our skin. Nothing harmful can pass into us that way."

Mack told me what the gray had said to him.

I looked the gray in the eyes and chimed in, "Yeah, but you spend a lot of time bathing alone. Have you ever thought of bathing with a friend?"

"It is not something that we would do."

"Yeah, but you should try it. It leads to other things."

Chapter 22

We returned to Center Earth and reported to Queen Igua's secretary that Mack's medicine had been found by one of the Draconian grays whom she had sent along to help us. Or, maybe to spy on us. Actually, the gray had found the bottle of medicine exactly where Mack had dropped it from his trousers leg as he made his way around the rock to send a covert transmission to the FBI.

"Queen Igua would like you and Mr. LaSalle to join her at a reception for a guest representing the Royal Family of Ummo," she told Mack.

"Thank you. It will be our pleasure to attend," Mack replied. "When should we arrive?"

"The reception is already in progress. You should hurry so as not to disappoint Her Majesty."

We were dressed to dig for buried stuff in the snow, not to greet some royal yahoo, but Mack insisted that we go anyway. He said, "We can always make excuses for our appearance, but never for standing up the queen."

One of the secretary's Draconian grays led us to the reception, held in "the library." There were no books. On

Draco, a library is a room where stories and documentaries are played out as 3-D holograms, though only at ten percent of life size. When Mack and I arrived, the story of the Draconian victory over the Silicon Warriors of Center Earth was being played.

I guess that we missed most of it, because the Silicon Warriors were evacuating in damaged tureens for their home planet and the Draconian global anthem was playing. Queen Igua's eyes were watering, so it must have been a tear-jerker.

"Oh, wonderful," the queen exclaimed through the translation device that hung like an amulet around her scaly neck, "you have arrived!"

"We apologize for our tardiness, Your Majesty," Mack said. "We had business in the snow outside. Please excuse our appearance, but we feared that if we cleaned up prior to coming, we would have missed meeting the honored guest."

"Come, come!" the queen insisted. She turned to the tall gentleman from Ummo and said, "Commander Waam, permit me to introduce two outstanding American supporters of our New World Order, Agent Smith of the FBI and Mr. Sandy LaSalle of Hollywood." She turned to me and asked, "That is near Colorado, isn't it?"

"It's in California, Your Majesty," I replied, "but in Draconian travel time, it's almost next door."

Waam bent down to shake our hands. "It is a pleasure to meet you both," he said, "although I believe that Agent Smith and I were in a meeting together in Astana eighteen months ago."

"Perhaps so," Mack replied, "but perhaps longer ago."

One of the queen's entourage, also wearing a translation amulet, said, "I was there with both of you. It was three years ago at the meeting where His Excellency first discussed Agenda Twenty-One. He was in the container of an older woman."

"Yes!" Waam exclaimed. "That was it!"

"Yes! I remember," Mack replied. "Thank you."

"Ambassador Conger," the lizard said, bowing his head slightly.

"Thank you, Ambassador. You have an excellent memory."

"You were from the FBI, representing the American President, Agent Smith. I believe that he had a more important engagement in Hawaii, I think playing golf."

Mack's face bore surprise at the ambassador's remark. "I'm sure that you must be mistaken about our president's agenda that day, although he often does play golf."

The ambassador changed the subject, ever so slightly. "Your president has not made as much progress as we had hoped," he said.

Waam raised his eyes at Mack. He knew how Mack felt about the president and was clearly wondering how Mack would handle this accusation. Mack smiled at the ambassador and said, "Our American President has to work through both houses of our representative Congress, which is often difficult to do when they are led by opposing political parties. However, he has proclaimed numerous Executive Orders that have lightened the NWO's task. Among them are further gun control, redistribution of wealth, imminent domain over private property, and social justice. Best of all have been the appointments of more than twenty czars, unelected officials who have been placed into powerful positions of authority without the normal, lengthy vetting and hiring processes. Their efforts have practically guaranteed the subversion of the American economy so that its eventual collapse will ensure easy implementation of the NWO's global government. The USA is almost twenty trillion dollars in debt. Did you know that the entire stockpile of gold, silver, and platinum held by all the governments of Earth amounts to only sixteen trillion dollars?"

"This is all good, if it is as you say it is. Will the upcoming change in leadership bring all this progress to an abrupt halt?

"Mr. Ambassador, the grand plan is being implemented in the USA, in spite of the impending change in the country's president during the upcoming elections. Soon, the two top candidates will be NWO members, at least if the female candidate isn't indicted and replaced by some unanticipated billionaire. The grand plan will eliminate the two-party system by having no candidate owing allegiance to any large lobbyists. Regardless of who wins, Agenda Twenty-One will move into full swing."

"Gentlemen, I believe that the queen should be privy to some of this conversation," Waam interjected. "Not to share these details with her is not in your best interest."

"Commander Waam," the ambassador replied, "I am about Her Majesty's business and she will know all that I have learned."

"I shall personally assure Queen Igua that the American government is fully prepared to perform its role in the emergence of the New World Order, Mr. Ambassador," Mack said assertively. "We await only His Excellency's command."

Chapter 23

As the reception ended, Mack and I were invited by Waam to dine with him in the Ummite Residence, a small embassy that was situated approximately two blocks from the queen's suite.

Unlike the queen's facility, Waam's had the gigantic doors and furniture that one would expect when its residents are all between eight and ten feet tall.

"I thought it best to dine here because our facility is constantly swept for eavesdropping devices, and special electronic signals disrupt any listening by distant devices. Thus, we may talk freely," Waam told us.

"It's so good to see you, Waam," I said. "That ambassador doesn't particularly care for Americans, does he?"

"That is his job, to keep NWO allies on the edge, always feeling suspect and unworthy. He performs it well, doesn't he?"

"I was definitely feeling the heat," Mack said.

Waam sat down on an ottoman and went right to business. Mack and I sat across from him on a sofa. "I received your message, Mack. It was forwarded by the

FBI, but, unfortunately, I was already at Center Earth when I received it. I have sent word to have a small plasma warhead altered and delivered here via diplomatic courier. It should be here tonight or tomorrow. This is a dangerous game that you are playing."

"Altered?" I asked.

"Yes," Waam replied. "In addition to its plasma, it has been altered to include a small hydrogen device, similar to the American hydrogen bomb. It will be very effective for its intended purpose."

"We want to take out the Central Sun that warms and powers Center Earth," Mack said. "We think that its destruction might drive the reptilians back to Draco and buy us more time to stop the NWO's agenda. It should certainly delay it."

"I think we should find a reason to leave Center Earth and knock it out on our way out the door," I said.

"If you do that, we will all be marked men," Waam replied. "Representatives from all members of the Galactic Federation reside in embassies in Center Earth. What you are suggesting will kill many if not all of them."

Mack's communicator pinged. He checked his message and said, "I have been ordered back to DC. It seems that Center Earth has been identified as the possible target of a terrorist attack. I have no choice but to obey orders, gentlemen. It appears that I have to catch a hop back to DC."

"This is suspicious timing," I told them. "The warhead isn't even here yet, but the FBI already knows that it's on its way."

"There must be a leak, either in the FBI or in Montano Antilia," Mack said.

"Are you suggesting that an Ummite might be the source of the leak?" Waam asked.

"My communication went to the FBI and then to

you. You contacted your staff about the warhead. The leak can only be in those two places."

Waam didn't look happy about Mack's conclusion, but he knew that Mack was right about it. The question now was whether the queen had received a similar warning. We didn't have to wait too long for an answer. Queen Igua sent word to the Ummite Embassy that she would like to meet with Mr. Sandy LaSalle at once.

Mack decided to accompany me to the queen's office building. We were greeted by the queen's secretary and I was asked to wait. "Agent Smith, your presence has not been requested," the secretary told him.

"I'm here because I've been called back to Washington by my superiors. I need to catch a shuttle as soon as possible, and I am hoping that you can arrange that for me."

"You're not alone. Many of the ambassadors and their staff are leaving Center Earth over the next few hours." She handed Mack a small plastic device. "I will arrange passage for you. Please carry this communicator and remain inside Center Earth until you hear from me. That device will vibrate when I have information for you."

Mack thanked her. Before he left, he shook my hand and said, "It was nice meeting you Sandy. Hopefully, we will see each other again."

I knew exactly what he was getting at. The queen's request was strangely timed, so we both figured that I might soon be providing nourishment for the Draconian grays.

A few minutes after Mack left the office, a tall green lizard with pink edging around his lips came in and was permitted immediate access to the queen's office. I had seen lips like his somewhere before, but I couldn't remember where. I figured that his was a unique species of

Draconian. Two minutes later, Queen Igua announced that she was ready to see me.

The queen's secretary opened the door and announced my presence.

"Come in, Mr. LaSalle," Queen Igua said through her translation amulet.

I bowed slightly and said, "You asked to see me, Your Majesty?"

"Yes, Mr. LaSalle, I wanted you to meet Dr. Siggist Anguilla."

I raised my hand in greeting to the lizard who had walked through the outer office while I was waiting for my audience with the queen. I was surprised when Dr. Anguilla took my hand, but instead of shaking it, he lifted it to his nostrils and sniffed. He nodded to the queen.

"Dr. Anguilla was present at Livermore when His Excellency's migration into his new container was disrupted and his electrical essence was kidnapped."

I stepped backward, looking at Anguilla. "What are you saying?" I asked.

Dr. Anguilla looked me in the eyes and said, "When you passed me at the Her Majesty's reception yesterday, your scent smelled familiar. It was not until this morning that I recalled where I had smelled it before. It was in the broadcast studio at Livermore, and your scent was that of the Interrogator who destroyed His Excellency's new container. I accuse you of being that Interrogator."

"You're out of your mind!" I exclaimed, challenging his accusation. But I knew that I had been outed. "Your Majesty," I pleaded, "I just donated three million dollars to the construction of the Hollywood Rebirth Center!"

"My staff checked you out, Mr. LaSalle. You have pledged money, but you have not provided it. In fact, your partner is now trying to find an alternate source of funding because you have disappeared and your contact information is bogus. In fact, we would like to know where the equipment intended for Hollywood has been taken. Apparently, the shipment was hijacked."

"Your Majesty, I have not yet delivered the construction funds to Simone because I was summoned to come here by His Excellency."

"Your lies will not work here, Mr. LaSalle," the queen replied.

The queen raised her hand into the air and four Draconian guards entered the room. If I had had my 1911, I'd have taken a couple of them out before they killed me, but I had nothing to use to defend myself, and they were too imposing to try to out-muscle.

"Escort this man to the scow," the Queen ordered, "and schedule him for crystallization"

Whatever that was, it didn't sound like something appealing.

The guards took me by my arms and lifted me from the floor. I was literally carried out the door of the queen's office and down the hallway to an elevator. I tried kicking at the lizards, but to no avail. One guard passed his thee-clawed hand over a metal plate, and the elevator door opened. They pushed me into the elevator and then stepped in themselves. I was smashed against the back wall. They didn't seem to care.

When the elevator door opened, we were in some sort of garage. The guards lifted me again and took me to a filthy rectangular vehicle that looked a bit like what it was, a garbage tureen. While one guard opened a hatch, the others ripped my clothes off, and then threw me inside. I stood up, but before I could figure out a way out of my predicament, I was grabbed again and cuffed naked to a piece of scrap metal. The lizards left me, closing and locking the hatch as they did.

I felt motion and knew that the Draconian barge was

in the air. It was then that I noticed that the air inside the barge was getting colder. After a few minutes, my stomach felt motion again, and I knew that the barge was coming to a stop. I heard a loud scraping noise, a metal upon metal squeal, and then the sound of trash falling into a pile somewhere.

A hatch inside the barge opened. A lizard wearing dirty coveralls walked in. He inspected the plastic ties that bound me to the scrap metal, and then pushed me and the metal into the middle of the room. He then walked to the side of the room, connected his safety belt to a hook on the wall, and turned to look at me. As our eyes met, he said, "Enjoy becoming an ice crystal!" He then touched a button, and suddenly the scrap metal and I were falling into the frigid air of outdoors Antarctica.

I hit the snow on the edge of a large trash pile with a thud that took my breath away. The impact caused the scrap metal to bounce and twist violently. The plastic ties tore savagely into my wrists, but suddenly broke free from the scrap metal. It was too cold for me to survive for more than a few minutes, too cold to breathe deeply, and just too fucking cold. Maybe thirty below zero. I thought of Mona and how much I loved her. I was pretty sure that if she ever saw me again, I'd be a frozen cadaver and she would be there to identify the body. "Good bye, baby," I said aloud.

The wind was blowing wildly. I stumbled against it to the side of the trash pile. Beneath a piece of sheet aluminum was an assortment of plastic bags full of trash, some full of meat products and other paper. I climbed under the aluminum and in between the bags to get out of the wind. Because the garbage had not yet lost its air temperature, its warmth felt great. I curled into a ball to preserve my upper body heat, and I figured that that would give me maybe five minutes of life, tops. After a minute, I began shivering, then I felt numbness in my outer extremities. Soon I became tired, very tired. *This is what dying is like*, I told myself. *It ain't all that bad.*

Chapter 24

The queen's secretary touched a button on the console at her desk. Immediately, the small device that Mack Smith had placed into his trousers pocket began to vibrate. Mack hurried to the secretary's desk.

"Agent Smith," the secretary told him, "Unless you have made other arrangements, Her Majesty and His Excellency cordially invite you to ride with them back to Astana in her private Tureen."

"Outstanding. Please advise Her Majesty that I am delighted to accept her offer."

"Her shuttle leaves in thirty minutes from Hanger Fourteen. Be sure to get there ten minutes early."

Mack thanked the secretary and found his way directly to Hanger Fourteen. There was no time to stop for luggage, and whatever he left behind could be replaced for only a few dollars.

⁊⊙⊱

On the journey back to Astana, Mack, Queen Igua,

and His Excellency were discussing Astana. "The buildings there are incredible," Mack said. "It's the perfect
place for the headquarters of the NWO."

"My new palace will be constructed there, as well,
just a few hundred yards from the World Congress," Hitler told him. "The plans are almost complete. From the
air, it will appear in the shape of a swastika."

"Excellent," Mack replied.

"Did you know that the Swastika is an ancient symbol for the swirling direction of spiritual energy?"

"No, I didn't. That's very interesting, Excellency. I'll
have to do a Google search."

Queen Igua was bored with the conversation and
changed the subject. "Did you notice the extent of the
activity in the entrance as we prepared to leave Center
Earth, Agent Smith?"

"No, Your Majesty," Mack replied. "Is a special
event taking place?"

"Many embassies received warning today that the
Resistance may be planning a terrorist attack at Center
Earth. Because of the events at the Lunar Artifact in the
recent past, by this evening only a very few ambassadors
still will be dwelling at their residences."

"Really? I was totally unaware."

"We caught at least one member of the Resistance,
but he is no longer a problem."

"That's good. We don't need another incident like
Livermore or the Lunar Artifact."

"Perhaps more members of the Resistance may have
found a secret way into Center Earth. Like many who are
departing, we sense that there may be trouble brewing
here and feel that it is timely to make a temporary exit."

"This seems like another delay, Your Majesty, and
our grand plan has been delayed too long."

Hitler agreed. "We should already be hip deep in the

pandemic, and Her Majesty's forces already should be preparing to emerge from their subterranean facilities. The delays have been exasperating!"

"And what about your plans, now, Your Majesty?" Mack asked. "How will you ensure your safety from the Resistance?"

Hitler spoke before the queen, which is something that she generally did not like. "We will both stay in Astana for now, probably in our quarters in the subterranean facility," he said. "We will be living there on a permanent basis very soon. Have you visited your shelter, Mr. Smith?"

Mack lied, sort of. "I like to spend weekends there when living in DC. It's only a fifteen minute ride away on the TAUSS. When the pandemic is released, I will be very comfortable there." In truth, he had only been there for one weekend and found it terribly claustrophobic. He hoped that he would never have to live there with his wife for several months. He would almost rather die.

ഏഃഏഃ

The queen's tureen arrived in Astana just in time for a national celebration. Two astronauts had just landed in Kazakhstan after orbiting in the international space station for a year. Mack joined Queen Igua and His Excellency in the reviewing stand as a parade passed by the multitude of people who had turned out to cheer the country's heroes.

At the end of the parade, Mack thanked Queen Igua and Hitler for the ride to Astana and for the interesting conversation. "I wish you both safe harbor until the pandemic," he said. An hour later, he caught a hop from Astana to Rota, Spain, and then another from Rota to Andrews Air Force Base. From there, he traveled by military limo to Washington, DC and FBI headquarters.

Shortly after the parade, the Kazakhstani astronauts met with the queen in a private room, where they could debrief in private.

"We bring special news, Your Majesty," said the team leader. "The special NWO surprise has been readied!"

"How many missiles are we talking about, Colonel?" the Queen asked.

"Six missiles bearing four multiple nuclear warheads each have been prepped and are ready to launch at His Excellency's command. They will launch from the space station and streak toward Earth, exploding fifty miles above major cities in all hemispheres and resulting in widespread electric system destruction caused by the electromagnetic pulses associated with their nuclear explosions."

"Excellent!" Hitler exclaimed. The queen smiled widely. Hitler added, "Earth's communications systems will be fried, and we will use the Your Majesty's gravity wave communications system to issue orders to our troops and supporters. It will be the only functioning mass communication system on the planet."

The queen asked, "Soon, will it not be time to order the pre-selected survivors into the subterranean facilities, so that we can release the pandemic?"

"Yes!" Hitler replied eagerly. "With no communications available, those on the surface will have no concept of the magnitude of the pandemic nor any way to combat it. Then, when our troops arrive to save the day, the masses will willingly accept our rule!"

Hitler clasped forearms with Queen Igua and spun her in a circle. "The day has come at last!" he exclaimed. Turning to his aide, he ordered all international Rebirth

Centers to begin preparations to relocate to underground shelters. "However," he said, "all migrations must continue. Convey to all Center Directors that it is important that every selected individual be fitted with the chip that will connect all humans into the telepathic network so that they can receive messages directly from NWO Command and utilize the knowledge held in other brains for the common good of the survivors in all subterranean facilities during and after the pandemic."

Chapter 25

Mona felt a bit nauseous, she thought probably from eating the bacon that she had cooked two days ago and had stored unwrapped in the meat bin in her refrigerator. "I should have known better," she muttered to herself. She went to the kitchen sink and began rinsing the breakfast dishes and putting them into the dishwasher. Something just wasn't right.

From the upstairs she could hear the sounds of Stella stirring after her morning nap. In a few minutes, Stella would find her way down the stairs and into the living room, where she'd play quietly with her dolls until it was time for lunch.

When she had put the last glass into the dishwasher, Mona walked into the living room and plopped onto the sofa. Instinctively, she closed her eyes and cleared her mind, which was relatively easy to do when alone. Soon, she opened her mind to receiving images and impressions, as was taught during her Remote Viewing classes. She was definitely getting better at it, as Sarge had attested.

The impressions that she felt this morning were

about Danny, who still hadn't contacted her in several days. The impression that she felt was of being naked and freezing cold. She was certain that she was feeling what Danny was feeling. As her anxiety increased, the impressions stopped coming. That's the way it was with Remote Viewing. Attachments made the transmission of feelings more difficult, if not impossible, and Mona was as attached to Danny much the same as any woman could be to a special man. He was the love of her life.

Sounds of soft steps upon the carpet told her that Stella was awake and now beside her in the living room. She then felt Stella's hands on her knees. Stella was definitely here and was seeking attention.

Stella pulled herself onto the sofa and then she climbed onto Mona's lap. "Mommy okay?" Stella asked.

"Mommy is worried about Daddy," Mona replied, opening her eyes. "He hasn't called in a few days, and that just isn't like him."

"Daddy cold," Stella said.

"Can you see Daddy?" Mona asked.

Stella nodded.

"Can you tell me where he is?"

Stella shook her head.

"Can you show me where Daddy is?"

Stella nodded. She turned herself on Mona's lap and said, "Mommy sleep."

Mona wasn't sure what Stella wanted her to do, but then it struck her. "Do you mean close my eyes, honey? Do you want Mommy to close her eyes?"

Stella nodded.

Still sitting on Mona's lap and facing Mona, Stella put her open fingertips onto her mother's temples. Mona closed her eyes and tried to empty her mind of the anxiety that filled it. Instantly, images flooded into Mona's consciousness. She saw Danny, lying under a piece of shiny metal. He was naked and cold. Then she saw Waam, discovering Danny, covering him with an article of clothing, and carrying him like a baby into the warmth of his tureen. Danny was going to be okay. But he was still cold, very cold. Was she seeing the present or the future? She couldn't be sure.

Mona tried to send Danny energy to warm his body. She told Stella, "Make Daddy warm, honey."

Stella removed her hands from Mona's temples. The images stopped pouring into her brain.

Mona opened her eyes and asked, "Stella, can you help make Daddy warm?" Stella nodded. "Please help Mommy make Daddy warm, honey. Please help Mommy make Daddy warm."

Stella placed her fingertips on Mona's temples again. "Warm," she said. "Warm."

As Stella was saying "Warm" over and over again, Mona saw herself giving birth to a little boy, whose eyes were like Stella's. Now the morning's nausea suddenly made sense. "Those bastard lizards made me pregnant again!" she said aloud.

Stella looked at her Mommy. "Mommy has baby," Stella said, pressing her finger into Mona's belly.

"Bastards!" Mona said again.

Chapter 26

Soon after Mack and Dan Arrow had left his embassy for Queen Igua's offices, Waam received word that a special diplomatic courier was waiting for him at his tureen. "Excellent," he said. He immediately took the embassy's elevator to the garage area and took a hover car to the hangar where his tureen was stored.

The courier snapped to attention when Waam exited the hover car. "At ease, soldier," Waam instructed. "Where is the package that you've brought me?"

The courier took Waam into his small two-man tureen, opened a secret compartment, and handed Waam a cardboard tube that was six feet long and eight inches in diameter. "Sir, I believe that this is what you asked for," he said to Waam.

"Yes, this appears to be the item. Who else knows that it has come here?"

"Only those who constructed it, Commander."

"Are they trustworthy?"

"Sir, yes, sir! I'd stake my life on it."

"You already may have, trooper," Waam replied.

The young courier looked quizzically at his Commander and then he asked, "Do you have a message or package to be returned to Montano Antilia?"

"No. You are finished here. Have a safe flight back to Italy."

The courier saluted. Waam carefully backed out of the small tureen and carried his prize into his own military tureen, paying little attention as the courier's tureen hovered and then left the hangar. Once inside his own tureen, he shut the ramp and busied himself installing the missile into its special launch tube. The installation was quick; however, ensuring that the computer guidance system communicated effectively with his own computers required that he run a special program. It would take close to an hour.

While the program ran, Waam sat reading scrambled messages from Ummo Command. He was advised that an important message had been downloaded from the communication device that had been taken from Dr. Cassini. In brief, the broadcast message advised all Rebirth Centers "to take necessary steps to relocate to assigned subterranean caverns within thirty days." Obviously, something big was going to happen, and Waam was pretty sure that it was the release of the global pandemic. Where, though, and what would it be?

As he sat contemplating the message in the pilot's seat of his tureen, Waam noticed a massive garbage scow passing overhead. It was moving very slowly and silently, its pilot being careful not to damage other craft or to strike support beams as he maneuvered his vessel toward the exit from Center Earth. When the shadow of the scow passed beyond his tureen, Waam's communication device alerted him that the computer chip that had been inserted into Dan Arrow's tattooed forearm was leaving Center Earth.

"Something's not right about this," Waam said

aloud. He hit the ignition on his tureen. The quiet hum let him know that the drive was warming, and then a single chime told him that it was ready to go. He placed his fingers into the handprint on the control panel, and the tureen slowly rose and glided quietly toward the exit, following the scow. To avoid being seen, Waam flipped a switch and his cloaking device did its thing, making the tureen invisible to the naked eye.

Waam followed the garbage scow at a safe distance, until it reached its destination, the Draconian dump, located a few clicks less than five miles from the entrance of Center Earth. Holding his tureen steady against the brisk wind, Waam watched as the scow released its payload onto the existing pile of frozen garbage. Of interest, the scow sent a smaller pile of waste, as though someone had used a push broom the clean up the bilge before shutting the hatch and returning to the central hangar. Waam couldn't be certain, but he thought that the smaller pile may have included a human form.

When the barge had finished unloading its smelly cargo, it left the dump. Waam slowly hovered over the newly dumped scrap until he located the source of the beacon from Dan's identification chip. He landed close to the location, opened his ramp, and began looking for Dan. The wind was howling and it had begun to snow.

Holding his communicator, Waam moved through the debris until the signal was at its strongest, and then he began to dig through the scrap with his bare hands. "There he is!" Waam said aloud when he saw a human figure huddled in the fetal position beneath a sheet of aluminum. Waam tossed the aluminum aside. The wind picked it up and it tumbled on its edges for a hundred yards before it fell flat into the snow. Seeing that Dan was naked and unconscious, Waam then removed his own jacket and wrapped it around him. He then picked

Dan up and carried him back to the warmth of his tureen. Even for an Ummite, walking against the wind was difficult and Waam's own body began shivering from the cold.

Back inside the tureen, Waam removed the jacket and placed Dan on a table, where he could be warmed under a plasma lamp. Twenty minutes later, the heat brought Dan back to consciousness. Still shivering, Dan sat up and thanked Waam for saving his life. Then he asked, "Are all of your people out of Center Earth?"

Waam nodded.

"It's time to do that place in."

Waam concurred. Returning to his contoured pilot's seat, Waam guided his tureen back to the entrance of Center Earth. He waited for several minutes, while a convoy of tureens exited the facility, before he floated into the main area and hovered over an open field about a mile from the first buildings of the city.

"It is a beautiful setting," Waam told Dan.

"Beauty is as beauty does, Waam," Dan said.

Waam nodded. Using his large left hand, he tapped on a small keyboard, setting the coordinates on his missile for the Central Sun, which was glowing several miles above. "I cannot do this," Waam said. "Many humans remain here to keep systems running."

"But I can," Dan replied. He reached above Waam's head and depressed the red launch button.

As the missile left its tube, Waam turned his tureen and quickly exited the entrance, narrowly missing an NWO tureen that was entering. As the NWO tureen disappeared into the tunnel, it was greeted by a hurricane of burning gasses which consumed it and everyone on board. Although Waam had reached the mouth of the entrance, the concussion from the explosion flipped his tureen from behind and sent it spinning a few yards above the water which was pounding the icy shores of Antarctica. It took a moment for Waam to stabilize his craft, and then, after setting the coordinates for a small village in Virginia, he took Dan back home to Mona.

Chapter 27

We were somewhere over Miami when Waam's communicator pinged. He held it to his ear for a moment. "Just a minute," Waam said into the receiver, "I want to put you on the big screen." He hit a couple of buttons, and a screen appeared on the inside wall of his tureen. "Can you see us?" he asked. The screen flipped for a moment and then Mack's face filled the screen.

"Where are you?" Mack asked.

"Just north of Miami," Waam replied.

"What about Dan? How did it go with Queen Igua?"

"I'm here," I replied, stepping into the camera so Mack could see me. "Let's say that she gave me a cold reception, but Waam is taking me home, where things should go better."

"You'll never guess, but I caught a ride to Astana with Her Majesty and our old friend."

"Hitler?" I asked.

"Yeah. I wanted to take him out, but between the queen and her entourage of guards, I couldn't do anything without committing suicide."

"Too bad," I replied. "Did you get any info that will help us ferret that bastard out of hiding?"

Mack nodded. "They plan to stay in Astana for a couple of months. We're going to have to find a way to do the deed over there."

That was definitely going to be harder.

"There's more, though. I caught a couple of hops and I'm now back in DC. I've been going through my emails and I thought you'd both be interested in a report that I received from our research division."

Waam laughed. "They always find interesting things, Mack, even if the information is so out of date that it is useless."

"Well, this is timely. It seems that a research team has been conducting autopsies on lone wolf terrorists. Unexpectedly, they discovered that the last six of them had small computer chips located in the frontal lobes of their brains."

"Part of the Hive?" I asked.

"I think so. But here's the zinger: They've always deemed the chips to be non-functional, but they got special permission from a terminal inmate at Sing Sing to insert one into his brain. When they did, the chip sprang back to life. They called NASA in to test the device, and NASA has been able to trace the faint signals that the chip receives to a single location in the stratosphere."

"So, now we know at least one location from which the signals are being sent to the Hive by the NWO—" I exclaimed.

Mack interrupted me. "Just a minute, guys," he said, looking at his cell phone. "There's major news breaking on all the wires. A major earthquake has occurred in Antarctica. There are Tsunami warnings for Cape Town and Tasmania. Also a tsunami watch for Melbourne."

"Can't imagine," I said.

"There's more." Mack paused for a few seconds while he read the wire report. A simultaneous earthquake has hit the Indian Ocean. A Tsunami is headed toward Indonesia."

"I hadn't expected that," Waam said.

"Did you guys do it?" Mack asked.

"Do what, Mack?" I asked.

"Did you nuke Center Earth? That's the only thing that I can think of that would cause an earthquake in Antarctica. It's essentially a seismologically stable continent."

"Well—" I began to say, but Mack cut me off.

"Wait a minute," he said, holding up his hand, palm side toward us. "I just received a communique from Astana. Waam, are you sitting down?"

"Of course," Waam replied.

"You need to know that the NWO has put you on the international terrorist watch list. Their message includes your picture. They are accusing you of being the lone wolf terrorist who destroyed Center Earth. They want you alive. You are going to need to disappear, and I'm not sure that Ummo is going to be a safe place for you."

Waam immediately checked to be sure that his tureen was cloaked. "What about Dan?" he asked.

"The communique doesn't mention him. But you have a price on your head, Waam, and every bounty hunter in the galaxy is going to be looking for you."

"Yes, I see. I think my day-to-day life is going to be challenging from now on."

"I'm so sorry, Waam," I said.

"It's okay. It was a calculated risk, and I was aware of the ramifications. I am now an outlaw, a known member of the resistance. My superiors are not going to be happy with me, and they may not protect me."

Mack told us that he had been called into an emergency meeting to discuss the two earthquakes and the role the FBI was going to play in providing assistance to relief workers.

We said goodbye and Waam shut down his communicator. He didn't want to hear from anyone, especially his superiors on Ummo.

The final ten minutes of our trip took us from southern Georgia, USA to Villagio Ibrido. He circled the Villagio to scope out activities of law enforcement before landing in my back yard.

"Thanks for saving my life, Waam," I told him. "Would you like to stay here for a little while? We have an extra room, and Mona will cook you anything you'd like, especially when she hears about how you saved me."

"Thanks, but no. I would stick out like a sore thumb. Besides, too many Villagio residents are associated with the NWO. I would not be safe here for long."

As I stepped down the ramp to the green grass of my back yard, Mona opened the back door and hurried out, Stella in her arms. "Danny! Stella told me that you were coming! How are you? I saw you freezing in the snow!"

We kissed, and Stella kissed my cheek while I was busy with Mona's lips. Obviously, Mona had a lot to tell me, and I wanted to spend some time in her arms. It was good to be home.

Chapter 28

Mona put Stella into her bed and came back down the stairs to me. "She'll sing for a while, and then she'll fall to sleep. She sings herself to sleep every night now, Danny. It's kind of neat."

"You like being a mother, don't you, baby?" I said.

"She's more and more remarkable every day. You'll see. Over the next few days, she'll do things that you'll wish you could do. Her skills and comprehension seem to grow at a faster rate every day. I think that Mack was right about the fact that she'll be miles ahead of us intellectually by the time she's ten. Maybe even eight."

"The thought of having a genius for a child is kind of weird, Mona. I mean, I'm just a regular guy. How am I going to relate to someone who's smarter than Einstein?"

"I don't think she cares how smart we are or how limited our skills are. She loves us the way any daughter loves her parents. And you—you're her daddy. There's just something special between little girls and their dads."

"She kissed me on the cheek when I was kissing you," I said. "It was kind of sweet."

"She misses you when you're gone, Danny. And she

knows how much I love you. If it weren't for Stella, I'd never have been able to see you in the snow."

"How did she do that, baby?"

"She can see things that we can't see. Some of it is in the present and some of it is in the future."

"The future?"

"Yeah. I was worried about you because you hadn't called me, so I tried remote viewing to see where you were. I was having difficulty concentrating, so Stella put her hands on my temples, and it was like a video was turned on inside my head. I felt the cold that you were feeling, and I actually saw Waam pick you up and carry you into his tureen, but I saw it before it happened. I think she wanted to let me know that you were going to be okay."

"That's amazing. Do you think I'd see the future if she did that to me?"

"Maybe. It was like a gift for me to know that you were alive and that you'd be okay."

Mona took my hand, pulled me off the sofa, and led me upstairs. We looked in on Stella, who was deep in sleep, and then we went into our bedroom and closed the door. Mona gave me one of those passionate kisses that let me know how lucky I was going to be. Then she undressed me, kissing my chest and belly, and tickling my thighs with her fingers.

"What the fuck is this on your forearm?" Mona asked abruptly.

I figured that my lovemaking session had just ended. "Something that Mack gave me," I replied. "It's supposed to wash off in a few days." I was lying. She studied that damn NWO tattoo for a moment and then started exploring my body tentatively with her hands again. I tried to get our reunion back on track. "I missed you, Mona. I don't like being away from you," I whispered.

"Shut up," Mona said, pushing me onto the bed. She undressed and climbed on top of me. She wanted to be in control, so I relinquished it to her. She was gentle, and when I finally erupted, it was like we were one.

We lay motionless in bed for maybe half an hour. I drifted in and out of sleep until Mona finally spoke.

"Danny?"

"Yeah, baby?"

"There's something else."

"What's that?"

"When Stella let me see the future, I saw something else."

"What did you see?"

"I'm pregnant. Those bastards made me pregnant again, Danny. They won't leave me alone. This time I'm having a little boy."

"I know."

"What do you mean? How do you know? Do I show already?"

I smiled. "No. I had one of those abduction experiences. It was almost a dream, but it seemed so real. Those alien bastards milked my sperm like I was a cow. I couldn't move, like I was frozen still. Then I saw that you and Stella were there in the tureen with me. Stella was walking around, but you were lying on a gurney beside me. They stuck a needle into your abdomen and impregnated you with my sperm."

"I'm guessing that it was no dream, Danny. It must have really happened. If they impregnated me with your sperm, then I definitely want this little boy. I've already seen him, and he does resemble you, except that he's handsome."

"Hey, wait a minute," I said, poking Mona in her tummy. She giggled and pushed away from me. I pulled her back to me and kissed her breasts. She let out a little moan that let me know that it would be okay to make love to her again. Only this time, I was in control.

ᏫᎦᎦᎠ

In the early afternoon, I was playing foam ball catch in the front yard with Stella when a UPS truck pulled to a stop at the end of our driveway and the driver got out. "Are you Daniel Arrow?" the guy asked.

"Yeah."

"Sign here."

I used a stylus to sign his electronic pad. He returned to his truck, pulled out a large oblong box, and plopped it at my feet. "This came from the FBI," he told me. "It must be important."

He was gone in less than a minute. I read somewhere that these guys are given three minutes to deliver each package. If that's true, from where I stand, their work day would be an eight-hour sprint with a lot of frustration, especially during the early morning and late afternoon rush hours when cars just won't get out of their way.

I dragged the box up the driveway and into the garage, with Stella pushing it to help me. You gotta love kids. I told Stella, "We really shook that bridge!" It was something that had I learned from Mona, a story about an elephant and a canary walking across a bridge together. What I told Stella is what the canary told the elephant when they got to the other side. You get the point.

I used a box cutter and opened this unexpected package. It was a strange double telescope of some kind made under the Santilli name. I knew that it came from Mack, because nobody else from the FBI would give a damn about me, especially the ones who support the NWO.

There was no note, so I knew that Mack would be calling me, or else he would be coming for a visit. The one thing that bothered me was that anytime Mack showed up, it usually meant that he had something for me to do, and often at a high degree of peril. I mean, look, I just about lost my life in Antarctica thanks to one of Mack's crazy missions. And before that, I was almost cut up to feed the Draconian grays below Denver, and I was a hair's breadth away from death at the hand of Commissar Nargas on the Moon. So, Mack clearly had something up his sleeve and I knew I'd be learning about it in a short while.

Mack didn't let me down. He texted Mona and told her that he would be at the Villagio at dinnertime and wanted to know if he could mooch a meal. Given that he is her boss, Mona texted back, *Of course! There's always a place at our table for you.*

I hoped that she was cooking macaroni and cheese out of the box with lima beans, or something equally unappetizing, but she took steaks out of the freezer and told me that I had to cook them on the grill. "Mack likes his steak the way that you do," she told me. "Medium rare."

So, Mack arrived at six-thirty sharp, like he had been parked down the street, waiting for exactly the correct moment to ring the doorbell. I could tell that the paperwork in his hand had to do with the telescope, because across the top of the first page it said, *Santilli 150.*

We had cocktails. Well, Mack and Mona had whiskey sours, while I opted for a beer. Then I excused myself and cooked the steaks. When they were done, we all sat at the table, including Stella, who sat next to Mona so Mona could feed her the same meal that we were eating, except that Stella's went through a small hand-cranked food grinder before it found its way into her mouth. Given how intelligent she is, I'm sure that she couldn't wait for her teeth to come in so she could chomp down on a nice piece of charcoal broiled Angus rib eye.

Over dinner we discussed the pending emergence of the reptilians from their deep underground military bases, or DUMBS. Mack brought a copy of an internet article that he'd found about how an alien binary code had been cracked, first by a soldier who had touched a UFO at Rendlesham Forest in England, and, second, by a guy who translated a crop circle that looked like a response to a binary message that NASA had sent into space, alerting the galaxy that humans were finally attempting inter-steller communications.

"It's all been planned," Mack told us, referring to a strategically sequenced desensitization of human beings to the presence of aliens. "The translation of binary code proves that aliens are here: in the first case, communicating with each other, and in the second case, communicating directly with those who know binary code. Educated humans, especially scientists, will not be surprised but will, in fact, welcome their space brothers."

"You're sounding a lot like an NWO supporter, Mack. And then what will educated humans do when they find out that their space brothers were involved with killing off ninety percent of all human beings before they emerged from their DUMBs?" I asked.

"They'll feel betrayed," Mona said. "They'll know what I know…that their space brothers can't be trusted and that their space brothers only tolerate the existence of a few humans because it suits their ends. They'll know that somehow, and with the full agreement of our global governments, we humans gave ownership of our planet away to a bunch of unscrupulous lizards."

"Regardless," Mack replied, "news reports like these are targeted to prepare humans for the emergence, so they will not be shocked if the actual emergence occurs."

"That's the operant word, Mack," I said. "If!"

Mona asked Mack if he wanted an after-dinner drink.

"I'd love one, but maybe after Dan and I do some star gazing. You should join us, Mona."

"Maybe after Stella is down."

"Dan, that Santilli telescope is the latest technology. Have you tried it yet?"

"Not yet. I just got it this afternoon. What's so special about it?"

"I've never looked through one, but I think we should try it tonight. The Santilli uses concave lenses instead of convex, and what you actually see is antimatter."

"Antimatter?"

"Yeah. It's like propulsion…you know, for every action there is an equal, opposite reaction. It's the same with matter. For all matter there is an equal amount of antimatter. You can see matter, but you can't see antimatter. The Santilli telescope lets you see antimatter!"

"So, why is that important?" I asked.

"Santilli has found objects orbiting the moon and the Earth that are made from antimatter. That means that we can't see them with the naked eye or with conventional telescopes. Around Earth, they seem to hover above important military bases, as though the bases are under surveillance."

"This sounds interesting, Mack," Mona said. "I think you can count on me to join you in stargazing tonight. But first, I've got to give Stella a bath and put her to bed."

"Good night, Daddy," Stella said clearly.

"Say goodnight to Uncle Mack, Honey," Mona prompted, taking Stella into her arms.

"Goodnight, Uncle Mack," Stella repeated.

Mack blew Stella a kiss.

"Goodnight, sweetheart," I said. "I'll be up to kiss you as soon as Uncle Mack leaves." I hoped that he got the not so subtle message that I was sending.

Carrying Stella, Mona left the dining room and headed upstairs to run Stella's bath.

"So, is this telescope Italian?" I asked.

"American made," Mack replied. "Santilli lives in Florida."

It was nearing sundown, so I suggested that we head outside to set up the telescope while we could still read the directions in the fading light. Between the two of us, Mack and I managed to set it up in fifteen minutes. The interesting aspect of it was that it included a camera to take digital pictures of whatever we were looking at, which was good because we could study them closely after going back inside.

Mack adjusted the telescope, focusing on the moon. He used coordinates that he brought with him, wanting to see if invisible objects that Santilli had already identified were, in fact, really there. The camera didn't snap an instant picture but, instead, its lens stayed open for fifteen seconds. Then its screen popped on to reveal what the camera had found.

The first two pictures that Mack took, yielded nothing, but the third picture of the moon revealed a dark spot that was disk shaped. "Got one!" Mack exclaimed.

I looked at the screen. It looked like a human egg floating in fluid. "Are you sure about this?" I asked. "Is the lens dirty?"

"Through the traditional telescope, you see nothing, but through the Santilli you see objects. They're really there. Santilli's research has been corroborated by others. That pic is real."

Mona joined us. "She's singing."

Would you like me to go sit with her until she's asleep?" I asked.

Mona opened her palm. "I brought the baby monitor." She turned to Mack and asked, "So, what are you so excited about?

"This special telescope lets us see antimatter," Mack replied. "We've just taken our first picture of an invisible UFO. Santilli proposes that tureens like these collect antimatter in some manner and use it for propulsion by exposing it to matter and harnessing the energy that results from the explosion."

"This is getting too technical for me," I said.

Mona looked at the camera's rear screen, and then she told me, "Listen, meathead, you already know that alien technology is thousands of years ahead of ours. You've ridden in vehicles that are years ahead of anything we've invented on Earth. You know that lizards and others are using us for experiments. So, what's the big deal that some alien race has found a way to use matter and antimatter for propulsion?"

"Thanks, Mona," Mack replied. "I couldn't have found a better way to describe what's going on here." Mack fumbled in his pocket and extracted a small piece of paper. He moved the telescope forty-five degrees to the southwest and then typed coordinates into the telescope. He clicked the camera and waited fifteen seconds. When the screen lit up, it showed a white object with a long squiggly tail.

"What's that?" I asked, pointing to the tail.

"According to Santilli, the tail lets you know that the object is moving," Mack told us. "The ball of white is the object itself."

"What are we looking at?" Mona asked.

"Dan will be interested in this one, Mona. It's the source of the signal that is being used to direct the actions of the Hive. It's the main computer that joins all the NWO chips inserted in human brains together. It's our next target!"

I was really surprised by that. "You mean that if we take that object out, we destroy the capability of the NWO to send messages to people who have chips in their brains?"

"Exactly!"

Well, now I knew the reason that Mack had visited tonight. And I also knew what my next mission was going to be. He was going to strap my ass to a NIKE missile and send me to lasso the object on the camera screen and bring it back to Earth. Or something like that.

"Why can't the US Defense System take it out?" I asked.

"Other than the fact that we don't know who in the government we can trust?" Mona asked.

"First," Mack said, "the US Missile Defense System doesn't know that the object is there. The object emits antimatter rays that make it invisible to standard telescopes and radar."

"What about to infrared scopes?"

"They only see matter, not antimatter, and this object is cloaked in antimatter. Besides all that, the shields of the anti-matter craft would make it impervious to standard missiles. Waam's latest plasma weapon is probably the only thing that would do the trick."

"But Waam's a hunted fugitive," I noted.

"So, what does he have to lose by helping us?" Mack replied.

Mack pulled a communicator from a zippered pocket on his windbreaker. "Waam gave me this in case of emergencies. Given the recent orders from the NWO to relocate migration chambers to subterranean facilities within thirty days, I believe that we're facing an emergency." He turned the communicator on and punched in a special code. Within a few moments, Waam's face appeared on the screen. "Waam, it's Mack. I'm here with

Dan and Mona Arrow. How are you, my friend?"

"Well, thus far. I am being protected by a circle of friends and subordinates from Ummo. Fortunately, no enemies have found me, and my nights have been peaceful. What is on your mind?"

"Dan and Mona and I have been scanning the skies with a Santilli Telescope. You've heard of them?"

"Yes, a rudimentary antimatter telescope. First generation."

"Well, we've traced the signals that are being used by the NWO to control linked human brains, and we have established coordinates. Using the Santilli telescope, we have seen the object, so we know that it's real. I'll send you pics if you'd like."

"Just send me the coordinates, Mack. I'll use our own antimatter identification devices."

Mack texted the coordinates to Waam—scrambled, of course.

Waam confirmed the existence of an object at those coordinates. "It's a Drac 918 IT tureen," he told us. "It appears to be unarmed."

"Unarmed?" I asked.

"Yes. By using antimatter cloaking, the object is absolutely invisible to your military scanning and tracking devices," Waam replied. "It appears to be staffed by three humans and a Draconian. They apparently feel secure and see no need to waste precious resources defending the tureen. Given that you are only discovering it just now, they appear to have been correct in their assumption."

"Waam, is there any way that you could help us to disintegrate that tureen?" Mack asked. "We know that you're in hiding, but perhaps you could send one of your men to take us to the tureen and help us to blast it out of its orbit."

"You know that I have taken a vow not to harm any

human beings, not even bad ones. I could not ask my subordinates to do what I would not do."

"Waam," Mona asked, "would your oath obligate you to watch millions of humans die at the hands of only a few misdirected humans who are under the control of the Draconians?"

"Miss Mona, it is a fine line that I have been walking and a dangerous game. I must be loyal to my planet and my people."

"Waam," I said, "this whole plan, this New World Order, was cooked up by the Draconians with Adolf Hitler, one of the evilest men in modern Earth history. Supposedly, humans and lizards will be co-existing on this planet in harmony, but you and I both know that once the lizards are here on the surface, the destiny of human kind is extinction. And once humans are extinct, Ummites will be driven off the Earth once again. Can you let that happen?"

Waam was quiet for a full minute, obviously thinking about what we had said. When he finally broke the silence, he said, "I have not been innocent in the deaths of a few humans. Simply by providing the means by which a few humans have died, I have questionably compromised my oath. However, I cannot stand by and watch the Draconians implement a plan that will hurt humans. The enemy of my friends is my enemy."

"Then you'll help us?"

"Yes, I will convey you to the position of the object, but I will not be the one to destroy it if humans will be injured or killed in the process."

"Excellent, Waam," Mack said. "We'll do the deed."

"I will come to the Arrow's home before dawn. It is best to conduct this type of initiative at a time when those who monitor such activity are less alert."

"We'll have breakfast waiting, Waam. It'll be good to see you again," Mona said.

"Thank you, Miss Mona. I will be there by four in the morning, your time."

I groaned silently. It looked like Mack would be spending the night with us, which meant that Mona would make me wear some sort of pajamas instead of letting me sleep in my skivvies.

Chapter 29

Waam, Mack, Mona, and I had breakfast together at four in the morning. As we ate, we discussed our strategy for taking out the Drac 918 IT tureen. Then, at four-thirty, I kissed Mona goodbye, and Waam, Mack, and I walked into my back yard and climbed into Waam's cloaked military tureen. Once Mack and I were belted in, Waam lifted us off the ground, hovered for a second while his computers programmed the coordinates, and suddenly we launched into the stratosphere, a trip of less than sixty seconds.

Waam turned us toward the rising sun and sped toward our target. As we approached, Waam's scanners indicated that our presumptions had been correct. Other than its cloaking, the IT tureen was essentially unprotected. Its invisibility to telescopes and radar was its primary defense.

Suddenly an alarm went off inside Waam's tureen. "My scanners indicate that we've been spotted. The NWO has launched two fighter tureens from Astana. They are rapidly approaching. We have approximately twenty seconds before they are within firing range."

"For us to defend ourselves or for them to fire at us?" I asked.

"For them to fire at us. I have raised our shields."

"Can we fire at the IT tureen?" I asked.

"I have confirmed that one reptilian and three humans are inside the IT tureen. I cannot fire upon it."

"But I can!" I exclaimed. "Just tell me when."

"Anytime. The sights are locked on."

I pushed the red button on Waam's control panel and a brief whine drew my attention to the wall above, where I could actually see a ball of plasma heading directly at the location where the Draco 918 was hovering invisibly. Suddenly a ball of light erupted. It had to have been a direct hit. The Draco tureen became visible. We had snuffed out their antimatter collector. While I waited for Waam's plasma weapon to recharge, two escape pods were jettisoned from the Draco tureen.

"The target is now void of life," Waam reported. "The two NWO fighters have arrived. Prepare for combat."

"Here they come!" Mack cried out, pointing to the two fighters.

Thank God that Waam had raised his shields because within a split second we were hit by two rounds of liquid light from the NWO fighters. Waam's tureen shook violently, but we were unharmed.

Waam began flying in crazy directions in defense. "Always try to maneuver so that one tureen blocks the ability of the other to fire at you," he shouted. Suddenly, we were rocked again by a blast of liquid light. "Fire at will, Dan."

"Blast the bastard, Dan!" Mack shouted.

I watched the screen until my sights locked onto the closest fighter, and then I pressed the red button. Kaboom! It burst into a ball of flame that cascaded down toward Earth.

"Woohoo!" Mack screamed in a high-pitched voice.

"In a moment, I am going to streak past the IT tureen. When I do, fire backward at it!" Waam shouted to me.

I could see the IT tureen ahead of us, and we were coming up on it at lightning speed. The second NWO fighter was hot on our tail, about a quarter of a mile behind. He fired again, but Waam dived as the liquid light approached. It flew over our tureen and actually grazed the Drac 918 tureen.

"Okay, Dan, get ready!" Waam shouted.

Quickly, we zipped past the Drac 918. I set the sights on it and pressed the red button. A burst of plasma sped behind us and exploded the Drac just as the second NWO tureen was beside it. The NWO tureen was consumed by the blast. In spite of our shields, both explosions shook us violently, causing disruption to Waam's electronics. We were suddenly spinning.

Mack barfed onto the floor, and its smell permeated the inside of Waam's tureen.

Waam switched to manual control of our tureen. "This is only a sampling of what would happen if the Earth suffered an EMP," he told us. "When all electronics are dead, the easy day-to-day life that you know ceases to exist."

Waam set his controls onto autopilot, got up from his seat at the control panel, and opened a small cabinet door in the wall. "I think I can fix this," he said. He took a small tool in each of his massive hands and began working on something inside the cabinet. When two orange lights began blinking on the panel beside him, Waam nodded. "Excellent! We are cloaked again!" He closed the cabinet door and set course for Italy. "We are limping home," he told us. "There I can get the necessary repairs to be able to take you safely back to your Villagio."

"Look, Dan," Mack cried, pointing toward Earth on the inner wall of the tureen. "Here come three more NWO fighters! Thank God they're arriving too late. If they had come a minute earlier, we'd have been toast!"

He was right about that. The three fighters blew by us toward the wreckage of the Drac 918 tureen without so much as an inkling of suspicion that we were flying back toward Earth. In aviation terms, I would call their passing a near miss, as they flew by within three hundred yards of us.

Our trip back to Montano Antilia took over an hour, so we were traveling really slowly. Waam communicated several times with the staff at his facility to prepare them for our arrival. When we touched down, a repair crew was waiting for us and was anxious to work on Waam's tureen as quickly as possible.

As soon as we exited Waam's tureen, a young officer stepped forward. "The NWO has been here looking for you, Commander," he told Waam.

"I suspected as much," Waam replied. "I did not send the projectile into the Central Sun, but I was present when it occurred."

"The Draconians have offered a reward of one thousand pounds of pure gold for information leading to your capture."

"So I am wanted but not yet a true desperado. Thank you for your loyalty, Gunno."

ⲉⲟⲉⲟ

After brief refreshments and a snack, Gunno took us to see Dr. Cassini. "We situated him in a hidden suite of rooms while the NWO interrogators were here looking for you, Commander," Gunno said, "but he has since been relocated to our best quarters for research and migration procedures."

"And how does he like his new facilities?" Waam asked.

"You'll have to ask him yourself, Commander. I believe that he is very happily situated."

We walked through several long corridors and then into a well-lighted area that could have served as the lobby of an expensive European hotel. "Through here," Gunno told us, pointing to double doors with six glass panels each.

When we entered the room beyond the double doors, we saw Dr. Cassini, speaking with an older woman who had difficulty communicating.

"She suffered a stroke a year ago," Gunno told us. "She has agreed to be migrated into the younger clone of a stranger until her own clone can be developed to maturity. In the short run, she will go from being eighty to fifty-five. In the long run, she will be in her early twenties, with the potential of a full life ahead of her."

"Potential?" I asked. "Why potential?"

"We can never predict when someone will fail to look both ways before crossing a street," Gunno replied.

He had a point.

Dr. Cassini looked up and recognized us instantly. He excused himself from the old woman and immediately came to greet us.

"It is nice to see you, Doctor," Waam said. "I trust that you are satisfied with the arrangements here."

"The facility is excellent, far better than I had expected. Would you like to see how I have laid it out?"

"Yeah, Doc. I'd like to see how it compares to the portable unit that was used at Livermore," I replied.

Dr. Cassini took us first to the migration room, where a single large unit was bolted to the terrazzo floor in the middle of the room. The control panel had been placed against one wall, and several cabinets stood against the others. The lighting was soft, and pictures of young children, puppies, and kittens adorned the walls. He told us, "I believe that this is the room where people feel the greatest anxiety because the removal of the electrical essence is the experience which most closely resembles death, and people, in general, fear death."

I nodded. "From what I recall, being born isn't a piece of cake, either."

Dr. Cassini looked at me in a strange way.

I clarified what I had said, "I mean, I don't remember being born, Doc, but I remember watching films of children being born. If it's an easy process, why are their heads often misshaped and why do they always cry?"

"Mr. Arrow," Cassini answered, "children cry to get oxygen into their lungs. It's the oxygen that turns the color of their skin from gray to pink."

"Oh."

"But you're correct. The birth process can be very difficult on the child. Many things can go wrong." Cassini motioned for us to move to the next room. "This is the lab where we manipulate DNA to remove genetic predispositions to cancer, Alzheimer's, and other diseases. We also modify gender, eye and hair color, height, and similar customer preferences. Then we grow the clones."

Cassini pushed a swinging door and suddenly I felt like I was back in subterranean Denver! Rising from the floor were several rows of cylindrical growth chambers. Most were empty, but half a dozen contained human bodies floating in bluish liquid and appearing in several stages of development. A shudder went through my body.

"This is the piece that I had not expected, Commander Waam," Cassini said, "and I am delighted with it. With this equipment, we are able to monitor the growth of as many as thirty clones simultaneously. It is absolutely state of the art. We believe that the period from conception to maturity can be reduced to only fifteen months."

"So," I asked, "whose clones are you growing in those tanks right now?"

"Two are the clones of a middle aged woman, funded by her three children. One container will be for her, and the twin will be for the unfortunate woman whom you saw when you first entered the Rebirth Center. Three are clones of the famous action hero, Nevada Ritter."

"Why three for him?" Mack asked.

"Why Hollywood stars? They are among the few who have the ready cash to be able to afford migration on demand. As the availability of this process becomes known within the Hollywood community, it will be routine to migrate a star from one container to another. In the case of two or more cloned containers, if the star is injured, filming can continue almost immediately. In the case of aging starlets, plastic surgery will almost disappear because their aging containers will be replaced by newer more perfect containers."

"Doc, I have a special request," I said. "After a suitable clone has been grown in the near future, would you please ensure that Billy Powers is in the queue to receive it. It has to be pro bono. He is a man who was in his early fifties when the Draconians migrated him into the container of an eighty-year-old woman. Worse than that, he has to bathe in protein fluids once a day to keep the container alive. More than anything, he deserves to be given the container of a younger man."

Dr. Cassini looked at Waam. Waam nodded. Cassini then said, "Yes, Mr. Arrow, if you'll give me his contact information, I will schedule your Mr. Powers for migration into a new body within the next few weeks. Perhaps one of Mr. Ritter's clones would be suitable."

I liked the sound of that. I figured that Marlene Powers had been sleeping with an eighty-year-old woman long enough to be sick of it, and that she'd probably like the opportunity to sleep with Nevada Ritter. Hell, in real life, old Nevada could bed just about any woman on the planet!

∽∾∽∾

After our tour, Waam excused himself to check on the repairs being made to his tureen. Gunno escorted Mack and me to the communications center, where we were given access to private booths so we could make important calls. I don't know who Mack called, but I called Billy Powers.

"Hello?"

It was Marlene Powers. "Hi, Marlene, it's Dan Arrow."

"Oh, hello, Mr. Arrow! How are you? Billy is going to be sorry that he wasn't here when you called."

"What's he up to?"

"He's down at Meatland, buying thirty pounds of meatloaf mix and ten two-liter bottles of Gatorade. It's almost time for his bath, and he needs to have fresh ingredients."

"Well, Marlene, I have a question for you."

"What would that be?"

"What do you think of Nevada Ritter?"

"He's okay. I don't think much of his movies. They're too full of busty women who'll do anything to have a bit scene in a movie."

"No, Marlene, I mean what do you think of the way he looks? I mean, if Billy looked like Nevada Ritter, would you need to get drunk to sleep with him?"

"That's a leading question, Mr. Arrow. But I guess that Nevada Ritter's easy to look at and a woman could fantasize, if you know what I mean."

"Marlene, I want you to talk to Billy this evening. There is a strong possibility that I can arrange to have him migrated from that old woman's container into one that looks a whole lot like Nevada Ritter."

"You're teasing me, aren't you, Mr. Arrow? Did Billy put you up to this? I know he's very self-conscious about being an old woman, and he knows that I'm not into the lesbian thing. Did he ask you to feed me this line just to see what I'd say?"

"No, Marlene. In a few weeks, Billy is going to get a call from a Dr. Cassini from Italy. Dr. Cassini is going to offer Billy the opportunity to migrate into a new container. Billy needs to be prepared to say 'yes.'"

"Will he still have to bathe in that chopped meat slop? He smells awful when he steps out of it."

"As I understand it, Billy will be like he always was, and he won't have to bathe in blood and guts. He'll eat like everyone else and things will be normal for you both, except that he'll look like Nevada Ritter."

"I think I can live with that, Mr. Arrow. I think Billy will do back flips when I tell him."

"Just be sure that he does whatever Dr. Cassini tells him to do, and the two of you will be back to playing your old bedroom games, Marlene."

"Mr. Arrow, you've made me a very happy woman. Thank you so much."

"The two of you should join Mona and me for dinner when Billy is back in a man's body. Promise me that you will."

"It's a date!" Marlene said. I could tell that she was crying.

⸎⸎⸎

"Brave Hearts of Ummo, I must leave Montano Antilia for your safety. I do not desire for you to be held complicit in the crime for which I have been charged."

"Where will you go, Commander?" Gunno asked for all Waam's staff to hear. "Where will you be safe?"

"You cannot be guilty of knowing that which you do not know, Gunno."

Waam saluted Gunno, and then he saluted his staff. They all returned his salute. I could see tears in the eyes of many.

"Goodbye, friends. May you enjoy safe futures," Waam said to Mack and me.

Then he walked up the ramp into his tureen. The ramp closed behind him. Shortly, I could hear the soft hum of his motors coming to life. His tureen wiggled slightly and then slowly began to climb into the vibrating rock above our heads. I continued to be awestruck by the technology that permitted a solid object to pass through another solid object. But I had been a passenger in one and done that, so I knew that it was reality.

Before disappearing into the ceiling above us, Waam flashed his rim lights three times. His staff burst into cheers.

Chapter 30

Mack and I had been riding on the train from Uzbekistan to Astana, Kazakhstan, for almost twenty-four hours. If we had taken a commercial flight from Rome, it would have taken us six hours, but Mack was afraid that our arrival by plane would have been too obvious, especially if the NWO was looking for us. He was jumpy that someone might have connected us to Waam and, at the very least, might have held us for several days of painful questioning. So, we flew from Rome to Uzbekistan and then took the train to Astana. It was a twenty-eight-hour trip on a narrow gauge train track, unless a herd of goats blocked the rails, causing the train to slow to a stop. We were lucky, though. We were stopped only once, and that was at the border to Kazakhstan, where former Soviet border guards, now working for Uzbekistan, swept through our train looking for known terrorists. A couple of American tourists were of little concern to them.

Our goal in traveling to Kazakhstan was to try to locate and capture Hitler, who was hiding somewhere deep underground beneath the World Congress building in

Astana. That is, unless Hitler's plans had changed since Mack had ridden from Center Earth to Astana with His Excellency and Queen Igua. I felt like it was a fool's mission, perhaps even suicide, but I had been on fools' missions before and I had survived them. If anything, that has been my hallmark: somehow I manage to get my butt out of the worst possible predicaments, with little to show for it except a few scars.

When our train finally came to rest at the Astana station, I found it difficult to stand because my muscles were stiff from being in the sitting position for so long a ride. I stretched and tapped Mack on the shoulder. He had been sleeping for the last two hours of the trip.

"Wake up, Mack. We've finally arrived in the Emerald City."

Mack opened his eyes. "I've been sleeping, huh?"

"We're in Astana."

"Good, I think. I guess we have to go through customs and then we can find our hotel."

We each took our small duffel bags from the racks above our seats and found our way down the aisle to the exit. Once on the platform, we were directed by uniformed men to the Customs Gateway. I had nothing to hide except my past, so it was going to be an easy passage.

As we had planned, I was three people in line behind Mack, just in case there was any trouble. I watched as the inspectors checked Mack's credentials and rummaged through his duffel bag before telling him to roll up his sleeve so they could check his identification. The inspector waved a wand across Mack's forearm and then checked his digital pad before waving Mack on. Good! Waam's identification chip was working. Mack simply walked away and would meet me later at the entrance to the station, as we had planned.

The same process was used on the guy behind Mack, but not on the lady behind him. She was a tourist from the Netherlands and didn't have NWO credentials. I found that interesting. If we had come as tourists, we'd have had less hassle than as NWO members. Go figure.

When it was my turn, I handed the inspector my credentials. He set them on the stainless steel table while he rummaged through my duffel bag. Then he directed me to roll up my sleeve. I did as he asked. He moved the wand across my forearm, paused, and then checked my credentials. He waved the wand across my forearm again and checked his digital pad for a second time. He motioned to his right, where two large goons were standing, waiting for something to do. I guess I was it. "You are not Gretchen Ozborne," the inspector told me.

"That's obvious," I replied. "I'm Sandy LaSalle of Hollywood. I've come to meet with Her Majesty Queen Igua."

"Your identification chip originally belonged to Gretchen Ozborne, who died three months ago. It has been re-programmed, but its original program is still encrypted in it. You are a spy!"

"They must have given me the wrong fucking chip!" I complained.

But before I could say another word in self-defense, the two goons grabbed me and smashed my face to the floor. I was cuffed and dragged away to a holding tank until my real identification and purpose for being in Astana could be established. I knew that I was screwed.

The woman whom they sent to question me was a stiff. I mean, she was six feet tall and weighed maybe ninety pounds. Her face was unusually round for a skinny person, and her nose had wide nostrils. Her hair was pulled back into a tight little bun, and from the side, her head looked like a boxing glove. I mean, if she was the last woman in the bar at closing time, I wouldn't have offered her a ride home. Ever.

"What is your name?" she asked.

"Sandy LaSalle."

"What is your business in Astana?"

"I have come to meet with Her Majesty Queen Igua."

"There is no such woman in Astana."

"Yes, there is. She is dating His Excellency. And she isn't in Astana, she's under it."

"You speak in funny riddles, Mr. Whatever. We have no record of a Sandy LaSalle in Hollywood, California, USA."

"That's because I'm here, not there."

The door to the holding tank opened. The goon who came in wasn't smiling. His knuckles were covered in adhesive tape, so I knew what was coming. The woman with the boxing glove head nodded, and the goon pretended that my face was a pile of clay that needed to be softened. I remember about seven blows to my cheeks and jaw before I lost consciousness. The nice thing about blacking out is that you don't really know if somebody is still pounding the shit out of you. Until the smelling salts arrive.

The aroma of ammonia roused me to consciousness. Then my face enjoyed a bucket of cold water. I swallowed a little, hoping that it would help. It didn't.

"Now, Mr. Whatever, while you were asleep, we took a blood sample and some of your saliva."

It was that same round-faced bitch with the stick up her ass. I tried to open my eyes, but only one would open. I looked at her, and her expression didn't look any happier.

"Mr. Sandy LaSalle was a guest at the Bavarian Grove this summer. He was supposed to donate four million dollars for the creation of a Rebirth Center in Hollywood, but he welched on his promise and has not been seen since. He is presumed dead. The chip in your arm belongs to Gretchen Ozborne, a corporal in the NWO guard, also deceased. So here you are, very much alive in Astana, and playing the part of two very dead people."

I winked at her, but because I only had one functioning eye, she probably thought that I blinked.

"Your saliva matches saliva taken from the microphone at Livermore, California, where His Excellency's migration was disrupted. So, now we know that you are the man who caused the panic and who destroyed His Excellency's new container. What we do not know is your real name. We would like to you to tell us who you are. If you do, your death will be quicker and a little less painful."

I smiled at her and passed my tongue over my teeth. That's when I noticed that my right eye tooth was missing.

She nodded to someone behind me, maybe someone behind a two-way mirror, maybe not.

Then the door to the holding tank opened again. This time it was a lizard. The lizard looked into my one good eye and inside my head I heard him say, "I remember you from Livermore. You were that Interrogator who appeared on the screen after the fight broke out in the migration room."

I smiled at him, too. He didn't smile back.

He slashed at my chest with his three-clawed right hand. My flesh ripped open and blood began draining onto my lap. I screamed out in pain.

"Who are you and what is your purpose for being in Astana?" the skinny bitch shouted at me.

I didn't answer her. Even if I had wanted to, I don't think I could have.

The goon came into the room again and emptied a

salt shaker into the gashes in my chest. I cried out in pain. Then, one, two, three, he punched my lights out again. Thank God.

Ammonia brought me to consciousness again. Then the pain in my chest and my face came rushing back.

I felt the scaly claws of the reptilian grasp my jaw and turn my head. I opened my one good eye, but it opened only partially. The reptilian asked, "Who helped you to kidnap His Excellency at Livermore?"

I couldn't speak, but he didn't care. He forced my jaw open and used a tool of some kind to twist a tooth in my jaw until its roots snapped. The severed nerve, now exposed to the air, sent a rush of pain into my brain. The pain was acute.

The skinny bitch came back, screaming into my ear, "Were you involved in the destruction of the Lunar Artifact?" I tried to smile but exhaled through my mouth and splattered blood onto her face. "You nasty, disgusting fuck!" she screamed. "Were you involved in the destruction of Center Earth? Were you?"

I inhaled through my mouth. The cool air flowing over my tooth sent a volley of pain into my ear. The big goon touched something metallic to my nipples and a shot of high voltage electricity shook my body. I felt it momentarily, and then I seemed to slip outside of my body, aware that I was in pain, but not so bothered by it anymore. He sent another shot of voltage through me, and I slipped into the merciful darkness of unconsciousness again.

છબ્છ

With Stella's help, Mona was Remote Viewing at home again. She saw her beloved Danny in trouble. He was locked in a small room, suffering physical torture at the hand of those who wished to know who was in league with him. Mona could feel severe pain in her mouth and the dull ache of a bruised brain, a brain damaged by undefended punches to the cheeks and jaw. She felt the tingling of electricity in her torso. She sensed that Danny wanted to die to escape the pain. He was waiting for his body to let him go. Mona called the DC office and asked to speak with Mack Smith's secretary.

"This is Meredith."

"Meredith, this is Mona Casola."

"Oh, hi, Agent Casola. How is your special assignment going?"

"Not well, Meredith. I need to talk to Mack."

"I'm sorry, Agent Casola, but Mack is out of the office for a few days. Shall I have him call you when he gets back?"

"Meredith, Mack is with my husband. My husband is in trouble and I can't reach him. I need you to give me access to Mack's personal cell phone number."

"You know that's against the agency's protocol, Agent Casola."

"If Danny is in trouble, Mack may be in trouble, too. This is a very real emergency, Meredith. I need that number."

"I am sorry, Agent Casola, but Mack has given me express orders never to give his number to anyone, even in an emergency."

"Meredith, as his personal secretary, you can call him. Please call him and tell him that it is imperative that I speak with him. It is a matter of life and death."

"I'll see what I can do, Agent Casola."

Meredith hung up.

"Stupid bitch!" Mona shouted at her phone.

Five minutes later, Mona's cell phone rang. It was Mack.

"Danny's in trouble," Mona told him. She described what Stella had let her see and feel during her Remote Viewing session.

"I knew he had been held for questioning, but I hadn't realized that it was a hard-core interrogation," Mack replied. "This is not good. We're going to need to call in the reserves."

"I need to help with this, Mack," Mona said.

"And what about Stella? It'll be too dangerous, Mona."

"Fuck you, Mack. You know I'm good at field work. Hell, I'm one of the best field agents you've got. So, you've stuck me out here in Pleasantville and won't let me do what I'm best at. I swear to God, Mack, if anything happens to Danny I'm going to the media and I'm going to blow this whole thing wide open—the aliens, the NWO, Villagio Ibrido, and our government's involvement. All of it!"

"Calm down, Mona. You're talking irrationally. Can you arrange for someone to watch Stella for a couple of days?"

"Yeah."

"Do that. In the meanwhile, I'll make a few calls and send somebody to pick you up."

"Tell them to get here pronto. Danny could die at any minute."

❧❧❧

Waiting to hear back from Mack, Mona heard the neighbor's dog barking excitedly. She looked out her back window and saw Waam walking toward her door. She opened the door and ran to him.

"Waam, Danny is hurt and near death."

"Mack told me. I am here to take you to Italy. Are you ready to go?"

"Give me just a minute. I need to let the babysitter know that I'm going."

"Please hurry, Miss Mona. That dog will attract attention."

Mona ran back inside for a few minutes and then returned, carrying a small travel bag. In the small of her back she was packing her FBI issued Model 1911. Waam led her to his cloaked tureen, which was hovering in the circle of flattened grass beyond Stella's swing set, and escorted her inside. After Mona buckled her seatbelt, Waam lifted gently off the lawn and said, "This trip will take less time than watching a rerun of *Star Trek*."

"This is no time to kid around," Mona told him.

"I apologize, Miss Mona, but I thought some levity might ease the tension."

"Apology accepted. How fast will we be traveling?"

"More than twelve thousand of your miles per hour."

"Can you go faster?"

"Yes, but in the turbulence of your atmosphere, it is unwise."

"Push it, Waam!"

⁀ↄ⁀ↄ

The stop in Italy lasted ten minutes, just long enough for Dr. Cassini to enter the tureen and be introduced to Mona.

"Jesus, you look like Hitler!" Mona exclaimed.

"So, I've been told," Cassini answered.

During the flight to Astana, Mack spoke to Cassini and Mona via the large screen communicator on the inside wall of Waam's tureen.

"Dan is now being held in the brig in Astana" he told them. "He is being interrogated for ten minutes every hour, and then is dragged back to his cell when each interrogation session is over. So far, he hasn't given them any information. When they tire of this routine, they plan to terminate him."

Mona's eyes burst into tears.

"My plan is basic, but it might work. The two of you will go to the brig and escort Dan out. You'll bring him to Waam's tureen, which will be cloaked and waiting for you just outside the entrance."

"What about you, Mack?" Mona asked.

"I have to remain undercover. If you two are apprehended, then I will do what I can to free you."

"I want to kill the bastards who've done this to him!" Mona said, spitting onto her fist and then rubbing it with the palm of her other hand.

"Just don't let them kill you first, Mona."

Chapter 31

The two young NWO non-coms, one a sergeant and one a corporal, snapped to attention.

"At ease, soldiers," Hitler told them.

"Your Excellency, we had not expected you this morning," the sergeant said.

"I have come to see the spy that we are holding. Has he died yet?"

"No, sir, not yet, but his container has taken severe punishment."

"It is my understanding that our interrogation techniques have not yet worked on this man."

"I don't know everything that we've tried, but beatings, oral pain, and electrical shocks have been unsuccessful. Even to his testicles."

Mona winced at the thought of what Danny had been going through.

"This is Doctor Lacosa. She is an expert in chemical interrogation. It is much less destructive to the container and is often more likely to produce results."

"Will you escort us to the holding cell?" Mona asked.

"Yes, sir, ma'am," the sergeant replied.

Mona and Dr. Cassini followed the young military policeman through a locked door and down a concrete passageway to the cell where Dan Arrow, a.k.a. Sandy LaSalle, was being held between torturous interrogation sessions.

"Who has been in charge of the interrogation?" Hitler asked while the MP unlocked the cell door.

"Interrogator Haam."

"Why would Interrogator Haam destroy this container and risk the loss of the information that we seek, when this man's electrical essence could be migrated into another container and the interrogation process be continued?" Mona asked.

"Sir, I don't really know. But she seems to be angry at this man."

"We'll be fine, Sergeant," Hitler said. "This should not take long."

The sergeant left his supreme commander and the doctor in Sandy LaSalle's cell and returned to his post at the front door.

Once the MP had gone back to his post, Mona and Dr. Cassini went quickly to work. Cassini took a stethoscope from Mona's jacket and listened to Dan's heart. "He's weak and his body is heavily stressed," he told Mona.

The doctor then gave Dan's body a quick inspection. The gashes on his chest were an inch deep and infected. Two of his ribs appeared to have been broken. Several more may have been cracked. His nipples had been badly burned by electrical shock. His testicles had suffered similar punishment. At least ten teeth had been broken, and his fingernails showed evidence of sharp implements having been shoved between the nail and the flesh below. And his face, as Mona put it, was hardly recognizable.

Dr. Cassini shook his head. "I don't know how he has survived for so long. He must have experienced severe pain."

"Let's do as we planned, Doctor," Mona said. "I can't stand seeing him like this. I love him too much to let him suffer any more than he already has."

Cassini agreed. He instructed Mona to open the briefcase which she had been carrying. She did and handed it to him. Cassini removed the spline and opened it so that it looked somewhat like an umbrella that had been blown open by the wind. Since Dan was barefoot, Cassini removed his own shoes and placed them under Dan's neck. He asked Mona to hold the shaft of the umbrella so that the fingers of the spline encircled Dan's head, but did not touch the floor.

Cassini then opened his own coat and removed several wires and electrodes from its lining. He quickly placed the electrodes on Dan's chest and forehead, and then connected the ends of the wires into small ports in the briefcase.

"Are you ready?" he asked Mona.

"Yes," she said, swallowing difficultly in anticipation.

"Just be certain that the splines don't brush against the floor."

Mona nodded.

Dr. Cassini turned the locks on the briefcase, and the splines began to rotate around Dan's head. As they accelerated, Dan began breathing heavily. Mona looked at the doctor, but the doctor was listening to Dan's heart. "Hold the splines steady," Cassini said to Mona.

Suddenly, Dan stopped breathing. His chest sank and his one open eye just stared straight ahead.

Dr. Cassini removed the wires and stuffed them into his pockets. He closed the briefcase. "Your husband's electrical essence has been migrated into the portable storage unit. It is time to go. We have exactly twelve hours to get him back to Italy."

Dr. Cassini quickly put his shoes back on and stood up. Mona dropped the spline and took a handkerchief from her pocket. She wiped away the blood and sweat from her Danny's forehead and from around his eyes. She kissed his lips lightly then picked up the briefcase and quickly left the Danny's cell, following Dr. Cassini.

At the same time and at the entrance, His Excellency arrived at the brig, walking through the front door with the posture and confidence of an emperor. The two young MP's popped to attention again.

"Has Interrogator Haam arrived yet?" he asked the two MP's, without ordering them to "at ease."

"Sir, we did not see you leave the facility," said the Sergeant.

"I just arrived. Where is Interrogator Haam?"

"Your Excellency, we do not know where she is. Where is the doctor who accompanied you earlier?"

"What are you talking about?" Hitler asked.

The sergeant broke from his position of attention and struck the alarm button with his palm. Instantly, pulsating alarms began ringing throughout the brig. Hitler covered his ears with his palms. After a few moments, four reptilian guards, half a dozen NWO military policemen, and three Draconian grays in combat gear had assembled in the entry office.

"Something is wrong!" the sergeant exclaimed. "His Excellency and a doctor arrived fifteen minutes ago. Now His Excellency has arrived again, and we should expect Interrogator Haam at any moment." He pointed to one reptilian and an NWO MP and ordered, "Hold His Excellency for questioning."

Hitler's arms were grasped by the reptilian while the

MP placed Hitler in handcuffs. "You'll be executed for this insolence!" Hitler shouted. "I am your supreme leader!"

"Gag him," the sergeant ordered.

The sergeant and the remaining soldiers hurried down the passageway toward Sandy LaSalle's cell. Dr. Cassini and Mona came from the opposite direction.

"Someone has killed Sandy LaSalle!" Cassini barked. "Check everyone's forearm chips and arrest anyone who does not belong in the facility." The sergeant appeared puzzled. "What is the problem, Sergeant?" Cassini demanded.

"Hold them for questioning!" the sergeant ordered to two reptilians and two NWO MP's. Mona and Cassini were handcuffed and escorted to the entrance of the brig, but instead of entering the office, they were detained in the passageway.

The sergeant and his remaining NWO troopers entered Sandy LaSalle's cell. LaSalle appeared to be deceased. Although his body had not yet entered rigor mortis, he was not breathing and he had no pulse. They quickly returned to the main office.

"What did you do to the prisoner?" the sergeant demanded of Mona when he saw her in the passageway.

"He was deceased when we got there. I tried to revive him but he did not respond to CPR or to the shot of adrenalin that I administered. Your interrogator effectively terminated his container. Was she intentionally trying to hide something?"

"She will pay for wasting this opportunity to obtain information from a member of the Resistance," Dr. Cassini said in a haughty tone. "Why are we being held, Sergeant?"

"I apologize, Excellency," but it appears that we have two of your excellencies here at the same time. I must keep you under arrest for your own safety."

"Arrest the imposter!" Cassini ordered.

The sergeant told the two reptilians and NWO guards to remain in the passageway with Cassini and Mona. Then he and the others entered the office.

The moment that Hitler saw the sergeant, he brushed the gag out of his mouth with his shoulder and huffed, "I demand to be released at once. This is an outrage!"

"It seems that there are two of you, Your Excellency, and until I get to the bottom of this mess, you will have to do as I say, do you understand?"

"Arrest the imposter!" Hitler demanded.

The sergeant put his head into his hands for a moment, and then he contacted the palace. "Please tell Her Majesty that we have a situation at the brig that requires her advice and attention." He listened for a moment and then said, "Yes. At once, please."

Ten minutes later, Queen Igua entered the office, followed by several guards and council members. Her translator dangled from her neck on a golden chain. When she saw Hitler in handcuffs she ordered, "Release His Excellency at once!"

"Which one would you like released, Your Majesty?" the sergeant asked.

"This one!" she said pointing to the Hitler in the office.

"And what about this one, Your Majesty?" the sergeant asked, opening the door so that Queen Igua could look into the passageway.

The Queen peered into the passageway, where she saw Hitler and Mona in handcuffs. She turned slowly and looked at the Hitler in the office behind her, and then again at the Hitler in the passageway. "It appears that we have a situation, don't we, Sergeant!"

"Yes, Your Majesty. One of these gentlemen is His

Excellency, and I shall apologize profusely to him when his true identity is determined. However, until then, I wait upon Your Majesty's command."

"And what of the prisoner?" the Queen asked.

"He appears to be lifeless, Your Majesty. He is not breathing and has no pulse."

"And who is the woman in the passageway?"

"His Excellency introduced her to me as Dr. Lacosa, an expert in chemical interrogation. He intended that Dr. Lacosa utilize her expertise to gather information that traditional interrogation techniques did not obtain."

"Have you checked her valise, Sergeant?"

"No, Your Majesty, there has been little time to do anything in all this confusion. The sergeant marched across the passageway, took the briefcase from Mona and opened it. "It is entirely empty, Your Majesty!"

"Nothing, Sergeant? No syringes? No implements of death?"

"Nothing, Your Majesty."

"Bring it to me."

The sergeant handed the briefcase to the queen, who inspected and smelled it carefully. "It is indeed empty, and I smell nothing of chemicals in it." She tossed it into a trashcan beside the sergeant's desk.

The queen entered the passageway. "You seem familiar," she said to Mona.

"I'm FBI. And, I'm the mother of a hybrid child, Your Majesty."

"Indeed?"

"Yes, Your Majesty. Commissar Nargas was the father."

"And the child?"

"She lives with me. Your doctors check her regularly."

"And what are you doing here?"

"As an FBI representative to the NWO, I accompanied His Excellency to interrogate Mr. LaSalle in our way."

"Better than our interrogation procedures?"

"Perhaps he would have been less resistant if interrogated by a human who could be a friend."

"Are you a friend?"

"He was dead when we found him, Your Majesty."

"But are you a friend?"

"I am a friend of Mack Smith's. I report to him."

The queen ordered that the other Hitler, the one in the office, be brought into the passageway. He was brought into the space abruptly and fought the reptilian who held him.

The queen turned to the real Hitler, "Your Excellency, what would you have me do with them?"

Dr. Cassini replied first. "Throw the imposter into the feeding tubs, Your Majesty!"

"He's mine to terminate!" replied the real Hitler.

"This is, indeed, perplexing," the queen said. She turned to one of her councilmen and told him, "Summon Colonel Smith. He is somewhere in the city."

While they were waiting, the real Hitler began to protest about being held suspect. "I have been with you for several months now, Your Majesty. How can you doubt me?"

Cassini kept the ball rolling, saying, "He was planted by the Resistance several months ago, Your Majesty. Undoubtedly he has become familiar to you. I had hoped that Mr. LaSalle or whoever he really is would tell us what this imposter's agenda is and when he hopes to implement it. I fear he intends to assassinate you as part of his plan."

The real Hitler lunged at Cassini, grabbing at his throat with his cuffed hands. They fell to the floor, scuffling and accusing each other of being the imposter. At the queen's command, two reptilian guards pulled them apart, holding each man upside down by an ankle.

"Quiet them!" the queen commanded.

A third lizard placed a small round disk on Hitler's neck and pressed its center. Hitler instantly fell limp, rendered unconscious. The lizard repeated the procedure on Dr. Cassini, rendering him, too, unconscious.

The queen looked at the sergeant and said, "Now we'll have some peace while we determine how to differentiate between the two. We cannot forget, Sergeant, that they both may be imposters."

Chapter 32

So, how will we solve this puzzle, Your Majesty?" her viceroy asked.

"It is indeed a conundrum, Viceroy. I cannot trust my nasal receptors because I have been in the company of one Excellency for several months. If it is true that he is the imposter, then my nostrils are not to be trusted."

"There must be another way, Majesty."

The queen drummed her claws on the teakwood table. "Viceroy, I think I have the way out of this puzzle. Have His Excellency's dog brought to Astana at once!"

"His dog?"

"Yes. Dogs are unwavering in their loyalty to their masters, and their noses are keener than even mine! The dog will know its true master because even identical twins have different scents. His Excellency's hound is in Denver. Have it here within the hour!"

⁀ↄ⁀ↄↄ

Mack Smith came to the brig to see the two Hitlers and to see if he could help Queen Igua differentiate between the real and the imposter. At least that is what he told the guards.

Without telling them that the queen would soon be using a dog to identify the true Hitler, Mack chatted with each captive about experiences they had shared together.

"What am I to do except to play this game out to its end, Agent Smith?" asked Dr. Cassini, handcuffed to a table within his cell.

"You are doing a great job, Doctor. The queen is unsure which one of you is the imposter. If we play our cards right, you may be the leader of the human division of the New World Order."

"It is not a role that I wish to play."

"But if you don't continue with this charade, you will be dead within an instant of their discovery that you are the imposter."

Mack handed Cassini an Italian chocolate protein bar. "You should eat this to keep up your strength," he said.

Cassini took the bar, unwrapped it, and bit into it. After swallowing the first bite, he asked, "How is Agent Casola?"

"She seems fine, although she has been incarcerated temporarily. The queen has taken special interest in her because her seed was fertilized by Commissar Nargas and she is now part of a larger experiment on the raising of hybrid children. I believe that she will remain safe. They haven't realized as of yet that she is not a physician."

"What will happen next?"

"The queen has something up her sleeve. If I can find out what it is, I will try to prep you for it."

"Thank you, Agent Smith."

Mack left Cassini and went into the next holding cell, where His Excellency was similarly handcuffed to a table.

"Your Excellency," Mack said to the real Hitler, "I am certain that Queen Igua has your best interest in mind. I truly believe that she thinks she is keeping you safe from harm at the moment."

"I have been with her for the past few months, ever since the Lunar Artifact was rendered uninhabitable. She should know who I am, if only from the conversations we have shared about the future of the New World Order."

"She fears that the imposter may have fed her misinformation that would cause her to make bad decisions. However, she has a plan that will expose the imposter for who he is."

"And when she discovers who I am and I am empowered again, I will execute that guard who treated me like a common criminal."

"He is only a noncom who is trying to do his duty, as directed by yourself, Excellency."

"He is still a dead man."

Fumbling in his pocket, Mack said, "You should keep your strength, Your Excellency. I have an Italian protein bar, if you'd care to eat it." Mack handed Hitler the small bar. "They tell me these are excellent. You'll have to be the judge."

Hitler took the bar and tasted it. "They are not bad, although I prefer the sweeter chocolate that the Americans manufacture." Hitler finished the bar and handed Mack the wrapper. "You are a good friend, Agent Smith. I will not forget that when I have the throne in my grasp."

"Thank you, Your Excellency. I am undeserving of your favor."

Mack said his farewells and assured His Excellency that whatever the queen had in mind would expose the true imposter. After exiting the brig, Mack pulled the empty wrapper out of his pocket. He found the small red dot that he had placed in the R of the word PROTEIN.

Yes, the one that he had given to His Excellency was the proper one, the one that had been laced with snake pheromones. Mack smiled and crossed his fingers for a few seconds, hoping that his plan would work.

ᙓᙡᙓᙡ

Three hours had passed since Queen Igua had ordered that His Excellency's pet dog, a German shepherd named Blondi VII, be brought to her in Astana. A tureen had been dispatched to fetch the dog, and it had finally returned. The viceroy brought the dog on a leash to Her Majesty. Queen Igua tried to pet Blondi, but she barked violently and showed her teeth. "A one-man dog?" she asked the Viceroy.

"Perhaps," he replied.

The queen ordered that all the captives, both Excellencies and the woman, be brought to her Royal Chamber. Three of her council members were present, and two representatives of the NWO—Mack Smith and a Chinese ambassador named Wu. In addition, four members of her royal guard, giant reptilians in full armor, were present. All dignitaries stood to the right of the queen.

The captives were last to enter the chamber. The viceroy ordered her guards to hold Mona to the left of the queen. Dr. Cassini and His Excellency were taken to the left center of the chamber.

Queen Igua rose from her throne and walked to the center of the room. "Now is when the imposter will be exposed," she said. "Uncuff the prisoners," she ordered. When a guard had removed the cuffs, she nodded to the viceroy, who clapped his hands. Two Draconian grays brought Blondi into the room. When he saw her, Hitler smiled.

Queen Igua ordered that the dog be released. Cassini

clapped his hands and said, "Come here."

Hitler bent down on one knee and wiggled his finger on the floor. Recognizing her master's posture, Blondi ran to Hitler, then she suddenly backed away, barking. She then went to Dr. Cassini and sniffed his hand, wagging her tail. Still, she seemed unsure. She trotted back to Hitler and then suddenly backed away growling, showing her teeth.

The queen nodded to a guard to terminate Hitler, but before the guard could press his breast plate, Hitler broke free, charged the queen, and spun around her, grabbing her from behind. He held her forehead in his left hand and pressed the back of her scaly head against his chest. In his right hand he pressed a box cutter, that he had hidden in his clothes, into the queen's throat.

"You stupid bitch!" he screamed, "would you deny me my rightful destiny?"

"Don't hurt the queen!" her advisors shouted in horror.

"Shoot the imposter!" Cassini shouted.

Not one to be held against her will, Queen Igua raised her right leg and brought it down heavily onto Hitler's shin, sliding it down to the top of his foot. Hitler screamed in pain, and in instant reaction, he cut her throat with the box cutter.

Queen Igua grasped at her throat and gasped for air. Blood spurted out in rhythm to the beat of her heart, painting the floor and splashing red liquid onto the shoes of her viceroy.

As she crumpled to the floor, blood gushing everywhere, Hitler's face turned to horror as he realized what he had done.

Immediately, Queen Igua's Royal Guards sent three volleys of liquid light at Hitler, severing him into four pieces. His container flipped and spun smoking to the floor. Two guards turned and sent volleys of light at Dr. Cassini, terminating him as well.

Mack and Mona froze and raised their hands. Two guards reached for their breastplates to terminate the humans, but the queen's two advisors shouted, "Stop!"

The guards paused momentarily and then turned to send a volley at Mona. "Stop! Don't shoot!" the queen's viceroy pleaded. "We need the humans as witnesses to this event. Their testimony will preserve all of our lives."

The guards stood down, recognizing the peril that they, themselves, might be facing at the hand of the Galactic Federation's Grand Council.

The viceroy ordered Mona freed and remanded her to Mack's custody until her video testimony could be recorded and transmitted to Draco and to the Galactic Federation. The viceroy then ordered two reptilian guards to cover her majesty with a cloth and transport her container to the hospital for official verification of her death. And last, he ordered the Draconian grays to "Clean up this disgusting mess and prepare their excellencies for the feeding tubs."

Chapter 33

W e have to hurry," Mona said to Mack. "The last
time I saw it, the briefcase was in a trashcan in
the office at the entrance to the brig."

"We can only hope that it's still there," Mack replied. "How many hours do you estimate are left before it
can no longer hold Dan's electrical essence?"

"Dr. Cassini said that the charge would last for
twelve hours. It has been at least nine, and perhaps more.
We are close to the drop-dead mark."

Mona and Mack walked as fast as they could without
running, so as not to arouse suspicion. The brig was a
healthy quarter of a mile from the Royal Chamber. As
they hurried along, sirens began to wail, and the flags on
all official governmental buildings began being lowered
to half-mast. "Queen Igua is officially deceased," Mack
said.

When they reached the office at the brig, one NWO
soldier was at the desk. "Have you heard?" he asked as
they came up to his desk.

"Yes, Queen Igua is dead," Mona replied.

"Worse," the soldier told them. "His Excellency has

been assassinated by the Draconians. I fear that there may be riots among the troops of the New World Order."

"Can you help us?" Mack asked. "We're looking for a briefcase that we left here a few hours ago."

"Where did you leave it?"

Mona pointed to the empty trash can that was against the wall behind his desk. "It was in that trash can."

"I think I remember it. The trash was taken out two hours ago. It could be in the incinerator by now."

"Where is the incinerator?" Mona demanded.

The soldier pulled out a map of Astana and pointed to a round building with a tall stack, on the east side of the city. "They placed the incinerator there because the prevailing winds come from the west, so the smell of burning garbage and soot never drift in the direction of downtown." he told them.

"Can we have this map?" Mack asked.

"Sure."

Mack grabbed Mona's hand and pulled her out the door. He started to turn down a walkway that headed west, but Mona stopped him. "Waam!" she said excitedly. "He may still be here!" Mona led Mack back to the brig and then out onto the grass in front of it. "Can you call him?" Mona asked.

Mack hurriedly removed the communicator from his coat pocket and punched in Waam's number. "Waam, it's me, Mack…Yes, I'm with Mona. Where are you?…We need your help!"

"I see you," Waam replied. "I am fifty yards from you. I will turn off my cloaking."

Almost instantly, Waam's tureen became visible, a dull gray Ummite military fighter resting on a diamond shaped flower garden on Nurzhol Boulevard, the "Radiant Path."

"There!" Mona said, pointing at it.

A man and woman who were peddling bicycles along the boulevard fell off their bikes when Waam's tureen suddenly appeared. The woman began shouting, "We're under attack! We're under attack!"

A reptilian guardsman who was standing beside an intersection fired a burst of liquid light at the tureen from his helmet, but it simply ricocheted to the ground.

Mona and Mack ran to the tureen as its ramp descended to welcome them. As they ran up the ramp, Waam closed it behind them and re-cloaked his tureen.

Mack showed Waam the map and pointed to the incinerator. "We have to get there, pronto!"

"That should be no problem," Waam replied. "It is only two of your miles away."

Without asking his passengers to buckle up, Waam lifted his tureen into the air and glided it east, toward the edge of the city. He circled the incinerator and settled his craft fifty yards from the truck entrance. He lowered the ramp, and Mack and Mona were gone before it touched the concrete surface.

When they entered the interior yard, four trucks were unloading trash onto a concrete platform, where a large vehicle was lifting buckets full of waste and dropping them onto a conveyor belt. The belt climbed at a forty-five degree angle almost two hundred feet into the air to the top of the building, where the garbage fell into the perpetual fires of the furnace.

"Where do we start?" Mona asked, breathlessly.

"At the conveyor!" Mack replied.

They ran to the man who was operating the conveyor belt. When he turned, Mack shouted, "Stop the conveyor!"

The man hit a kill switch and the conveyor abruptly halted. He turned toward Mack and said, "This had better be good."

"We're looking for the truck that recently picked up trash at the brig," Mona said. "It's a matter of life and death."

The man pointed to a truck that had already dumped its load and was readying to pull out.

Mona stopped the driver.

"Whadda ya want, lady?" the driver asked.

"Is your entire load on that conveyor?"

"Yeah, except for the stuff that's already gone into the incinerator."

Mona ran to the conveyor belt and climbed onto it. Mack joined her.

"It's a black briefcase, Mack, about twelve by fifteen and maybe three inches thick."

They began picking through the trash, and as they did, they moved higher up the ten-foot wide belt. After ten minutes, Mona began to feel as though their search was fruitless. "How will we ever find him, Mack?" she asked.

The man who controlled the belt shouted up to them, "You've got one more minute before I have to start the belt again. More trucks are coming and you're gonna cause a backup!"

Mona squealed in disbelief and began searching more quickly.

After a minute had elapsed, the conveyor operator shouted again, "I meant it, lady!" He hit the button and the conveyor slowly began moving toward the top of the building.

"Come on, Mona!" Mack shouted at her. "We have to get off of this thing!"

"No! I have to find Danny!"

Mona continued picking through the trash. The conveyor operator touched another button, causing the belt to lurch. Mona fell backwards onto the conveyor. As she struggled to get up, she saw the corner of the black brief-case sticking out from under a clear bag of trash, about ten feet above her on the conveyor. She began crawling upward to get it. Suddenly Mack was beside her. "No, Mona," he shouted. It's too dangerous! It's too near the top!"

Mona slugged Mack, pushing away from him and climbing upwards. As the briefcase reached the top, Mona lunged for it, grasping it by the corner with both hands. She could feel the -conveyor stopped. Mona rolled backwards, pulling Danny's storage unit to her chest.

"Mona! Mona!" Mack shouted up to her. "It was Waam! Waam saved us!"

Mona looked down toward the conveyor operator's station. Waam was holding the operator by his collar, dangling him in the air. He waved at Mona and smiled.

"Waam, I think I love you!" Mona shouted down to him.

She stood and began to pick her way through the garbage to the bottom of the conveyor. She stumbled twice, but never let go of her beloved Danny Arrow. At the bottom of the conveyor, horns began honking as drivers of trash laden trucks wanted to unload their vehicles and complete their runs before the end of the day.

Within five minutes, Mack, Mona, Waam, and the briefcase were in Waam's tureen and heading back toward Italy. Three miles before the Kazakhstan border, however, an NWO fighter tureen approached from the right, firing two bursts of liquid light. An alarm went off inside Waam's tureen. The tureen's shields automatically rose. Instantly they were struck by the two blasts. Waam's tureen shook violently, sending Mack and Mona into the interior walls. The briefcase carrying Dan flew to the floor, slammed into the center console, and popped open.

Mona screamed and dived for the briefcase, slamming it shut, and locking it. She pulled it to her chest, sobbing. Mack helped her to her feet and strapped her into a seat for the remainder of the flight.

"Draconian pilot!" Waam shouted. "This one is mine!"

As they approached the Kazakhstani border, the NWO tureen sent another volley of two bursts of liquid light. One missed Waam's tureen and one was deflected by its shields. Waam dived and rolled several times. The NWO tureen followed each maneuver. But, when Waam passed over the border, the NWO tureen turned away, not permitted by Galactic Federation law to fly horizontally into air space unfamiliar with tureens. Waam sent a burst of plasma at the tureen, and it blew to pieces in a fiery explosion behind them.

Chapter 34

Waam delivered Mack and Mona to the guest garage at Montano Antilia, and then bid them farewell. "I cannot remain here while I am still a wanted commodity. It places my staff at risk of prosecution for harboring a galactic felon," he told them.

Mona asked Waam to bend down. When he did, she gave him a kiss on his cheek. "That's for continuing to save our lives, Waam. Someday you'll receive a medal for all you've done for the Resistance."

"You humble me, Miss Mona."

After Waam took off for his unknown hideout, Mona said, "I'm certain that we have less than an hour to save Danny, Mack. This battery that Dr. Cassini developed has just about reached the end of its life expectancy."

With the assistance of Colonel Gunno, who was now in charge of the Ummite facility during Waam's absence, they found their way into the lab section where they were greeted by an Ummite doctor.

"Doctor Spann, this magnetic storage device was developed by Dr. Cassini," Mona said.

"Yes, I recognize it," Dr. Spann replied. "Have you completed its beta test?"

"I hadn't realized that this was a test, but I guess we have. The electrical essence in this device is my husband. He needs to be migrated into a new container. I don't think we have more than an hour of battery life remaining."

Dr. Spann attached the briefcase to a monitor. "Actually, Mrs. Arrow, you have fewer than eight minutes of battery left."

"Holy shit!" Mona exclaimed. "You have to help us!"

"I have two human containers left, one owned by Nevada Ritter, himself. It would be unethical to migrate your husband into that one. The other one has been promised to a Mr. William Powers, who is due here in several hours. I believe that your husband arranged that migration."

"You have to put him in that container and migrate Powers into something else."

"That would be unethical, Mrs. Arrow. However, I have an alternative to offer you."

"What would that be, Doctor?"

"I have a clone that is ready for migration. It is a Reticulan gray. They're the ones with…"

"Yeah, I know, the friendlier faces."

"This clone will have speech capabilities, Mrs. Arrow."

Mona knew that she had no choice if she was going to save Danny. "Yeah," she told the doctor, "let's do it. Please hurry!"

Dr. Spann gathered two assistants and had them set up the main migration unit. One checked the gauges and power supplies. The other placed a four-foot tall Reticulan gray container on the gurney. Dr. Spann placed the briefcase into the space normally occupied by larger to-roidal storage units, and then he connected the migration unit's wires into the ports on the briefcase. Glancing at the clock on the wall, Dr. Spann announced, "We are running out of time. Hurry with the placement of the electrodes!"

Once the electrodes had been properly placed onto the head of the gray by his assistants, Spann pressed a button. The machine made a very soft whirring sound. The gray container seemed to jump slightly, as though it had been shocked, and then it went limp.

"He's in the container," Dr. Spann said. "Bring me the defibrillator!"

One of his assistants brought Dr. Spann an AED unit. He set the charge for the lowest possible voltage, and then placed the paddles on the gray's chest. When he depressed the triggers, the gray's back arched. He hit the triggers a second time. The gray arched again. Dr. Spann placed his stethoscope on the gray's chest and listened. He smiled. "Your husband is now alive and well."

"Mrs. Arrow," Dr. Spann said, "it is unfortunate that your husband will be in a gray container because of the inconveniences it will cause for both of you. However, if you can bring me a few strands of his hair or something else than contains his DNA, I will begin the cloning process. In a brief fifteen months, he will have a new container into which he can be migrated and he will be better than new."

Mona reached into her pocket and pulled out the handkerchief that she had used to wipe Danny's face. "This contains his blood and sweat, Doctor. Will that do? If not, I will find some of his hair, even if I have to pull it out of the shower drain back at home."

"This appears to be all that I'll need. I'll see if we can extract the DNA before you leave for home."

"Thanks, Doctor," Mona said.

"Doctor Spann, the container is moving," an assistant said.

Mona went to Danny's side. The gray's eyes opened. He broke into a smile.

Chapter 35

I felt like I had been asleep for a hundred years. The last thing I remembered was having two more teeth cracked and my nuts zapped with electricity. Then I saw Mona. She was standing over me with a worried look on her face.

"Hi, baby," I said. "How about a roll in the hay?"

Mona knew that I was kidding. She told me later that my voice sounded weak and high pitched, and that that was going to take some getting used to. But she didn't tell me that then.

"Danny, this is Dr. Spann," Mona said. "He's one of Waam's staff members. You're in Waam's underground facility in Italy."

Dr. Spann spoke. "Mr. Arrow, to save your life we had to migrate you into a new container. Your wife gave me some of your bodily fluids from which we will extract your DNA. We will then integrate your DNA into donor cells from a Catholic priest. In fifteen months, we will migrate you back into your own body, except that you will be in your mid-twenties and all of your scars will be gone."

"Sounds good," I said, still trying to piece everything together. I looked at Mona and said, "Help me up, baby."

Mona put her hand under my head and gently lifted me to a sitting position. I didn't realize how strong she was. It was then that I looked down and saw my legs. They were thin and spindly, and their color was grayish blue. "What the fuck?" I exclaimed in disbelief. "What did you do to me?"

"It's the only container they had available, Danny!" Mona explained. "We had eight minutes to save you. There was no other choice!"

"Aw fuck!" I complained. "I think I'd rather be dead!"

"Fifteen months, Danny. That's all it is, just fifteen months!"

"Fifteen months of not eating, Mona! I'm going to have to bathe in tubs full of raw meat and Gatorade!" The thoughts of being in a gray's container were overwhelming. I'd be small, weak, and hideous to look at. For fifteen months!

Dr. Spann interrupted. "Time is all relative, Mr. Arrow. Think about high school. Didn't it go by quickly? This is less than half that amount of time."

"It's fifteen months, Doc!"

"Yes, and that's only a quarter of the time it took to clone a container three years ago. This new cloning is based upon the work of a group of your scientists at the Venter Institute who collaborated with Reticulans and Pleiadeans to create artificial DNA that actually reproduces itself! That gave them the ability to synthesize all sorts of things. We can now manipulate DNA to fashion a container to have just about anything its recipient could want."

Mona whispered in Dr. Spann's ear, but I couldn't hear what she said. Spann smiled and replied, "Of course,

Mrs. Arrow. Would there be anything else?"

"No, Doctor. I'm otherwise happy with him just the way he is."

"What did you ask him to do, Mona?"

She just smiled at me.

"Mona?"

"I asked him to increase the size of your Johnson by twenty percent."

"Jesus H. Christ, Mona!"

She broke out laughing at me.

I lifted the hem of my hospital gown to check out the size of the male apparatus on this container that I was in. "No penis! Am I a female, Doc?"

"No, Mr. Arrow. You have no sexual organs of any type. Grays are asexual. Since they are a manufactured species, they have no need to reproduce."

"I have the need to reproduce, Doc. I love reproducing."

"You have the memory of needing to reproduce, but that will fade in a few days. You should have no sex drive in less than a week. In fact, you won't be bothered by those hormonal drives at all."

"Mona, I can't do this," I complained. "I demand to be migrated into something else!"

"We can always put him back into a toroidal container until his clone is ready, Mrs. Arrow," Dr. Spann said.

"That won't be necessary, Doctor. He'll get over it. He always acts this way when something doesn't go the way he planned. In a few days, he'll be thanking you for saving his life."

❧❧❧

Later that day, when I had come to grips with my

situation, Mona had a chance to share her concerns with me. It was then that I realized that my being a gray alien wasn't just about me.

"I'm worried about how Stella will feel when she sees a gray alien claiming to be her daddy," Mona told me. "Hopefully, she'll be able to see beneath the surface and know it is truly you."

"I'm sure she will, baby. Stella probably knows everything that has happened to both of us. She's tuned into that sort of stuff, isn't she?"

"We're going to have to learn to cope with this situation, Danny. We won't be sharing meals together, and we won't be having sex. That's going to be hard for me. I'm already missing you."

"The Powers have managed to figure things out, Mona. Maybe we can figure things out, too. I mean, if you close your eyes and pretend I'm me and in my real body, maybe I can do some things to satisfy you and to remind you of who I am."

"And you're going to have to stay in the confines of the Villagio, Danny. You won't be going into town because you would cause hysteria in the general public."

"You know, Mona, I could get used to that. I've spent less time in the Villagio since we moved there than I have all over the world on Mack's crazy agendas. He won't be able to send me any place for fifteen months. You, Stella, and I can get real close, you know, bond better, if you know what I mean."

"Yeah," Mona said, "we can do this, Danny. As long as we have each other, there is nothing that we can't surmount—even a visit from my mother!"

I envisioned Mrs. Casola pulling up to our home, ringing the doorbell, and having me answer the door. I had to chuckle. Better yet would be if it happened to her dad. He never liked me, anyway.

Chapter 35

Mona helped me into the tub for my first protein and fluids bath. I felt like some kind of invalid, but I guess it was good that she did that, especially if this new container that I was in went weak and she had to draw a bath and put me in it.

"That isn't so bad, is it?" she asked after I settled up to my neck in the lukewarm fluid. As gross as it sounds to be submerged in ground meat and Gatorade, the container seemed to enjoy it, sort of like being hungry and taking your first bite of a hamburger. It makes you feel kind of instantly satisfied.

"So, what happened while I was being pummeled in Astana?" I asked. "How did you get me out of there?"

"I was remote viewing with Stella, and I saw what was happening to you," Mona said. "I was able to reach Mack, and he connected with Waam, who came and got me in Virginia. He flew me back to Italy, where we picked up Dr. Cassini, who agreed to pretend to be Hitler so we could get you out of there."

"I never saw you, baby. I never knew you were there."

"Danny, you were dying. Stella let me see that. And they were going to torture you to death if they could. Waam flew Dr. Cassini and me to Astana. We went to the brig, and everybody thought that Cassini was Hitler, which is how we got to you. He checked your vitals and could see that you were slipping away, so we removed your electrical essence and stored it in an invention of his, a magnetic storage unit that looks like a briefcase."

"So you killed me, so to speak?"

"You were dying. We decided to save your life, but not your body."

"So, then what happened?"

"Well, the real Hitler showed up, and he and Dr. Cassini got into it. Queen Igua didn't know which one was real, so she brought in Hitler's pet dog. Mack had given Hitler a candy bar that was laced with snake pheromones, so when Hitler reached out to his dog, it just barked at him. But, somehow Hitler got loose and killed Queen Igua—"

"She's dead?"

"Yeah. He slashed her throat."

"Grizzly."

"Yeah. And then her guards cut him and Dr. Cassini down with light weapons. I don't think the lizards cared much for Hitler, so since they weren't sure which one was Hitler, they cut them both down."

"Wow! How did you and Mack survive?"

"They needed us to testify to the Galactic Federation about the incident. You know, who did what and when. We did that via video testimony. Then we brought you back to Italy."

"It sounds like things were hairy, Mona."

"It gets better, though, Danny. Mack told me that the Draconians and the NWO have terminated their alliance

because each blames the other for the loss of their supreme leader in this incident."

"Really?"

"Yeah. Apparently, the Draconians have withdrawn
to Draco to determine what actions they will take, the
most important being the coronation of a new leader to
replace Queen Igua. But smaller detachments of Draconian forces have remained in DUMBS to monitor the actions of the NWO."

"And what about the NWO?" I asked.

"Mack says that the NWO must convene a congress
of its allied nations to revise its plans for domination, especially with the loss of the Draconian forces and their
alien technology. All initiatives, including Agenda Twenty-One and the pandemic, have been put on hold for the
foreseeable future."

"Do you think we've finally defeated them?"

"In the news this morning, it was announced that
Great Britain has voted to leave the European Union,
which many are claiming is the first sign that the NWO is
about to fall apart."

"We can only hope, baby," I replied, and then I
changed the subject to family. "And what about Stella?
Who's watching her?" I asked.

"My sister, Wendy. I called her for help when I saw
that you were in trouble."

"What was her reaction when she saw Stella's eyes?"

"I think she was a bit taken back by her eyes. She
asked a lot of questions. I had to tell her everything."

"Everything?"

"Yes, everything. The DUMBS, Nargas, the Livermore incident, the Moon. All of it."

"Are you sure that was wise?"

"Shit, Danny, she's my sister. We used to sneak out

of the house at night to smoke pot in our tree house. We don't have secrets."

"So what did she think when she learned about everything?"

"She was in shock and disbelief at first, but then when she saw what Stella can do, she began to come to grips with it. She realized that no kid Stella's age could do what she's already doing."

Chapter 36

Worried that he might fall and injure himself, Marlene helped Billy Powers down the three aluminum steps that led from the Ummite shuttle to the concrete floor of the hangar in Italy. As he negotiated each step, he lowered the tip of his cane to steady himself while his foot felt for the surface. Billy's container was now approaching ninety years of age, and it was clear to all who observed its motions that the container's strength, agility, and balance were all fading.

Dr. Spann had sent a nurse and an orderly to greet the Powers and to welcome them to the Montano Antilia Rebirth Center, housed temporarily in Waam's subterranean facility. The orderly opened a portable wheel chair and offered Billy a ride to the migration room.

"Yup," Billy said, "that would be nice."

"Thank you," Marlene added. "It's been a long day. We left our home in Olney at nine, which is a little early for Billy these days. The ride in your flying saucer was exhilarating. I can't believe that we got here in under an hour from Maryland."

Before taking Billy and Marlene to see Dr. Spann,

the nurse checked Billy's vitals. His pulse was regular, although clocking at ninety-two beats per minute, and his blood pressure was a little higher than she would have liked. "Are you excited?" she asked.

"Nervous more than anything," Billy responded. "I didn't volunteer to do this the first time, and it was a painful process. But before I was put into this old woman's body, I was a virile man in my late forties. I'm eager to get out of this thing and get back into something younger. Marlene didn't sign on to be my nurse maid, and I'd like to take her dancing."

"You're going to be just fine, Mr. Powers," the nurse replied. She nodded to the orderly, and the foursome moved quickly through the hangar and into the corridor that led to the migration lab.

When they entered the pleasant ambiance of the Re-birth Center, both Billy and Marlene seemed to relax a little. The nurse left them with the orderly and went to find Dr. Spann.

"How long have you been with this clinic?" Marlene asked the orderly.

"I have worked for Dr. Spann for two years, but on Earth for only four months. This Center just opened. You are our fourth customer, and our first pro bono."

A double door opened, drawing Marlene's attention. The tallest man she had ever seen walked into the room, looking very much like a doctor in his white lab coat. "Mr. Powers?" he asked bending over to shake hands with Billy.

"Yes. This is my wife Marlene."

"Have you eliminated in the past two hours?"

"Billy used the facilities inside the flying saucer, Doctor," Marlene answered.

"Excellent, Mrs. Powers." The doctor motioned to the orderly and then said, "Why don't the two of you come with me. I want you to see the container that will be the new you."

They walked back through the double doors and into the cloning room, where rows of empty glass cylinders were awaiting cells to develop into mature humans. Near the front of the room lay two Nevada Ritters, each wired to a machine that sent signals to the brain to keep the heart pumping and the lungs breathing.

"Choose," Dr. Spann said to Marlene.

"Oh, this is so difficult," Marlene replied. "Which one do you think, Billy?"

"It's like picking between two red Corvettes, sweetie," Billy replied. "They look the same, but one is likely to outperform the other over time. How do you know which one is best, Doctor?"

Marlene lifted the sheets and looked at each body. "I think you should take this one Billy. It looks like his thing is bigger."

Dr. Spann chuckled, "I assure you that they are exactly the same, Mrs. Powers."

"Give her the one she wants, Doctor. I want her to be satisfied. She's been through a lot in the past couple of years."

Dr. Spann tied a red tag on the big toe of the clone that Marlene had chosen, and then ushered the Powers back into the waiting room.

"Mrs. Powers, you will wait here until the procedure has been completed. When Nevada Ritter comes through that door, you can go home with him!"

"How long will it take? Is there a cafeteria?"

"He should be in his new container in less than half an hour, and ready to go home within an hour." Dr. Spann turned to Billy and said, "Come on, Mr. Powers, let's go prep you for the process."

Marlene bent down and kissed Billy on his forehead.

Her eyes were filled with tears. He raised a shaky hand and pressed it against her cheek. "I love you, poopsie," he said.

Dr. Spann and the orderly moved Billy from the waiting room to the migration room, where the state-of-the-art unit sat boldly in the center of the room.

"New technology?" Billy asked. "It seems newer and cleaner."

"Yes, it's brand new. It's much quicker and there should be no pain or discomfort." Dr. Spann said.

"Does it work the same?"

"It is based on the same principles as the older, original units, but its circuits are all printed superconductors. The pain associated with the process of the past occurred when the electrical essence passed through soldered wire junctures. Any such juncture causes resistance and heat, and the essence is susceptible to those sensations as pain."

Two nurses began working on Billy, removing his clothes and attaching electrodes to his head and chest. Then, one rolled the twirling magnetron arms into position such that they would spin around his head. She connected the wires and told the doctor that all was ready.

"Mr. Powers, as recently as two months ago, we would have migrated your essence into a storage unit and then we would have moved the storage unit into the migration unit. It was a two-step process. That is still necessary in the field. However, in this center, we have upgraded our technology, and you will simply move from point A to point B in a seamless process."

"Let's get it done, Doctor. This container isn't getting any younger and I don't want it to die before you migrate me."

"Close your eyes and enjoy your trip," Dr. Spann said.

When Billy closed his eyes, Dr. Spann pushed a button and the migration machine began to hum softly. After ten seconds, the container that Dan Arrow called Miss Powers went limp. Simultaneously, the cloned container of Nevada Ritter arched its back briefly. The nurses removed the electrodes from Nevada Ritter, and Dr. Spann placed the paddles of an AED unit on its chest and hit the button. The container twitched. Dr. Spann listened to the container's heart and smiled. "Success!" he said to his staff.

∽∾∽

Mona and I learned that Billy and Marlene Powers were at the Rebirth Center, so we decided to go see them. It had been awhile, and I was glad that Marlene had taken me up on the offer to have Powers migrated into a younger body. Hell, the poor sap deserved that, didn't he? Especially after spending the last year as an eighty-year-old woman.

Mona held my hand as we walked into the waiting room. Marlene was sitting in a love seat against the wall. When she saw Mona, she quickly came to greet her. "How are you, Mona? It's been so long!"

"Hi, Marlene. This is a big day, isn't it?" Mona said. "Are you excited?"

"I guess I'm nervous more than anything. What will Billy want with a middle-aged woman when he will be a young man, and very handsome? All sorts of women will be throwing themselves at him."

"From what I could tell when I last saw you, you two lovebirds only have eyes for each other. I wouldn't expect that to change," Mona replied. "Billy is a sensible guy and you two have been through a lot together. That's the stuff that makes great marriages."

"I hope you're right. By the way, where's Mr. Arrow? He's the one who arranged all of this for Billy. I want to give him a big kiss."

"You might want to try kissing my friend here," Mona replied, motioning toward me.

I shot her a dirty look. Then I turned and said, "Hello, Marlene," extending my thin, gray arm and three-fingered hand.

"I'm pleased to meet you," Marlene replied.

I tried to let her know who I was. "Marlene, we met in my office the day after Billy's body was classified as a suicide by the FBI."

Marlene gave me a very strange look of disbelief. "Oh my God, is that you, Mr. Arrow? How did you go and get yourself stuck in a body like that?"

"Thanks, Marlene. You're not making me feel a whole lot better about my situation."

She bent down and planted a juicy kiss on my cheek. I wiped it away because my gray container absorbs just about everything that it comes into contact with, and I didn't know if Marlene was carrying anything strange in her saliva.

"This is really a surprise, Mr. Arrow."

"It was a surprise for me, too. I just went to sleep and woke up this way."

"Well, Billy and you have shared a common experience then, haven't you?"

"This is only one of many, Marlene. How's he doing, anyway?"

"He's been in the migration room for almost an hour. The doctor told me—"

The noise of the door bursting open interrupted Marlene mid-sentence. It was doctor Spann and Nevada Ritter. "Howdy, ma'am," Ritter exclaimed, picking Marlene up by her waist and twirling her in a circle.

"Oh, will he always talk like a cowboy, Doctor?" Marlene squealed.

Powers planted a kiss on his wife that almost made me turn away in modesty. It was definitely a happy reunion.

"Your fantasy will become reality this afternoon, poopsie," Powers said. "Maybe a couple of times!"

Marlene squealed in delight again. Powers put her down. As she rearranged her dress, Marlene smiled. "I've always wondered what it would be like to make love to Nevada Ritter. I guess my wish will come true."

It was too much information for me. I could never understand why the Powers shared the secrets of their intimacy with just about everyone they met. But this time, at least, the image in my mind of Marlene in bed with a strapping young man was better than the previous image of her in bed with a woman who was old enough to be her mother. Maybe her grandmother. Ugh.

Marlene turned to Dr. Spann. "Doctor, since Billy is now so young, I'm wondering if I might have the opportunity to be young again, too. Maybe we could start a family. Do you have an extra clone of Marilyn Monroe?"

"Sorry, Mrs. Powers, but no female containers are available in Italy at the moment, and clones of deceased actresses are out of the question. For the time being, you will have to remain as Marlene Powers, married to Billy 'Nevada Ritter' Powers. Perhaps you would consider donating some tissue samples, and you could be migrated into a younger version of yourself in about fifteen months."

Marlene agreed.

"Good," Dr. Spann said. "Then you and Mr. Arrow can be migrated into new containers at about the same time. Perhaps it would be a good time for a reunion."

It couldn't come soon enough for me. Fifteen months seemed like it was so very far in the future.

Dr. Spann took Marlene and Billy into an examination room, where he could extract some tissue samples to begin the cloning process for Marlene's new container. Afterward, the Powers were going to rock the trailer in their guest room for the rest of the day. Well, that was my hunch.

Mona and I weren't going to get so lucky. My new container had no sexual organs and, as the doctor predicted, I was beginning to lose interest in sex, anyway. Already, I was beginning to live the life of a neutered dog. This is a dangerous situation for a woman like Mona. She does everything with passion, and our relationship is based upon that passion. I wondered how she would handle spending fifteen months in a live-in relationship with a three-fingered sexless creature who would offer no passion. This trial would test the mettle of our love. God help me.

Epilogue

About a month after my migration, Mack and I met to discuss the ramifications of my having nuked the Central Sun. According to NASA and the National Weather Service, the results were two-fold. First, the nuclear blast caused heightened pressures against the Earth's crust, which, in turn caused a major earthquake that resulted in a tsunami in Indonesia. Second, it caused a slight increase in global warming, because the heat of the blast increased the core temperature of the plasma in the Central Sun, such that the Earth's interior beneath the Pacific Ocean warmed by one degree. The end result of all of that is the largest El Nino in recorded history. The polar ice caps have begun to melt, and the number of violent tornados and hurricanes has increased. Oh yeah, and, a twenty-five-mile long crack has appeared in the Brunt Ice Shelf of Antarctica, forcing several research stations to relocate fourteen miles inland or risk floating out to sea. Some alarmists have blamed human use of fossil fuels for these effects, but I can't stand up and tell the world that it was my fault because it would make me a fugitive, like it did to Waam, and the world isn't ready to listen to a gray alien anyway.

The good news is this: Ummite scientists have calculated that within two years the Central Sun will have consumed the extra energy boost caused by the nuclear blast, and the surface temperature range of Earth will return to normalcy within three years. Until that time, weather will seem uncharacteristic of familiar patterns. So, the global warming advocates will have that long to create legislation to restrict human use of energy resources before we return to the freezing cold winters that will rebuild the polar ice caps.

By then, Mona will have had our child, her second, and I will be back in a cloned container which was made from DNA extracted from my own blood and sweat. I will look like I did in my mid-twenties, but my new container will have no physical scars. I can't speak for any mental scars that I might carry from the beatings I've taken at the hand of the New World Order. We'll have to see about that. On the plus side, however, they tell me that after I migrate into the new container, I will have the sexual appetite of a twenty-year old. I chuckle at that thought, because Mona thinks she had difficulty dealing with the juvenile side of me before I was migrated into this sexless gray container. I can hardly wait.

Dr. Gunno says that my clone is coming along and should be ready in about a year. That's good news. Marlene Powers is in constant contact with Mona, planning a major vacation and celebration for the day when she and I are migrated into our younger bodies. Marlene is anxious to be able to keep up with Billy's schedule of dancing, partying, and love making, and she is certain that regaining her youthful body will bring her that capability. She would know because she's already been there and done that.

I have unanswered questions, however, that keep me from sleeping at night. First, who was it among Waam's staff who leaked the information to the FBI and to the embassies in the Draconian's Antarctic subterranean facility? They were all warned about a pending attack, and that warning caused a mass evacuation on the day that we nuked its Central Sun. Waam needs to find the mole and pluck him or her from his staff.

Second, and more perplexing to me, is the question of who abducted Mona and me and impregnated her? She has no memory of the abduction, but her swelling belly is clear evidence that it did, indeed, happen. However, I vividly remember the abduction and the milking procedure that I underwent. I know that the abductors weren't Draconians because no lizards were involved and the grays who served as technicians were not the Draconian type. Instead, they had heads like dwarfs. Most of all, I remember the insect-like alien who was in charge of the procedure. Waam says that the praying mantis aliens are known as "The Watchers," and that they have supreme authority over all other life forms in our galaxy. Who are they? Who gave them that authority? And, why did they choose Mona and me to be part of their agenda? As soon as I'm back in my own container, I'm going to find out.

About the Author

Born in Massachusetts, Edward Baker traveled widely as a child because his US Marine father was transferred to new assignments across the USA on a regular basis. By the time Baker was twelve, he had crossed the United States three times. And at ripe old age of sixteen, he actually drove a stick-shift Ford across the USA, following his dad, who was pulling a small camping trailer behind the family station wagon.

An English major at Elon College, Baker earned a master's degree at Appalachian State University and a doctorate in Educational Leadership at the Graduate School of the Sage Colleges. After thirty-five years in higher education, and after retiring as the interim president of a public community college, he turned his attention to his first love, writing, while continuing to teach undergraduate and graduate courses on an adjunct basis at a private college in upstate New York.

During the warm months, Baker and his wife Edna reside in their cabin on Galway Lake, New York. During the cold months, they "hole up" in their winter quarters in Saratoga Springs, New York. When he's not teaching or writing, Baker is playing with his four grandchildren or working on a long list of renovations and construction projects.

Baker saw his first UFOs as a young man while camping out at Green Lakes State Park near Syracuse, New York. He saw his second while living on the beach at Emerald Isle in North Carolina, back when it was still a wild and undeveloped stretch of dunes. His first Black Opal book, *Dan Arrow and the New World Order,* is based on these experiences and on current conspiracy lore, combining the UFO mystery with national and international politics and the rumored agenda of the legendary New World Order. Baker says that the Dan Arrow books are fun to write because they permit him to delve into seemingly unrelated elements that mesh together into a fabric offering many clandestine possibilities.